Praise for Pajtim Statovci's

CROSSING

"A gritty, gut-wrenching and heartbreaking read."
—*The Post and Courier* (Charleston, SC)

"An excellent and evocative novel about the intersection of migration and gender." —*Library Journal* (starred review)

"Shocking. . . . The matter-of-fact depiction of numerous traumas intensifies the impact." —*Publishers Weekly*

"Poignant . . . powerful. . . . [A] searching tale of a young Albanian whose struggle to understand his sexual orientation and gender identity is interwoven with his struggle to survive in foreign lands." —*Booklist*

"*Crossing* will devour you; this is some fierce, dazzling, and heartbreaking shit." —NoViolet Bulawayo, author of *We Need New Names*

"Anyone who has ever known what it's like to leave home in pursuit of happiness and belonging will most likely love this tender, beautiful novel as much as I did."
—Imbolo Mbue, author of *Behold the Dreamers*

"Reading Pajtim Statovci's fiction is like entering a lucid dream: life and death intertwines in an intimate dance; the nostalgia for the past is akin to the nostalgia for the future. *Crossing* is a novel that dazzles and mesmerizes, and the reader, upon finishing, may have the extraordinary sensation that his or her own dreams have been scattered along the journey, beckoning for rereading."
—Yiyun Li, author of *Where Reasons End*

"Everything, and I mean everything, is threatened with devastation and loss, but Pajtim Statovci's prose, the quality of his seeing and remembering, promises to save an invaluable part for all of us."
—Amitava Kumar,
author of *Immigrant, Montana*

PAJTIM STATOVCI

CROSSING

Pajtim Statovci was born in Kosovo in 1990 and moved with his family to Finland when he was two years old. He is currently a PhD candidate at the University of Helsinki. His first book, *My Cat Yugoslavia*, won the Helsingin Sanomat Literature Prize for best debut novel and his second, *Crossing*, won the Toisinkoinen literature prize. He received the Helsinki Writer of the Year Award in 2018.

CROSSING

CROSSING

CROSSING

PAJTIM STATOVCI

Translated from the Finnish by David Hackston

VINTAGE BOOKS
A DIVISION OF PENGUIN RANDOM HOUSE LLC
NEW YORK

FIRST VINTAGE BOOKS EDITION, MARCH 2020

Translation copyright © 2019 by David Hackston

All rights reserved. Published in the United States by Vintage Books, a division of Penguin Random House LLC, New York, and distributed in Canada by Penguin Random House Canada Limited, Toronto. Originally published in Finland as *Tiranan sydän* by Kustannusosakeyhtiö Otava, Keuruu, in 2016. Copyright © 2016 by Pajtim Statovci. This translation originally published in hardcover in the United States by Pantheon Books, a division of Penguin Random House LLC, New York, in 2019. Published by agreement with Salomonsson Agency and Otava Publishing Company.

This translation has been published with the financial support of the Finnish Literature Exchange.

F |
L I

The Library of Congress has cataloged the Pantheon edition as follows:
Name: Statovci, Pajtim, author. Hackston, David, translator.
Title: Crossing / Pajtim Statovci ; translated from the Finnish by David Hackston.
Other titles: Tiranan sydän. English
Description: First American edition. New York : Pantheon Books, 2019
Identifiers: LCCN 2018034024
Classification: LCC PH356.S838 T5713 2019 | DDC 894/.54134— dc23
LC record available at https://lccn.loc.gov/2018034024

Vintage Books Trade Paperback ISBN: 978-0-525-56301-3
eBook ISBN: 978-1-5247-4750-3

www.vintagebooks.com

Book design by Maggie Hinders

Printed in the United States of America

Sometimes the facts threaten the truth.

—AMOS OZ, *A Tale of Love and Darkness*
(trans. Nicholas de Lange)

CROSSING

GOD'S RIB

When I think about my own death, the moment it happens is always the same. I'm wearing a plain, colored shirt and a matching pair of pants, cut from thin material that's easy to pull on. It's early in the morning and I am happy, I feel the same sense of contentment and satisfaction as I do at the first mouthfuls of my favorite meal. There are certain people around me, I don't know them yet, but one day I will, and I'm in a certain place, lying on my hospital bed in my own room, nobody is dying around me, outside the day is slowly struggling to its feet like a rheumatic old man, I hear certain words from the mouths of my loved ones, a certain touch on my hand, and the kiss on my cheek feels like the home I have built around me like a shrine.

Then one by one my organs give up and my bodily functions begin to close down: my brain no longer sends messages to the rest of my body, the flow of blood is cut off, and my heart stops, mercilessly and irreparably, and just like that I no longer exist. Where my body once was now there is only skin and tissue, and beneath the tissue there are fluids, bones, and meaningless organs. Dying is as easy as a gentle downhill stroll.

I am a twenty-two-year-old man who at times behaves like the men of my imagination: my name could be Anton or Adam or Gideon, whatever pleases my ear at any given moment. I am French or German or Greek, but never Albanian, and I walk in a particular way, the way my father taught me to walk, to follow his example, flat-footed and with a wide gait, aware of how to hold my chest and shoulders, my jaw tight, as though to ensure nobody trespasses on my territory. At times like this the woman within me burns on a pyre. When I'm sitting at a café or a restaurant and the waiter brings me the bill and doesn't ask why I'm eating alone, the woman inside me smolders. When I look for flaws in my dish and send it back to the kitchen or when I walk into a store and the assistants approach me, she bursts once again into flames, becoming part of a continuum that started at the moment we were told that woman was born of man's rib, not as a man but to live alongside him, at his left-hand side.

Sometimes I am a twenty-two-year-old woman who behaves however she pleases. I am Amina or Anastasia, the name is irrelevant, and I move the way I remember my mother moving, my heels not touching the ground. I never argue with men, I paint my face with foundation, dust my cheeks with powder, carefully etch eyeliner around my eyes, fill in my brows, dab on some mascara and coif my lashes, put in a set of blue contact lenses to be born again, and at that moment the man within me does not burn, not at all, but joins me as I walk around the town. When I go into the same restaurant, order the same dish, and make the same complaint about the food the waiter does not take it back to the kitchen but tells me the meat is cooked just the way I asked, and when he brings me the check he watches me as if I were a child as I rummage in my handbag and pull out the correct sum of money, then disappears into the kitchen with a cursory *Thank you*. The man within me wants to follow him, but when I look at what I'm wearing, my black summer dress and dark-brown flats, I see that such behavior would be inappropriate for a woman, and so I leave the restaurant and step out onto the street, where Italian men shout and whistle at me, at times so much that the man inside me curses at them in a low, gruff voice, and at that they shut up and raise their hands into the air as though they have come face-to-face with a challenger of equal stature.

I am a man who cannot be a woman but who can sometimes look like a woman. This is my greatest quality, the game of dress up that I can start and stop whenever it suits me. Sometimes the game begins when I pull on an androgynous garment, a formless cape, and step outside, and then people start making assumptions, they find it disconcerting that they don't know one way or the other, sitting on public transport and in restaurants, cafés, it irritates them like a splinter beneath their fingernail, and they whisper among themselves or ask me directly: *Are you a man or a woman?* Sometimes I tell them I am a man, sometimes I say I'm a woman. Sometimes I don't answer them at all, sometimes I ask them what they think I am, and they are happy to answer, as though this were a game to them too, they are eager to construct me, and once I've given them an answer order is finally restored to the world. I can choose what I am, I can choose my gender, choose my nationality and my name, my place of birth, all simply by opening my mouth. Nobody has to remain the person they were born; we can put ourselves together like a jigsaw.

But you have to prepare yourself. To live so many lives, you have to cover up the lies you've already told with new lies to avoid being caught up in the maelstrom that ensues when your lies are uncovered. I believe that people in my country grow old beyond their years and die so young precisely because of their lies. They hide their faces the way a mother shields her newly born child and avoid being seen in an unflattering light with almost military precision: there is no falsehood, no story they won't tell about themselves to maintain the façade and ensure that their dignity and honor remain intact and untarnished until they are in their graves. Throughout my childhood I hated this about my parents, despised it like the sting of an atopic rash or the feeling of being consumed with anxiety, and I swore I would never become like them, I would never care what other people think of me, never invite the neighbors for dinner simply to feed them with food I could never afford for myself. I would not be an Albanian, not in any way, but someone else, anyone else.

At my weakest moments I feel a crushing sense of sorrow, because I know I mean nothing to other people, I am nobody, and this is like death itself. If death were a sensation, it would be this: invisibility, living your life in ill-fitting clothes, walking in shoes that pinch.

In the evenings I sometimes hold my hands out before me, clasp them together, and pray, because everybody in Rome prays and asks God to help them resolve difficult situations. A thing like that can catch on so easily, and so I pray that I might wake up the next morning in a different life, even though I don't even believe in God. I do, however, believe that a person's desire to look a particular way and behave in a certain manner can directly impact the breadth of a shoulder, the amount of body hair, the size of a foot, one's talent and choice of profession. Everything else can be learned, acquired—a new way of walking, a new body language, you can practice speaking at a higher pitch or dressing differently, telling lies in such a way that it's not lying at all. It's just a way of being. That's why it's best to focus on wanting things and never on what might happen once you've got them.

When I first arrived in Italy I was sure I would be able to secure a job I enjoyed, I would meet a partner who loved me and start a family for whom I would be prepared to give my life. I was convinced that somebody would find me and see the potential I had, appreciate everything I could give to the world. I waited and waited, a year, a second and third, waited for these things to start happening, waited for someone to see my uniqueness, but the authorities and social workers didn't care for my plans and hopes, they scoffed at my dreams of studying psychology at the University of Rome, though I explained I'd read the basic texts many times. *Shouldn't you study a vocation instead?* they asked. *You don't even have a high-school diploma; most people your age have one of those, some even have a university degree,* they argued and sent me home to consider my limited options: a career in the construction or customer-service industry, a life not significantly better than the one I had left behind.

As time passed I realized that I no longer considered myself special or unique, and this is perhaps the worst thing that can happen, for this if anything will make a person passionless, this if anything forces one to believe in God. You clutch the branches you can reach, and settle for your destiny. Only then will you see the light, the fact that the lack of rights and opportunities very rarely leads someone to the fight for them.

Every day I spend in this city, in these different lives, is meaningless and insignificant, and for that reason all those years I have spent learning new skills and foreign languages I might as well flush down the drain. The most ridiculous thing of all is that throughout my childhood and my youth, I considered myself beautiful, talented, and intelligent—a combination of qualities that ought to guarantee success. I am quick to absorb information, I've never feared going the extra mile, I've always enjoyed the fact that the things I have studied are challenging, and I derive great satisfaction at being able to solve a tricky conundrum. I have never doubted myself or questioned my future success, because I have always practiced long and hard until I become the best at anything and everything I turn my mind to.

Yet instead I have entered a life in which I wonder how to erase myself from the world in the least painful manner. There are days during which I barely open my mouth, not even to thank someone or to say hello, days during which the only thing I am capable of doing is appearing like I know where I am going, looking like I belong in this city. This is not my life, these days are not mine. It is not me who obsessively washes stains of urine and excrement from around the toilet bowl in cafés and restaurants simply so that nobody using the toilet after me might think I'd left such a mess. That is someone else, a ghost living at the edge of my shadows.

. . .

One day I walk through the city center, along Via della Minerva, and to my left, the Pantheon looks like the hunched figure of an old Albanian man. The long, uneven cobbles plague my feet, making me step to the side and wobble along the streets like a millipede. Endless herds of tourists move through the city like a bubbling stream, it's always sunny, the street cafés are open all day long, impatient children stand scattered in front of the ice-cream stands like plastic bags in a junkyard.

I can't breathe because the air gathers into a sodden ball of wool at the back of my throat and the incessant noise of the piazza makes my concentration come in fits and starts, and when I place a hand on my moist cheek and scratch off the sweat with my fingernail it feels like peeling away a layer of skin.

I walk to the other side of the square, away from the crush of tourists, and wonder what the people in front of me are talking about. The few words of their conversation that I understand always sound like the ravings of a madman. They are probably talking about the same things as everyone else. One of them, perhaps the mother in her late thirties, is explaining that it's been a year since her mother died, and another one, her friend who is about the same age, explains that she has had a row with her partner because they disagreed about how best to discipline their children, then they weep and console each other, together they wonder what to do next, how to cope with their respective misfortunes.

People here have time to lick their wounds, to be traumatized for years about something utterly trivial—they have all the time in the world to think about the meaning of life from one day, one month, one year to the next, to wonder what they want to do, what kind of profession they wish to have, while in my homeland newborn babies die of a fever and malnourishment, men die of shots fired to uphold the family honor, and women fleeing from their husbands are killed by the bullets given to their husbands by family during their wedding celebrations. They are buried, and a new day dawns, and nobody has time to mourn for them, nobody will worry for a second about such matters, because nobody has the time to think any farther than tomorrow, and it would never occur to anyone to wonder whether I became like this because my father died when I was sixteen, or perhaps because my parents divorced when I was little, or maybe because I only learned as an adult that I was adopted. Because a hungry man thinks of other things altogether—the fat, the salt and sugar of his next meal—and when there is no food he starts to think about a time when suddenly standing up makes his vision blurry, leads to fainting and eventually death.

Are the Italians happier than the Albanians because they think so profoundly about themselves and their dreams, because they argue with such passion, with the kind of verve that carries them from one day to the next, a verve that doesn't even seem genuine but rather an attempt to conceal the fact that they don't know who they are or what they want though they spend their entire lives chewing over the same questions? It is this that forms the underlying power and the depth of their lives, and I can do nothing but despise it.

On the move again, I pull my tight polo sweater farther down, adjust the position of my padded bra, and tug up my denim shorts, which stretch halfway down my thighs. I look at the thin, beautiful women walking side by side, proudly wearing their summer dresses, and I envy them. I envy their names, Julia or Celia or Laura; I envy the way they walk in their stilettos, envy the pitch of their voices, the way they talk as though they have not a care in the world, their ability to give their current or future husbands children—things I will never be able to achieve, neither with all the hope in the world nor with the readiness to give anything for them. All I can ever have is a copy of their life, a photograph in which I look almost like them but not quite, a lie that must be created from nothing.

I arrive at the Piazza Navona, an oblong square with three ornately decorated fountains, the center one of which looks like a delicate Italian woman with its tapered obelisk standing proudly in the middle. This square too is full of tourists throwing coins into the fountains, though the things they wish for are probably laughable: they want their former beloved back or their partner to pay them more attention. Still, I understand them, because that is the way the old curse goes: everybody wants something they do not have, and everybody feels as though the lack of this one thing cannot bear the light of a single new day.

The Piazza Navona looks the same as the other squares in Rome: faded buildings erected around the cobbled square, the streets between them just big enough to fit through without suffocating; buildings that are lined so close to one another that the whole city seems like one enormous barrack; and the motorways surrounding it resembling barbed-wire fences designed to keep people apart. All of a sudden the buildings around me seem ominous, and the stones beneath my shoes seem to lick the soles of my feet as though they were ready to bite them off.

I manage to gasp a handful of air and continue on my way, tears falling from my eyes as though through a still, and for a moment I think it must be raining until I realize there is not a cloud in the sky. I arrive at the Ponte Umberto I; I stand at the top of the bridge and look first right, then left, at the Castel Sant'Angelo, which resembles a moldy orange; at the people incessantly taking photographs; at the green trees planted along the riverbank; at the flowing, almost misty waters of the Tiber, then I cross the street leading to the Piazza dei Tribunali and walk a short way forward until I reach the long tongue of steps leading up to the Castel, the only place where there are no longer any pedestrian crossings and the drivers dare to go a little faster.

I glance briefly over my shoulder and imagine that I won't have to wait for long, but several minutes pass until the tires of a large enough car whistle in my ears and I lunge into the road.

I

Tirana

1990–1991

THE MARBLES

I am fourteen years old, not very young but not old enough to be taken too seriously. I walk through the center of Tirana with my father, who smells of sweat. We pass Skanderbeg Square and Tirana's National Historical Museum with the mosaic on its façade depicting a group of Albanians in national costume holding high the Albanian flag and carrying guns, bows, and arrows. We arrive at an enormous intersection and before long we are scuttling along the side of the bazaar. Roasted-looking men have set up rickety stalls lining the streets, trying to sell passersby counterfeit watches, tobacco, Skanderbeg liqueur, and useless knickknacks: cigarette lighters, decorative souvenirs, mouth organs, and traditional instruments like the *çifteli* and the *tupan*.

My father pulls me along like a reluctant dog and I glance at the bazaar, which looks like a giant, colorful rug beneath which the merchants, their meat and wares, have been swept. Heat and moisture flood in from above and beneath, from all sides, and as I imagine the people pressing into the bowels of the bazaar about to suffocate, I am relieved that I don't need to be in there myself. The merchants address my father as *Sir,* and they call me a little sweetheart, trying to show off their wares, but we move quickly because we both know that anything can happen these days. I could disappear and never be found, snatched away in the clutches of a complete stranger, bundled into a strange van or sucked into the heat of the bazaar, where the hungry hawkers will tear out my organs and sell them in desperation, or something equally savage.

We walk on a few kilometers and arrive at another square, its edges lined with litter, and my father grips the back of his head. He is wearing a dark suit, complete with a waistcoat, the same suit he wears every day. He takes off his jacket and places it across his arm and continues rubbing the back of his head. I notice his white shirt is wet around the armpits and shoulders. The bus may arrive soon or it may arrive a while later, but we will wait, because I want to show you the fortress at Krujë, he says, squinting his eyes, clacking his jaw, and exhaling heavily.

My father looks handsome, smart, and dignified though the sweat is dripping off him as if someone has wrung a wet towel over his head. He has shaved and the light hitting his shiny leather shoes almost dazzles me, and when the bus finally pulls into the square my father seems startled; he grabs my hand and starts hauling me toward the bus. He gives the driver some money, then we walk to the back and sit.

I think about how happy I am in my father's company, and I can't for the life of me remember when we last spent time together, just the two of us. As I sit beside him I guess my happiness must have something to do with the fact that people are so rarely happy these days, that Enver Hoxha is dead and the city isn't the same anymore, that people in Tirana are so desperate that their woes crowd the walls and ceilings of their houses like the wrapping paper and empty cigarette packs that fill the gutters, that they spew from the drains and through the floorboards, out into the streets and into strangers' homes like floodwater.

My head aches, my father says eventually and he tries to open the window, but it is jammed shut. He slumps back into his seat and I sit quietly beside him. I am too afraid to tell him I feel terrified because the driver is accelerating like a madman with a death wish, up and up along the serpentine road winding its way across the mountainside. The narrow dust track is dotted with small rocks, dips, and bumps, and I am convinced the tires of the bus will burst at any moment. Every turn in the path is steep, and the driver seems to speed up as he approaches them, though he can't see if there are any cars coming in the opposite direction. But the ravines, maybe fifty meters deep, into which the bus is in danger of plummeting he most certainly can see. Doesn't he realize how close we are to dying? I wonder, looking at my father. He has closed his eyes and opened his mouth, and the onion-smelling stink of his breath fills the air between us.

We finally arrive, and my father grips me by the hand and sets off toward the fortress at the top of the hill, pulling me behind him, along a steep, cobbled path buzzing with visitors. A few stalls have been set up selling all manner of junk, handicrafts, sweets, rugs, and postcards. Once we have reached the top, my father wipes the sweat from his brow on his sleeve and begins pointing out the collapsed fortifications and isolated boulders, a mosque that I recognize from photographs, and the Skanderbeg museum standing like a gigantic cow, and we start walking toward it.

A white statue in the foyer depicts Skanderbeg and his troops.

I notice that Skanderbeg has huge, thick legs that bulge from beneath his chain mail like two barrels, he has a metallic helmet with an insignia portraying a goat's head, he is wearing a long cloak, his sword rests in his left hand, he has a thick beard. My father points at the men standing behind Skanderbeg and tells me that his army had more than ten thousand soldiers, among them one Lekë Dukagjini. The rules and commandments of the *Kanun,* which bears Dukagjini's name, need not even be written down since they flow through the veins of every self-respecting Albanian.

The museum is packed with artifacts, suits of armor hanging from the walls alongside crests and coats of arms from the time of Skanderbeg himself, tables and glass cabinets full of weapons that have taken human lives. Despite his headache and ever-increasing sweating, my father talks incessantly, like a deranged swarm of wasps. Hundreds of years ago the Turkish Ottomans forced their way into Albania and ruined our beautiful country, he explains, his voice booming. According to the practice of the *devşirme* infantry, the Ottomans rounded up reinforcements for the regiments of the Janissaries, and Albanian dukes were forced to recruit their own sons as a sign that they were prepared to obey the orders of the sultan. If they did not, the sultan might decide to snap the dukes' sons' spines.

One of the recruited boys was Gjergj Kastrioti, my father explains, and it was from this very place, the fortress at Krujë, that the Kastrioti clan ruled the land, he adds. Gjergj Kastrioti eventually took the name of Skanderbeg and succeeded in liberating his city from Ottoman occupation and defended it not once, not twice, but on three separate occasions. When my father recounts the story of how, as a sign of his victory, Skanderbeg raised a flag bearing his family's crest, a two-headed eagle, above the fortress at Krujë, I feel a profound sense of pride in my homeland and in Skanderbeg, and when my father tells me that we Albanians are the descendants of Skanderbeg and the ancient Illyrians, I give him my proudest smile.

Then my father says that Skanderbeg is the most famous Albanian in the world because he was less than ten years old— far younger than you are now, he adds—when he and his three brothers were sent to Edirne to enter the service of the sultan Mehmed the First and to be trained by the Ottoman army. The sultan wanted to school his prisoners, to raise them to be Turkish soldiers, and to convert them to Islam, but Gjergj Kastrioti did not yield to the sultan's will. He became a soldier the like of which had never been seen before, a military strategist, a warrior without equal who in a quarter of a century lost only two battles. Before long Skanderbeg returned to Albania with the intention of freeing the country from the Turkish occupation, something he naturally succeeded in doing, and nowadays, my father adds, his spirit rests across the land of Albania, the heart of an immortal man beats in the breast of the black two-headed eagle on the flag, and the red surrounding the eagle is the color of the endlessly shed blood of an immortal people.

My father also mentions Skanderbeg's wise and heroic horse, which loyally battled along with its master and which, legend has it, could gallop faster and farther than any horse has ever galloped. According to my father, after Skanderbeg's death the horse would not allow anyone else on its back, and for some reason this part of the story makes the greatest impression upon me. Perhaps the horse could see into the future and knew it had borne a man like no other, a man who will never die.

First the Turks came here, my father says, his voice and head lowered as if weighed down by a heavy crown, then the Italians when that fat guinea pig of a man Mussolini banished the cowardly Albanian king Zog, who took with him all the gold he could steal and fled to England, France, the United States, where he lived a life of luxury, and now my father seems almost angry. Then came the Germans, and then the rest of them. Everybody wanted to occupy this country, because this beautiful mountainous land is rugged and because the serrated ridge of its mountain peaks is—what else—the jaws of a predator, and oh how ready those jaws are to bite down on the neck of any people or nation. He stops and swipes his hands as though drawing himself an invisible path through the air.

We come to a halt at the top of the hill and admire the landscape, and the views from the fortress are breathtaking. Krujë looks like a rusty platter, the concrete bunkers built into the surrounding green meadows look like spaceships, and farther off the roads wind their way along the sides of the mountains like ribbons. My father says if we climb a bit higher we'll be able to see the sea, then he stops and scuffs the dusty path with the tip of his shoe. You won't believe how many good men have lost their lives here, how much blood this sand has sucked up, he begins, you cannot yet imagine how much bloodshed has taken place here, how many gods have died here, how many gods have disappeared in these mountains, buried by the interminable winter. He stops, and the pompous tone of his voice is starting to frighten me, because now I am trying to imagine what all those dead men must have looked like: they are lying one on top of the other, their limbs severed and their guts spilled on the ground like sticky, oily dough, the sand dusting their bodies like carelessly scattered flour.

As we walk hand in hand back down the hillside, my father stops at one of the vendors' stalls and buys me a set of marbles wrapped in a small cotton bag with a drawstring around its neck. To me, they seem outlandishly expensive, but my father doesn't care; he knows what he is doing and he is determined to get them for me, though for that money he could buy flour, salt, and sugar for a long time. As he hands over the money, he lets go of my hand, and all of a sudden I feel as though I'm very far away from home and my father is farther away still. *Fool,* whispers the man who took my father's money. My father doesn't seem to notice how he is being mocked, and it makes me so angry that I almost feel like leaping onto that despicable man's shoulders and clawing his eyes out, but instead I just glare.

I press the marbles into my pocket, feel their accusatory weight against my thigh as we waddle toward the town center like ducks, and when we sit down for a moment on the boulder near the bus stop, I give in to my desire and take the marbles out of my pocket. My father's brow looks like a joint of ham roasting in the oven. I examine the marbles: there are twelve in total, completely round, colored in shades of blue, green, turquoise, and yellow, and if you hold them up to the light all those colors shine at once. My father tells me that every marble in the world is unique. I nod and clench the marbles in my fist. My head hurts, my father says again, and he grips my hand between his own. His skin is rough, his short, stumpy fingers are moist like freshly harvested potatoes.

I'm not well, he says eventually, coughing, and I notice that he must be very hot because sometimes it looks as though steam comes out of his mouth every time he exhales. He pulls back his hand and props his elbows against his knees, and at that moment the marbles fall from my fingers and scatter across the ground, though I am not particularly surprised by what my father has told me. The marbles rattle against one another and strike the pathway, roll between the cobbles and across the sand surrounding the bus stop, and when my father says I have to be brave I understand why he has brought me here to tell me all these stories about Skanderbeg.

My father gives another cough. I begin gathering up the marbles and putting them back in their cotton bag, and when I cannot find the last one I turn my head to look the other way, burst into tears, and cover my face with my hands, for never in my life have I wanted so ardently not to cry. I stare at my shoes and look up at the women walking hand in hand in the distance, at the forest where I would like to flee, and suddenly I am unsure what to do with my arms and legs. I grip my father's hand and haul myself up against him, so close that I can feel the fever in his body. I am about to suffocate and I cry utterly inconsolably, against him, upon him, but my father isn't crying at all, he simply breathes in and out and coughs and pants and pushes me away with heavy hands, because he can't concentrate, and the bus back to Tirana pulls up to the stop.

In the bus my father is silent and his eyes are closed. I press my head against the back of the chair and bathe in the red of the setting sun, my mind as clear as the surface of the sea after a storm, and with an inexplicable sense of calm I look past my father and out of the window at the villages as they pass, at the bunkers built at the edges of the villages and along the valleys and mountains, and I no longer fear anything at all. I pull the marbles from my pocket, and when I remember the missing marble and the vendor's whisper I burst into tears once again, and for a moment the force of my sobs is almost too much to bear, but when my initial feeling of bottomless guilt eventually subsides and I tuck the marbles away, I am consumed by an urgent desire to say to the boy sitting across the aisle by himself, a boy far younger than me, that we are all going to die on this bus.

The boy looks at me as though I were deranged, then turns to look out the window. I watch him with the hungry eyes of a vulture: I can feel his body warming up, see as his imagination turns his thoughts to menacing visions, and a moment later I tell the boy that hundreds of people have died on these roads, some of them in traffic accidents caused by either the driver's mental instability or general lack of driving skills, while others perish from thirst after wandering across the mountains for days and weeks. The sand on these roads is ground from human carcasses and the foundations of the mountains are human bones, I say, and the boy looks up at me again.

This time his gaze is querying and helpless, his eyes dazed and glassy like those of a beaten animal. He buries his hands deep into his moist armpits. I'm certain we're going to die today, I tell him, my father said so too before falling asleep, we're all going to die, I say again, and I realize how thrilling it is to see the boy press his hands even farther into his armpits, to look at the way his feet are bulging from the tops of his dirty white sneakers as he clenches his toes, at the way he sits there biting his upper lip. You'll never see your family again, I continue as with one hand I grip my chin and with the other I hold the boy's shoulder.

At this the boy starts to cry, and his sobs are so ugly and grotesque that they attract the attention of an old man sitting a few rows in front of us. It appears the man has heard our conversation, as he fetches the boy, tells him to sit next to him, and slaps me square in the face as he might an attacking boar.

I taste the blood as it gathers in my mouth; my entire head is dizzied and I can still feel the force of the thump in my jaw.

I slip a hand into my pocket and squeeze the marbles with all my strength and press my other hand over my nose and mouth so that the rage consuming me doesn't wake my father. When we arrive my father finally wakes up and the man who slapped me walks up to him, tells him about what happened, and grips me by the shoulder. *If this little runt was my child I'd knock his teeth so far down his throat he wouldn't utter another sound.*

As the man shoves my head to one side, I can feel the bitterness on my face and I am unsure whether it is because of my disgust at the man's touch or my shame at being caught. When my father answers the man by staring past me and asking in nothing but a whisper for me to be a good boy, I feel light and clear, though the marbles rolling between my fingers and palm are slippery with sweat.

We step off the bus; it is as dark as the far side of the moon and my father seems almost unconscious as he clambers from the bus and staggers along the streets of the black city like a disoriented drunk, and he doesn't care to hold out his hand for me anymore, and I realize, too, that I would not take it if he did—so ashamed I am of him.

———

My mother has made peppers stuffed with rice and ground beef. There's homemade yogurt, olives marinated in lemon juice, fresh cucumber, and boiled eggs pickled in vinegar, but my father barely takes any, even though we never eat so lavishly. He grabs a chunk of bread and pulls it to small pieces but still scarcely touches his food.

We eat in the living room around a white sheet laid out across the floor. My father is lying down, and after only a few mouth-

fuls he rolls onto his stomach and drags himself with great difficulty to a mattress placed by the wall so that half of it forms
a backrest and the other half a seat. Your father is tired, my
mother explains, her voice pained, and looks at my older sister,
Ana, who asks how my day was, and I do my best to pretend I
am not about to dive into the food laid out in front of us and
wonder why they are behaving as though this were a perfectly
normal day, as though we ate like this every day, as though my
father didn't exist, as though he weren't upset that his favorite
food would be left uneaten.

It was nice, I answer between mouthfuls. My mother fetches
a blanket for my father, who has started to snore, and now that
I have stuffed myself full, I ask if I can be excused. I want to tell
my best friend Agim all about Krujë and Skanderbeg and show
him my marbles. We live in the same two-story house with
a general store on the ground floor and two identical apartments on the floor above. A living room, a kitchen, two bed-
rooms, and a hallway, the bathroom cordoned off with a set of
curtains. We look identical too, almost, and sometimes people
mistake us for twins.

I greet Agim's mother and father, a man who speaks very
seldom and who doesn't get along with my father because they
disagree over politics. I don't know much about it, but I know
that Agim's father hated Enver Hoxha while my father swore
and continues to swear by the name of the PPSh, the Communist party Hoxha led for forty years. Agim's father believes that
the hundreds of thousands of bunkers Hoxha put up around the
country are the work of a paranoid lunatic who believed that
other countries were planning to invade Albania. But nobody
is interested and nobody ever will be interested in this forsaken
country, this prison for insane leaders, this asphyxiated people,

Agim's father says. Nobody cares about this rotten country, this land the shape of a lump of shit being kicked by the heel of Italy's boot. Once, when Hoxha was still alive, the men of the Sigurimi came to the door and took Agim's father away, kept him under arrest for several days, and accused him of fraternizing with the capitalists and disseminating capitalist propaganda. He never spoke about his time in prison, but from his battered face and his limp we could all tell he had been beaten, and when Hoxha eventually died of his various illnesses and power was transferred to Ramiz Alia, Agim's father celebrated like many others.

I knew what might happen to anyone who opposed or stood up to Hoxha and his regime, because Agim and I had often thought and talked about it. The same things happened to thieves, to those who tried to hide their wealth, or to those who didn't inform on known capitalists. They were thrown behind bars to rot, then they were executed as a warning to others during elaborate ceremonies in the city square. We had never been to a public execution because we were too young, but we knew that talking about Hoxha was forbidden, asking questions about him was forbidden, he was unassailable, distant and out of reach, yet he was present in every minute that passed, in the air we breathed and the ground beneath our feet, and we know there are places where Hoxha continues to exist—in the words and phrases people say to reach back into the past, in the hats that men lift from their heads before saying a prayer of thanks, *Thank God that time is behind us, thank God that man is dead and buried,* they say, placing their hats back on their heads without understanding that, in this gesture too, Hoxha lives on.

I am walking toward Agim's bedroom when his father suddenly answers my greeting from the living room and asks how my father is doing. Well, I reply, somewhat taken aback, because never before has he addressed me with so many words about my father or his well-being. To my even greater surprise, he stands up from the floor, walks over to me, and places a hand on my shoulder. Give your father my best regards, he says, and I promise to do as he asks and continue toward Agim's room, upset, as I get the impression I am the last person to hear about my father's illness.

Agim is a year older than me but much smaller. He eats irregularly and only a little at a time because he doesn't want to grow too big. We go to the same school, and he is by far the best student. He studies foreign languages and picks things up easily, and though he wants it to look like he doesn't need to put in the slightest effort, I know that he studies hard because he and his father go to the library every week, and his father picks out the books that Agim reads in the evenings. Sometimes he reads to me. Often I find it hard to keep up because the stories are so terribly metaphorical and I seem unable to interpret them like Agim and his father, with whom Agim has passionate discussions about them.

One of his favorite stories tells the tale of an old man who goes on a long fishing trip and who, after encountering many misfortunes, is forced to return home without a catch, powerless, and when Agim had finished reading it he said it was a wonderful, sad book telling a story of desire, of a man who has given everything he has to give yet who must still accept that desire alone rarely leads to the realization of desire. Yes, I said, looking him in the eyes, I must read that book someday, I said, looking away again.

In another of his favorites, animals begin taking control of a farm they have commandeered from a drunken old farmer. Then there's a revolution, Agim explained, enthralled, both his hands clenched into fists, his eyes and mouth wide open. Then the pigs that started the revolution get into an argument, and the counterrevolutionaries are either killed or chased from the farm. He nearly frothed as he said this. Imagine, Bujar, the animals form a totalitarian society. With this he brought his account to an end and presumably imagined that I would be as excited about this as he was, that I would see the same connections as he did, but instead he had to explain to me what the word *totalitarian* meant and that this is what it used to be like in Albania not so long ago, and when I replied by saying that animals can't talk, he didn't show me his frustration or disappointment—he never did—but patiently explained everything again.

Agim understands things like this, and even the most complicated words flow from his mouth the way water bubbles in a brook. Agim knows a phenomenal amount—details of the lives of important people whose names I can barely remember; he writes flawlessly and his handwriting is beautiful, and sometimes I feel ashamed by my own ignorance, especially when he asks me my opinion about things that I would never dream of thinking, questions like *Do you realize how narrow-minded it is to think that there are only two genders in the world, two types of people, men and women?* Then he might state as simple fact things that nobody else would dare say out loud, things like *All religions are the same,* or *Women are far more intelligent than men,* or *English is the simplest language in the world.*

Each morning we walk to school together and in the afternoon we walk back home, and on dark evenings the journey frightens us so much that we walk hand in hand or run, because at home and school people are constantly telling us how dangerous Tirana is these days. Children are abducted from their parents' arms, they are drugged to make them fall into a deep sleep, and when they wake up again, if they wake up at all, if their organs haven't been cut out and sold, they are already far away, they have crossed an ocean and find themselves in a dark room, cold and alone. At times the dangers of the outside world and the weapons people own make us wonder what could happen if you're not careful enough, if you don't keep an eye on your own shadow.

You could be shut away in a mental asylum, a place where the deranged staff give the patients electric shocks and force them to swallow poison. You could end up like the Christians living in the north of the country who are tortured to death, those poor, wretched men and hopeless women who are left dangling upside down, the blood running to their heads, or whose feet are singed with a red-hot iron. Even thinking about such things makes us quiver as though someone were wiping us around the neck with a cold, wet towel; it shocks us so much that we can only wonder how disturbed a person needs to be to even think of doing things like that to another human being.

Agim is sitting by himself in the middle of the room; he has placed a set of cards on the floor and is playing *zhol* against himself. *Do you want to play?* he asks. I nod and sit down opposite him and look at his delicate face and slender body. He has tied his long black hair in a bun and pulled on a shirt belonging to his little sister and a pair of tight long johns that run along the contours of his thin legs. He looks just like a girl, and when I tell him so Agim smiles, his lips pressed tightly together, and holds out his long arms like a satiated fox, though my intention is to make him understand that this is why people beat him and call him names at school. Why don't you dress more normally? I've asked him so many times. Why don't you wear clothes like mine?

I'm sorry about your father, Agim says, and the words come from somewhere so deep within him and with such difficulty that he is almost moved by his own condolences. Then he deals the cards and we start playing. I take the marbles from my pocket and show them to him. He admires them for a moment and suggests we use them as stakes in the game and that we play rounds of *zhol* until one of us has six marbles, and I smile because now there is a perfect number of marbles for the game.

As the cards hit the carpet we talk about everything, about the time we stole pears and pomegranates from the yard behind one of the nearby houses and how we climbed up the hillside and threw stones at the passing buses and the tramps wandering along the road with their mules, how we once stuck a long stick into a snake's nest and how we were almost bitten, about the time we climbed up Mount Dajti in the pouring rain and we were so tired that we crawled into a bunker and fell asleep in each other's arms, though we were afraid the wildcats, wolves, or bears might attack us during the night, and how the following morning we awoke to the smell of pine trees and gazed out across Tirana where the buildings looked like balls of dust and the roads resembled a labyrinth of rivers, and how we spent the whole day exploring the waterfalls and caves along the hills of the mountain and how we kicked thrown-away plastic bottles and pieces of litter into the ravines and to the side of the pathway, out of sight. We'll be together forever, says Agim eventually, and I reply by telling him that he is my best friend and will be my best friend for all eternity.

As we sit there playing, Agim asks me what I want to be

when I'm older. I don't know, I reply after a moment's thought, and my cheeks begin to blush. *If you could choose, what would you be?* he repeats and I mutter something indistinct. I don't know, a policeman maybe, I manage to say, or maybe a lion, I say when he falls silent. We both laugh. At least a lion doesn't have to think so much, I try to argue, pulling a card from the deck. You can be anything you want to be, says Agim, as long as you work hard enough. I can help you, he says and gives me a warm, benevolent smile, and the blush on my cheeks disperses because I know that with his help things will surely work out, with his help—if only I could have a tiny fraction of his intelligence— I truly could be anything I wanted.

What about you? I ask. And now Agim starts to talk, and he talks at great length, almost without stopping for breath, as though he had planned his question knowing I would eventually ask him the same question too. I don't know either, he begins, I haven't decided yet, there are so many options, a surgeon perhaps, or a lawyer, he adds and closes his eyes for a moment—and I'm not sure whether he is thinking about the future or whether he is hoping for a joker from the pack. But that would be too easy, he says eventually, and I look at him in bewilderment from beneath my eyebrows. I mean, to become something you could become through hard work. Anyone can be hardworking, he adds.

"I want to be talented at something," he says with a note of sadness.

"But you're talented at everything," I respond, looking at him all the more confused.

He interrupts me. "No, it's not the same thing. I want to be able to sing or draw or run very fast," he continues, snatching a mouthful of the next piece of conversation. "I want to be unique. I want to have something that nobody else has. Do you understand?"

"Yes," I say, nodding my head, all the while keeping my eyes on the pack of cards, though I don't understand him in the slightest because as far as I can see a person is always unique, always sounds and looks like himself; there are no two people alike, not even fully identical twins.

I am the first to get six marbles, and I have the feeling that Agim let me win. Then Agim stands up and skips to the other side of the room, light as a fairy, opens the wardrobe, and begins rummaging through his sister's clothes. He pulls on his little sister's sleeveless red shirt as though I weren't in the room at all and asks whether we can play husband and wife. Again I look at him in bewilderment but I agree; I stand up and say that he must be the woman and I am the man. That's right, he replies, placing my arm around his lower back and his own arm around my neck.

He begins walking me through the room, and I realize he wants us to dance. I imagine that Agim is a woman, and it is so easy for me, so effortless, that I realize I am like Skanderbeg, and that the most impressive parts of my father's stories were neither Skanderbeg's glorious victories in battle nor his horse, neither the size of his army nor the breadth of his patriotism, but his ability to imagine. For years Skanderbeg hid in the dark, he lived his life in perfect silence, in the shadows along the walls of ornate palaces and imposing gladiatorial arenas, all the while allowing his immortal thoughts and his faith to simmer like a slowly bubbling stew. He was a snake who withdrew into his burrow to lie in wait for his prey until finally he gripped his sword as a sign that the years of waiting and imagining had come to an end.

Agim sniffs at my hair and places his head in the crook of my shoulder, then he stops and asks me to lie with him on the mattress. As I lie down next to him he crosses his legs and stretches one of them up toward the lightbulb dangling from the ceiling. The room is small, its walls yellowed and the paint flaking, the dark-red carpet smells like old socks, and in the small window is the reflection of an Albanian flag hung on the wall.

"I think my father is going to die soon," I say.

"I think so too," Agim says. Again he tells me he is sorry and squeezes my hand tighter, then presses tighter against me and kisses me on the cheek.

ALL MY FATHER'S STORIES

When I was little my father used to tell me stories about Albania and Kosovo, about Albanians who overcame their fears and looked the most dreaded beasts in all legend right in the eye, of clowns who gambled away their house because they believed the word of a wretched Serb—tales of the landscape of his childhood and youth, a place to which he returned in his stories with a sense of longing for what he no longer had in his new homeland. He told stories about his family and school, of his brother with whom he used to sleep in the hallway of the house, of his father and mother, whose lives were nothing but a cycle of sowing and reaping the harvest, of the bitter winter nights with no electricity that he spent studying by the light of a flashlight, of the teacher who was in the habit of beating all the other pupils except my father, because he was as diligent as a mule.

He told stories of houses that had once been homes but that today were nothing but ruins, of men and women who had

turned their backs on their hometowns because their foundations, filled with land mines, had turned them into cemeteries,
of the dead who were never found and the lost who didn't want
to be found, of places that he wished might mean as much to
me and Ana as they did to him. And we listened to him, spell-
bound, because his stories were peppered with incredible events
and magical creatures, like any story worth telling always is.

Long before the start of my own story, my father moved
from Kosovo to Albania. He completed a degree in business
at the University of Pristina and moved to Tirana, a city he
considered enormous, because he didn't believe in Yugoslavian
socialism, in Tito, or in the idea that Yugoslavia could survive
the pressure of all those religions, languages, and cultures. *People that different cannot live side by side, that's how it's been and that's
how it'll always be,* he said to his family, who opposed the idea
of his moving away. In Albania they speak the same language,
my father told them, pure Albanian, not some bastardized
tongue, and there's more work over there, Hoxha has grown
the economy and increased the standard of literacy. Besides,
Tirana isn't even that far away, my father continued, and eventually convinced his family. *I am a strange bird, always changing
location, free as a two-headed eagle,* my father said to us happily,
holding out his arms like wings and bursting into a volley of
cawing laughter.

My father told us how he met our mother, the love of his
life, in a park in the granite center of Tirana. It was the beginning of August but the air was still scented with the freshness
of May. My father had been to a job interview, where he had
been asked a series of questions, and already he was ashamed of
the answers he'd given.

He was handsome and swarthy, dressed smartly in clothes a

man should wear when the person interviewing for the job is none other than the bank manager himself, and he was walking toward a woman. She, meanwhile, was on her way home from lunch. She too was beautiful—dark haired, brown eyed, her face round. She was wearing a long, dark-brown dress with sleeves, black sandals with rounded tips, and a black silk scarf, which she had wrapped around her shoulders. She had been enjoying lunch with her father, ordered her favorite dish—sardines marinated in lemon juice and served with coleslaw—and had sat stroking her hair as she listened to the demands of her father, who worked in a government ministry.

My mother's father wanted his daughter to get married as soon as possible; he had even lined up a group of possible suitors for her, because he was afraid he might lose face if she remained unmarried for too long. On that occasion, just as on the occasions before, my mother hadn't dared tell him she wanted to make her own decisions about her marriage; she was annoyed at herself and decided to deviate from her usual route and walk home through the park instead.

That woman's face is so expressive, so milk white—that's what my father thought as he saw her stand up straight next to the fountain, and that man's eyes are the color of chestnuts and full of woe, thought my mother as she saw him approaching across the park. He was walking steadily from the direction of Bajram Curri Boulevard and soon crossed Lumi i Lanës, the river running through the city. She turned into the park from the direction of Myslym Shyri Avenue; to his eyes she moved with the grace of a gentle sea creature. The sky rising up behind the man looked like a sheet of crystal, and the grandness of the government buildings behind the woman sighed with Enver Hoxha's immortal presence.

Then they passed each other. A second later the man came to a stop without fully understanding why stopping felt so necessary, for in the course of his life he had walked past thousands upon thousands of women who would have been more than willing to walk by his side. When the woman heard him stop, she stopped too.

"What is your name?" the man asked as he turned to look at her tall, slender back.

The woman waited without turning.

"My name is Afërdita," she replied, then turned, and upon noticing that the man was still smiling, she continued. "And what is your name?"

"My name is Afrim," he replied, smiling. "It begins with the same letters and means almost the same as your name."

The woman began to smile. Afrim, *closeness,* and Afërdita, *daybreak is close.*

And so they met, the way people meet in the most classical of stories, in a park as the sun beats down at the sweltering height of summer. They were two random passersby who lived in the same city, separate from each other and unaware of each other until a single moment brought them together, and after that they never stopped thinking about each other, or being in each other's company, and nothing was ever the same again.

They went to restaurants and the movies, took walks together and visited museums. My mother learned that my father came from a modest family. He was born to a family of poor Kosovar farmers, the second son in the Communist hierarchy, the third child. Her family, on the other hand, was full of diplomats, doctors, lawyers, and professors, and they lived in a desirable location in the center of Tirana.

"I am destined to do something special with my life," he

once said over dinner in a restaurant and took her hand. "That's why I moved here."

She could feel the softness of his skin, like a ripe banana, against her own; she listened to his self-assured way of speaking and fell in love with him. After convincing the woman's father with a story of how a farmer's son grew to become a bachelor of business, they were attached to each other like opposite poles of a magnet, and eventually he took her to the altar. He began working in a bank and came home each evening via the grocery store, where he bought the woman a can of sardines and some lemons, which she used to season the sardines, and they ate them on slices of corn bread.

A few years later they had a daughter and, at the woman's request, gave her the name Ana. *All across the world people know this is the name of a beautiful woman,* she argued. *Besides, it is in the name of this beautiful city.* The woman remained at home to look after their daughter and the man went to work. He could not have been prouder of his wife and daughter—and of the fact that he was able to be the breadwinner.

After another few years the woman began to yearn for another child, and the man barely noticed when she decided that the boy's name should be Bujar. *It is a good, traditional Albanian name,* she said, defending her decision. *Besides, the letter B comes straight after the letter A.* And that is the story of my family. The four of us formed a unit of which my father was as proud as one can be of something so wholly average.

In a story set at the dawn of time, a wise old man gave his three sons the task of building a sturdy wall around a fortress at the top of a hill, to protect the fortress and the town around it from external threats. In a single day the brothers built an enormous brick wall, but inexplicably the wall collapsed during the night. The following day the brothers built another wall, this time of stone, but when they returned to the site of the wall on the third day, they saw that once again it had collapsed.

That day an old man walked up to the top of the hill and gave the hapless brothers a piece of advice. He explained that the wall would remain standing only if a woman was buried alive inside it. This could not be any woman; it had to be one of the three brothers' wives. The wise old man told the brothers that the task had come from God himself and that the wife to be sacrificed would be the one who served their meal that evening.

At this point in the story my father lowered his voice, clasped his hands together, and seemed to savor his next words. On their way home that evening, the brothers agreed that none of them would tell their wives what the old man had said. Still, the eldest of the brothers, Durim, warned his wife and told her to tell a lie and say she was unwell. The middle brother, Dardan, did the same, while the wife of the youngest brother, Diar, who kept his word, prepared a meal and served it to the three brothers.

After the meal, Diar's wife, Rozafa, was told that she was to be buried alive so that the wall built at the top of the hill would remain standing. Rozafa agreed to this, but on one condition: she demanded that she be left a few small holes in the wall and that a rope be strung between the wall and her little boy's cradle. Rozafa's final wish was to be able to rock her son.

The brothers agreed to Rozafa's demands, and on the fourth day they bricked her alive inside the wall. They left Rozafa two small holes: one she used to breathe, and through the other she stuck out her hand and rocked her son's cradle until she died.

Her son grew into a great warrior, and as time passed Rozafa was buried deeper and deeper inside the wall; her skin turned to moss, which to this day grows across the surface of the wall, and her hair grew into an enormous vine that swaddled the wall like a blanket around a sleeping child.

God, a man with a big white beard who, as I sat listening on the floor, I imagined looked just like Skanderbeg, nodded contentedly at Rozafa's sacrifice and created the rain from her blood. He plagued Durim, Dardan, and their wives with sickness and childlessness, and when they died he did not let them enter the Kingdom of Heaven. From the milk of Rozafa's breast God created the color white, and from her maternal love he created all that is good. In return for her sacrifice, Rozafa was granted eternal life in Heaven. Her body is the very bricks and mortar of a wall that will not come asunder, and her soul has been given eternal rest in God's heavenly paradise, where Rozafa was reunited with her loved ones.

Another story my father used to tell us was that of a young boy named Ilir Jakupi, who lived in a remote village in the countryside more than a day's walk from the nearest village and three days' walk from the town. Ilir was a quiet, sensitive boy, clumsy and with bad posture, a boy who enjoyed spending time by himself, and his timid character was a terrible disappointment to his parents, Arian and Fazlijë, whom God had cursed by giving them twelve daughters and a son whom their relatives mocked, calling him the thirteenth daughter.

One day Ilir's father asked the boy to accompany him on a trip into the town; together they were to fetch enough salt, sugar, and flour to feed the family during the winter months.

Throughout the long journey, Ilir's father told his son stories of Albanian heroes, of an Albanian man's self-respect, which must be defended to his final breath, of an Albanian man's honor, the offending of which was the greatest sin of all, and of the responsibility an Albanian man must shoulder for the dignity of his family.

On their journey home they stopped at an inn owned by an old man. His father sat at the counter and Ilir sat next to him, and his father ordered them both a portion of bean stew. When the innkeeper handed them the plates, the clumsy Ilir gobbled his food as though he had not eaten for days. He ate so hastily that his plate fell to the floor, and so it happened that Ilir managed not only to soil the inn's creaking floorboards but also the boots and trousers of the man sitting next to him.

The other guests in the inn jumped to their feet despite Ilir's profuse apologies. The men gathered at the scene of the crime to assess the situation. They asked for Ilir's name, and Ilir knew it was best to answer them immediately, to give them his name and his father's name, and the man covered in bean stew introduced himself too: his name was Kreshnik Kaqibegu and his father's name was Fatos Kaqibegu.

"Well, that's that," said one of the men, a rifle slung over his shoulder.

"Yes, that's that indeed," said another, pointing a blackened finger at the stew now spilled across the floorboards. "It's a sure thing."

"No doubt about it," chimed a third, stamping his right foot on the floor.

"God be with you," said a fourth and looked up at Ilir's father, whose face was deathly white and ridden with shame.

After completing their investigation, the group of witnesses came to the conclusion that Ilir Jakupi had offended the honor of Kreshnik Kaqibegu and the whole Kaqibegu family, and with this Jakupi's family was in debt to the Kaqibegus. Once the offended family had set the price of the debt at five strong horses or the life of Ilir Jakupi, the head of Ilir's family, the esteemed Arian Jakupi, began weighing up the possibilities this situation offered. For days he walked around the garden outside his house like a fish swimming at the bottom of a pail.

Three days after Arian Jakupi had decided that the Jakupi family would repay the debt by giving the head of their only son to the Kaqibegu family, Kreshnik Kaqibegu shot Ilir Jakupi on the mountainside. As he approached Ilir Jakupi's dead body and propped the barrel of his rifle against the boy's lifeless cheek, as was the custom, the mountains began to whisper in Kreshnik Kaqibegu's ear, telling him that the debt had not yet been repaid.

When the Kaqibegus realized that the blood of Ilir Jakupi was not the sacrifice of a true man but was instead nothing but the scheming of a coward cursed with a useless son, they declared to the Jakupi family that the debt had not yet been paid. Through his obscene scheme, Arian Jakupi had brought endless shame on the whole family, and when Kreshnik Kaqibegu arrived at the family home and shot him too, the shame of the Jakupi family was so unbearable that the men of the family decided the only option was revenge—not for Ilir or Arian's sake, but for the sake of the Jakupis' lost face.

Bathing in glory, the Kaqibegu family accepted the Jakupis' vengeance, and with that the two families entered *gjakmarrja,* a vendetta, an endless cycle of revenge. Kreshnik became the *gjaksi,* the murderer whose blood would have to be shed next. He attended the funeral of Arian Jakupi, where he was not to be touched by any of the men of the Jakupi family, as for the day-long period of *bessa* no blood could be spilled. Kreshnik Kaqibegu enjoyed a meal with the Jakupi family after the funeral and looked at the women dressed in black who had arrived from the neighboring villages as they wept, pulled their hair, and scratched their faces, and watched as the blood flowed down their cheeks and onto their black clothes throughout the funeral, for they were not allowed to wash in the village or on the journey home, and with a sense of immense pride Kreshnik Kaqibegu swore to himself that he was ready to die, though he knew that this meant the Kaqibegus and the Jakupis would be in a cycle of *gjakmarrja* for decades and generations to come, for as long as there were men left to avenge the previous killing.

"Never do as Ilir Jakupi did, and never do as Arian Jakupi did, but behave like Kreshnik Kaqibegu and the men of his family," my father declared as the moral of the story. "For, as Kreshnik knew, certain things are larger than a single human life, certain things are worth more than the blood of a few men. The family's honor is one of them. That and a man's self-respect, his name, and how he bears it."

———————

In my father's story, death was preceded by the sun, for it was the sun that ultimately killed him. It had shone within him so long that it had filled his brain and organs with tumors, and eventually there was such an immense amount of sun within him that he had to be placed in the bosom of the earth where the sun could not shine upon him ever again, and it all felt utterly silly—to die of something as mundane as sunlight.

At the hospital they discovered that he was in the advanced

stages of cancer, which had taken root in his brain, stomach, intestines, and liver. *Nothing lasts forever,* he said at the dinner table. *The beauty of our life is that it ends, that is how it is meant to be, the old make way for the young and for all the children yet to be born, who will make the world a better place,* he continued, looking first at Ana, then at me, before asking us not to shed a single tear over something so banal and natural. *Besides, I will never truly die,* he said, placing his right hand on my head and his left hand on Ana's head. *I am here, wherever you are.*

Once he had said that, Ana closed the window. Her night-gown brushed the floor as gently as a horse's tail, and I pulled my legs up tight against my chest, and when she returned to the table Ana did the same. All of a sudden it felt as though the floor were bustling with danger: shards of glass, ravenous lions, unpredictable land mines, or the darkened, moldy guts of the dead, and if you stepped on them, the liquids inside would run along the soles of your feet like leeches.

My father was so relaxed about his illness that we were unable to prepare ourselves for what the following months held in store; when he talked about his illness to us and the guests who flowed in and out of our home, he appeared in seemingly good health. He woke early in the morning and slavishly went to work, and there seemed to be no room in his life for illness, and that's why I began to suspect things weren't quite the way my father had told us, because when he had the strength to discuss it he appeared almost intoxicated at the idea of what his impending death would mean for his loved ones and for him too, how it would change his mode of existence, how it would change the way people saw him and related to him. Through sickness he attained a level that he would otherwise never reach: everybody would listen to him, everybody would bring him whatever he wanted, and he could bathe in other people's attention, which was a mixture of pity and empathy.

When my father eventually began to feel exhausted, to vomit on the bed and over himself, he no longer thought in quite the same way, and when my mother no longer had the strength to carry him to the bathroom or the shower and his nausea medication no longer had any effect, he simply stopped getting out of bed altogether, the same bed where he died a few months later because, in addition to his honor and dignity, the sun had taken away his ability to swallow.

Over a period of months we watched as my father died, slowly withering like a tree. At times we felt as though he would never leave us and at others it seemed that in a matter of minutes he would slip into a sleep from which he would never wake.

Every day was exactly like the day before. We woke up at the same time as my father, we made him breakfast, tidied our rooms, went to school, came home again, and told him what had happened at school, and he listened until he no longer remembered who we were. Then he fell asleep and we fell asleep too, and as he lay there cloaked in sickness there was so much I wanted to tell him, such as all the times I had lied to him without being caught, that every now and then I had pinched money from his wallet, but I never did, and suddenly the time for atonement and absolution had gone.

One afternoon, when Ana was still at school and my mother was grocery shopping, my father beckoned me to his bedside. He wanted me to help him into the wheelchair and to wheel him over to the window so that he could look out at the street. I moved the chair close to the bed, locked its wheels, pulled the old urine-smelling blankets from above him, and, gripping his wrists, placed my arms beneath his armpits and hauled him up against my chest like a sack of potatoes. My father was ungainly; he had wasted away to nothing but a skeleton and his hair had grown so long that he looked like a mop, and when he moved his limbs they cracked as though his bones were breaking from the strain.

I pushed him up to the window and remained standing next to him. My father was slumped in the wheelchair because he was no longer capable of sitting upright, and the force of gravity made his lower lip droop so much that spittle dribbled onto his shirt. He then asked me to go into the hallway and bring him a cigarette. I took one from my mother's pocket though the doctors had forbidden my father to smoke, and though my mother would have torn me to shreds if she'd seen how easily I gave in to him, I lit the cigarette for him and held it up to his lips at regular intervals. After only a few drags, the filter was so wet that no smoke could pass through it, and when my father realized this his upper body began to shake, and for a moment I thought that this is it, the moment has come, he is going to die right here by my side, right now, to die of the cigarette I have given him. But he didn't. He simply wept.

I want to smoke, he began as the cigarette fell from his mouth into his lap, and from his lap onto the floor, *and walk, I want to walk and run and drive a car and ride a horse and write a novel,* he said, his voice hoarse. Then he stopped thrashing and turned his head to look at me, and I was unable to say anything to him as his voice slid along my neck like a slimy worm, all the way down to my lower back, and all I could do was clutch his arm and stroke his hairy skin as I felt his limp gaze on my face.

There's still so much life in me, he said, and once he'd said it I ran back into the hallway and this time I fetched the entire pack of cigarettes, and when I returned I was out of breath though I had taken only a few steps, for on the way I had thought what might happen if I didn't return to him with the cigarettes but crept up behind him and wrung his neck. Instead I stood beside him and lit a new cigarette each time the previous one became so sodden it was useless. My father's breath was heavy as lead and his irises followed the people loitering in the doorways of the house opposite; he watched an old woman with a loaf of fresh bread beneath her arm, a man waving to the owner of the store beneath our apartment, the mountains rising up in the distance, and the houses set along the hillside, shrouded in sand and dust, houses that looked like the heads of drowning people, and he looked up at the gaps in the clouds where the last beams of sunshine hung and cascaded to the ground like a woman's hair.

It happened in the early hours. That's when it normally happens, or so said the doctor who was looking after him, because in the morning we are at our calmest, and our brain releases a hormone that slows down our organ functions and eventually stops them altogether. Apparently the vast majority of terminally ill patients die in the early hours, when nobody is there to see them; it is as though the body were in some sense aware that its final moments will be private and lonely, that they are not intended for the eyes of the living.

Perhaps this is why the living keep death at arm's length, shutting it somewhere outside like a bag of rubbish, why the deceased is immediately whisked away and quickly taken to a morgue situated in the basement of a local hospital; the body is hidden out of sight, after which it is locked in a coffin and the coffin is then lowered deep into the darkness of the ground, and with that death is once again shifted a notch farther away, though in fact it is creeping closer all the time. That's what we do, though if you think about it rationally you would expect death to be put on display for all to see, because it affects every living being on earth.

I remembered my father once saying that at the moment of their birth every person is allocated a finite number of heartbeats, and as I sat at his bedside waiting for his breathing to stop, as I soaked another towel in warm water, I thought I might witness the moment when he raised his hands and sketched a great, beating heart above the table.

"It depends on the individual how they want to use their heartbeats," he had continued, taking a breath. "If a person becomes agitated, if he falls in love, if he becomes angry or upset, if he is grieving or easily frightened, if he does too much exercise or drinks too much alcohol, if he cares too much about what other people say or even if he doesn't care for other people at all, it will put a strain on his heart."

His hands were the size of giant rocks and his speech sounded like boiling water, and at times it seemed as though instead of talking he was on the verge of throwing up right into my lap, and remembering this made me feel very odd because it was almost impossible to imagine that soon my father's resonant voice would never be heard again, that nobody would see his passionate, gushing gestures ever again. Never again would he do the things that were so characteristic of him, so recognizable, like coming home from the bazaar with a gigantic hunk of meat, throwing it down in the middle of the living room so that it thudded to the floor like a boulder hurled into the water, and he wouldn't tell us that he got that lump of meat in exchange for only a chocolate bar and a can of lemonade. *Fat idiots will do anything when they're hungry.*

I remembered how serious and peculiar my father's expression was as he told me this, his eyes half open, his mouth taut, his lips pressed tightly together, as though he were carrying out the most important task in his life, telling me the one story toward which all the other stories he'd told us had been just a buildup. But when I changed his sheets or adjusted his pillows, when I moistened his dry, sandy mouth with a soft cotton swab, I began to understand that my father's stories weren't building up to anything at all, because there was no rhyme or reason to them whatsoever. People didn't wear out their heart by worrying or doing exercise, children weren't kept alive by simply rocking their cradles, and the rain wasn't created from the blood of a woman bricked into a wall, no woman's skin can turn to moss, and Tirana is not a place where people meet the way my mother and father did.

And I realized that my father was a liar, just like all storytellers, and that at the crux of my father's stories was not God but the lack of God, that and a megalomania born of the fear of dying, which in turn is fed by a person's deepest emotions and the singular desire to live forever. This became crystal clear to me during his final days, when I realized that my father was so terrified of dying that he began calling out God's name, not to ask Him to end his suffering but to allow him to live longer. But God didn't respond to his prayers, didn't care about his pain or about us, just as my father didn't care about us either, didn't care, for instance, about how much it upset me when he asked me to leave the bathroom, where I had only barely managed to carry him, because he wanted to do his business without me watching, didn't care how much it frustrated my mother and sister when he emptied his bowels into the bed and the only way to get rid of the smell was to wash the sheets many times in near-boiling water, because God wasn't there when my father died—the Devil was.

I haven't done anything I was meant to do, said my father, and my mother reminded him, *We have two beautiful children. The children,* he scoffed. *Anybody can have children,* he continued, turning on his side, and I sensed the bitterness in his movements, in his legs, which he used to kick away the blankets, in his twitching eyelids and itchy neck, in the palm of his hand, which he clenched into a fist, and in his crooked mouth, where his spiteful words became lodged in his limp jaw muscles.

Throughout his final days my father sobbed, either against my mother's shoulder or alone in his bed, and in his half-closed eyes I could see how much worse the fear of death felt than the pain itself, and all my mother was able to say to him was *I love you, Afrim, forever and ever. Whenever you're ready, you can let go. Don't be afraid, and don't worry about me or the children.* And I stood behind the door and heard it happen, his final breath like the sound of the rain stopping, my mother's silent weeping, the scratch of her hand against my father's skin, and I could sense the life escaping from my father's body in a single exhalation, sense how it disappeared into the room like a whisper, a word that doesn't matter, and through the slat in the doorway I watched my mother as first she blew her nose, wiped her eyes on her wrists, then stood up from the edge of the bed and fetched a blanket to cover my father's face, a face devoid of all expression and color, and I remember thinking I will never forget what a dead man looks like, that a dead body looks as though nobody has ever lived in it.

"Oh God," said my mother once she'd covered my father and sat down beside him on the bed. *"O zot,"* she repeated, standing up again and walking to the other side of the room to look at him, her hand in front of her mouth as though an unpleasant smell had just wafted in.

Perhaps my mother called out to God because she didn't know what else to say, or because she had sensed the same thing as me, the devastating distance that had suddenly opened up between her and my father, the act of theft that death commits, and the agonizing sense of rush that the deceased exudes into the space where life ends.

THE FUNERAL

The day after my father's passing, we set off in a bus that wound its way along the mountainous roads that join Albania and Kosovo, their path like a trickle of water constantly changing direction. My father's last wish was to be buried in the village near Pristina that he had left, never to return, and which we were now visiting for the first time.

As my father's illness progressed, my mother contacted my uncle Adem, my father's only brother, who worked as a builder. In her final letter, posted only a week before my father passed away, she wrote of my father's wish to be buried in Kosovo. *Afrim is very ill, and the doctors have told us to prepare for his death. It makes me sad that I will meet you under such circumstances, but we will all attend his funeral, and we will arrive in a few days, a few weeks at most.*

Accompanied by his two sons and my father's cousin, my uncle met us at the bus station in a tractor and a car. As he laid eyes on us for the first time, he kissed me on the cheek and Ana on the forehead, shook my mother's hand and offered his condolences, then his smile melted into a faint sobbing that he tried to smother by speaking only in single, sporadic words.

They carried the coffin from the storage space beneath the bus, placed it on a trailer attached to the back of the tractor, and covered it with a tarpaulin. Ana started to cry and I wasn't far behind, as my uncle was the spitting image of my father: he moved in the same manner, the way he wiped his hand on his shirt was the same, his small front teeth and flappy earlobes, the way he ordered his sons and cousin about, and the image of him I'd constructed through all my father's stories corresponded to how he was in reality, like my father's double.

My uncle told his sons and his cousin to drive carefully and sent the tractor on its way, then led us to a small restaurant situated at the edge of the bus station and owned by a friend of his. Inside, the white tiles on the floor and walls were covered in smudges, the leather upholstery of the chairs torn, the air a mixture of corn and cooking fat. You must be starving, order whatever you like, said my uncle after gesturing us to our seats.

We were indeed ravenous, as the journey from Tirana to Pristina had taken a long time. We ordered burgers and *qevap*, coffee and lemonade, and as we waited for our food and during our meal my uncle told us about my father, about the time when he and my father were young and inseparable, and as I listened to him it felt as though my father were still alive because my uncle sounded so unmistakably like my father and because the stories he told could have been stories about me and Agim. He wasn't just my brother, he said wistfully, he was my best friend too. I'm sorry he left you so early, but you know that he's in heaven now, and that is a better place, a place like no other.

At the end of our meal, the restaurant owner walked up to our table, placed his right hand upon his chest, and offered his sympathies. *May the deceased meet you again in heaven,* he said, and he refused to accept any payment from my uncle. When the owner returned to the back room, my uncle left some money on the table and led us to the car. Ana and I went into the back and my mother sat in the passenger seat.

We drove out of the town center, which felt incredibly small. In Kosovo the ground was dry and everything looked unfinished—the buildings, the houses, the roads, nothing had been cared for. Miserable-looking stray dogs skulked along the streets, the pavements were awash with litter. Rubbish spilled from the doors of newspaper stands and shop fronts as it might from a dumpster, and it seemed the streets were swarming with even more children and gypsies selling sweets and cigarettes than in Tirana. On the outskirts of town the houses were not only farther apart from one another, they were also smaller and more incomplete, most of them housing multiple generations while still lacking windows and doors on the upper floors.

The Serbs want to get their hands on this place, my uncle explained to my mother, who had spent the entire bus journey giving us a blow-by-blow account of the desperate situation in Kosovo. Increasing numbers of Kosovar Albanians were fleeing the Serbian aggression and heading for neighboring countries and Western Europe. *Milošević should be beheaded,* my uncle continued, allowing his eyes to take in the panorama across the mountains and valleys behind the windshield. *So many people have lost their jobs, their livelihoods, everything,* he said. *I'd join the KLA in the blink of an eye if my back wasn't in such a bad way. This is a truly saddening, desperate time for all Albanians,* he continued, *always feeling as though something terrible is going to happen, and keep happening. Every day someone around here loses his life. Did you know, nowhere in Europe has a nation been so scattered as the Albanians?*

Ana looked out of the window, and I looked at the back of her head and at my mother, who was solemnly nodding in time with the cadences of my uncle's speech, and the image of the Albanian people that he conjured up settled in my mind like a chapter in a tragedy spanning the millennia. All hope seemed to be erased from the Kosovars' minds. It was as though they lived in fear of tomorrow, and they were angry, angry with the Serbs, angry with the Croatians and the gypsies, and I wondered what would have to happen, what would have to change, how many wars would have to be fought by my uncle and his brethren, people who dreamed of a great, invincible Albania, in order for them to be content and proud. How can you be proud of something you haven't achieved yourself? I wondered.

When we finally arrived at my father's family village and its modest houses, we were greeted by a large crowd of people we'd never met before and who followed us around long after we'd been introduced to one another. It felt as though my mother, my sister, and I were precious museum items, so eager were people to examine our clothes, our haircuts, and the way we spoke. The Albanian spoken in Kosovo was completely different from ours; it sounded childlike and unsure of itself. People here used strange words, they called a plate a *tanir* instead of a *pjatë*, and a drinking glass was called *bardak* instead of *gotë*. Everyone was terribly religious and they were always talking about God, and they stared at us like strangers, especially my mother, who didn't dress like a Muslim woman. They behaved as though they were my father's true family instead of us, as though we were responsible for the fact that one of their own had decided to leave them behind.

There were no indoor toilets, so everybody had to go about their business in an outhouse in the garden, which meant that the entire garden smelled of feces. I remember feeling disgusted by the nearby vegetable patch and by eating its produce because my thoughts inevitably turned to the ground in which the food had grown. The people were poor, they smelled bad and talked incessantly, nobody seemed to have a job or anything in particular to do, everybody had yellow teeth and damp stains beneath their armpits, and as I looked out across the meadows where my father had walked and the houses in which his family lived I wasn't remotely surprised that he'd wanted to leave, because there was no room to breathe out here, there was no escape.

My uncle informed me that I would have to stay by his side for the duration of the forty-day *pamja*, because the local men would want to visit not only him but me too, the son who would continue the deceased's line. Otherwise people would start talking, he explained. The women would be in the house too, but during those forty days it would be inappropriate to communicate with them. And I remember looking at my mother as she interrupted my uncle and told him I could go wherever I wanted and talk to her whenever I wished. When I saw how vehemently my uncle stared at her, I said I was sure it wouldn't be a problem.

My father was buried the day after we arrived, and probably more than five hundred men gathered in and around the pavilion erected in my uncle's yard, and inside the house was almost the same number of women. As the clock approached midday my uncle and my nearest relatives fetched my father's white coffin from the cellar and carried it into the middle of the yard, whereupon the imam, whose presence had been requested, informed us that it was time for the womenfolk to bid their farewells. At this the women formed a line near the coffin and began walking counterclockwise around it, some whispering, some touching the coffin. Once the women had filed indoors it was the men's turn, and we formed a similar line and paced around my father's coffin, which was wrapped in the Albanian flag. After this the coffin was lifted and placed in the middle of the trailer attached to the back of the tractor.

My uncle clambered up onto the trailer and held out his hand to me. *Jump on board,* he said and pulled me up. I sat down opposite him, my father resting between us, and there was barely enough room for both of us to squat on the edges of the trailer. Then he gestured to his boys, who were in their twenties, to jump in too. *Place your right hand on the coffin,* he said and gave a whistle, and with that the tractor revved its engine and began transporting us at walking speed to the graveyard half a mile away, a cortege of hundreds of men winding along behind us.

I felt as though someone had hit me on the back of the head with a shovel and thrust icy hands into my gut, so violent it all seemed—the scuffed surface of the coffin and all the men I had never met but who had flocked to my father's funeral as though it were an outdoor concert, and at times it felt as though all those people were happy that my father had died because it gave them an excuse to get together and share news like *Did you hear about that baby that Ratko Mladić and his troops set on fire in Bosnia, or how the Yugoslav federal army tortures and imprisons innocent people, robbing sons of their fathers and wives of their husbands?* And I was proud of my father because it looked to me as though he was right when he said that people who are too different from one another can never live side by side. As far as I could see, Kosovo and the whole of Yugoslavia was in chaos, a strip of land inhabited by primitive cavemen, a place I wanted to shut outside myself because the stories people told about it felt too shameful, though no representatives of my people were guilty of any of these atrocities.

We—the deceased's next of kin—carried the coffin to the edge of the grave, and all around us hung the smell of rotten fruit, mature cheese, unwashed feet; my father had been festering in the warm coffin for days. The imam stood at one side of the coffin and we remained at the other, me, my uncle and his two sons, and the men behind us spread out across the cemetery like a smudged black blanket.

In his dark-blue suit and the embroidered hat that covered his bald head, the imam began to speak about how frivolous death can be, a matter of chance, and how we would all be reunited with my father in heaven. Then he said something I could no longer understand, held his hands above the coffin, and blessed it by shouting *Allahu ekber* three times, and his low, resonant voice glided down into the meadows and back up again.

Planks had been placed at the edges of the grave to help lower the coffin to the bottom. The grave looked bleak, the roots of various trees and plants jutting from the earth; it was dark and colorless, and the idea that this could be someone's final resting place felt somehow wrong. Once the coffin had been winched down into the grave and the planks pulled back up, my uncle handed me one of the shovels standing propped in the loose soil that the deceased's relatives then began to cast back into the grave.

As I shoveled soil and watched the white coffin disappear bit by bit, I felt an enormous sense of relief, similar to that I'd felt when my father had died but different nonetheless. It was neither gratitude that he no longer had to suffer nor liberation from having to watch him suffer but a sense of calm, of waking up after a long night's sleep. The fact that we had carried out my father's wishes by bringing him to his final resting place—and that he no longer had to wait in the luggage compartment of the bus or in the cellar—brought the incompleteness surrounding his life and death to a close. There was nothing left to say, nothing to explain, nothing to reason or understand. Instead there was emptiness, silence, a dark void in the middle of a day drenched in sunlight, the sound of men breathing heavily as though they were witnessing a solar eclipse and were afraid of entering a world of endless dusk.

According to some beliefs, the deceased's soul remains with us for forty days, in a state between life and death, and this is why the *pamja* is held. For the duration of those forty days the deceased's soul visits all the places it had once experienced life. The soul exists in the moonlight and the mercilessness of the sun, it resides in the cooling breeze that dries a sweaty face at midday and as night falls on skin pimpled with goose bumps.

For forty days the soul knows that it is welcome back home. It would mingle with the guests at the family's remembrance service, sit on people's shoulders, rummage through their pockets, and listen to all the stories people tell about it, and it is the job of the living to make sure that any words used to describe the deceased and stories told about him are uplifting and praise his greatness, his honesty and nobility. When the soul sees how many people have arrived to share the family's grief and when it hears that the stories told about its life are all good and sees the pain and the sorrow begin to fade from the minds of its relatives, then the soul is ready to leave behind the world of the living and move on.

For us, those forty days were filled with conversations that resembled one another. People arrived, walked up the hill to the house with the pavilion erected outside it, greeted us, bid us farewell and left. Everybody said exactly the same thing. People came from far away, hundreds and hundreds of people, even some people who hadn't known my father at all; then they left and the next people arrived, and at every turn I had to watch my words, I was allowed to inquire about the men's health only in a certain way, I wasn't allowed to cry because people would say the deceased's son was deranged with grief, I wasn't allowed to smile because people would say the deceased's son was happy about the tragedy, and all the while, through all the expressions of condolences and meaningless conversations, my father was sitting on my shoulder, invisible.

I hope you will find him again in heaven.
Death is a natural part of life.
You mustn't grieve, the same fate awaits us all.
This life is worth nothing at all; only the next life is worth something.
God's blessing to you, sweet boy.

After forty days I was sure that my father had left my shoulder a proud man. I could feel his departure in my muscles, in how loose my arms and legs felt, in the slowness of conversations, the unceremonious, inexplicable sense of absence, like standing alone in an abandoned house.

We said goodbye to my uncle and other relatives, and my mother swore that from now on we would visit one another more often, though we all knew in some way that this would be our last meeting, and my father was no longer present in that conversation either.

We were extraordinarily tired and didn't have the strength to talk to one another on the journey home. My mother asked me how things had gone with my uncle. Fine, I said offhandedly, resting my forehead against the bus window, and I don't think I had ever seen a night as dark as this. I thought about the tractor journey, the planks in the grave; I thought about what our lives would look like from this moment onward, how long my mother would live, whether she might become ill like my father and how long I'd have to look after her; I thought about Ana, wondered whether she'd ever find a husband and who would decide whether the man was upstanding enough; I thought about where I could find a job; and I thought about what death must feel like, is it like falling asleep, like dreaming an endless dream, or something else altogether—and all of a sudden I was so angry at my father that I could have killed him with my bare hands if he'd still been alive. That's what I thought, and then I began to cry and wished for the bus to topple over and roll into the gaping mouth of the ravine like a cigarette end thrown from the window.

THE RED SHOES

After we arrived back in Tirana we couldn't carry on like before; we didn't know what to say to one another or how to live, how to use all the time my father had left behind. We'd become so used to my father's illness that living and getting on with our lives now seemed tactless, almost an insult to my father's memory, so we all retreated into our own worlds. The city was becoming increasingly restless, but I couldn't bring myself to think about it and focused on thinking about my father, concentrating on special moments with him, like when he was sick and weak, grasping at the remnants of his humanity and saying things like *Take me outside right this minute, I've been lying indoors all day,* or when he would angrily say to my mother, *I'll fetch my cigarettes by myself if you don't bring them to me right now,* though he knew perfectly well that this would have been impossible.

Perhaps I wanted to keep him alive that way, or perhaps I felt remorse that I hadn't behaved more appropriately, that I hadn't said what should have been said, that I hadn't stopped my father from bringing shame upon himself and his surroundings.

Because after his death everything I had done for him felt like a mistake, all the words I had spoken to him felt wrong, all my deeds felt wrong, the way I scoffed at his ridiculous threats and laughed when he thought I was somebody else, the way I angrily swore at him as I washed his backside and another handful of diarrhea spattered on my wrist.

The days felt thick and viscous, the hours like honey dried to the bottom of a jar, our food was bland and we didn't eat much, and we would sit staring at the spot on the floor where my father had eaten his meals until eventually my mother stood up and covered the spot with cushions.

Although only one of us had gone, and we were no longer the same people, everything had changed, and everybody—the kids at school, the people in our neighborhood and extended family—thought we were so downtrodden by all that had happened to us that we started to behave as though it were all true and didn't make the least effort to get on with our lives. One moment you are breathing and speaking and the next you are festering deep inside the cold earth, unable to move or form cogent thoughts.

My father's death was most difficult for my mother, because for her my father meant much more than he did for me and Ana: he was a husband, the father of her children, the object of her passionate love. She shut herself in her room and came out only to eat and go to the toilet. During the day the sound of weeping filtered through the walls and at night we kept hearing her talking, as though she were in the room alone with my father. I saw Ana less and less; she stayed out late and left early in the morning, and because nobody was there to watch out for her comings and goings I was sure the silly girl would lose her life one day. I spent most of my time with Agim, told him my every thought, cried with him, laughed with him. I ate at his house too—just as little as he did, because it would have been impolite to take more.

In Tirana people had begun gathering in the squares to demonstrate. Families were suddenly starving and there was no food in the stores. Ramiz Alia gave speeches in which he praised Enver Hoxha and vowed to continue the tradition of the PPSh, though under pressure from the intelligentsia he conceded that this must happen in association with Western Europe and that through this, he promised, a new golden age would grace this land. But nothing had changed the way it was supposed to, nobody was able to move forward, people were suffering, and the newspapers ran stories about the country's colossal financial difficulties. I withdrew from the conversations taking place around me, didn't know what to make of predictions based on the value of the lekë, and didn't comprehend the ins and outs of financial terminology. All I understood was that the situation was dire, and the rest of the time I spent living, trying to survive.

People began filling the streets, each more emaciated than the next, loitering in parks and in front of shops, people queuing at the gates of the city's churches and mosques in the hope of food aid. Entire families abandoned their homes and illegally forced their way into the gardens of international embassies because they thought this way they would be granted a visa out of the country. We heard that people were moving to Greece, Germany, France, Kosovo, Macedonia, and Turkey—anywhere they could get to. Children in the neighborhood spilled into the streets selling anything and everything their families owned, girls barely older than me swarmed outside hotels and along roads with lots of traffic, selling themselves for money, and it was only now that we began to realize how poor we were, how poor the entire country was, how the whole of Albania was considered the black spot of Europe, a surreal place with no direction, no sense, a place about which nobody knew a thing.

We lived in a place that time could not reach, in an insignificant chunk of land where rational thought could not be heard. It was as though nobody had bothered to tell us until now of the circumstances exerting force upon us, and that in turn made it feel as though we didn't matter at all.

Europe's rubbish dump, Europe's backyard, Europe's largest open prison—the comparisons changed daily. The newspapers wrote of life in Germany after the fall of the Berlin Wall— the Germans had gotten themselves back on their feet, their people were unified again—while in photographs the French, the English, and the Swedish looked so pure, so well-to-do, that the shame I'd begun to feel in Kosovo grew so big that it shrouded the world I knew, everything, people who considered themselves decent and upstanding yet who stole one another's property and stabbed one another in the back at the first opportunity, my yellowed teeth, and the scruffy clothes I was wearing.

I was grateful that my father wasn't here to witness the chaos in which the whole country had been engulfed during his illness, for he would have spat at it as he would the face of a coward, and instead of cancer he would have died of disappointment and the ravaging flames of his own rage because, for the first time in his life, he too might have been ashamed to call himself an Albanian.

One day Agim told me that, while I was in Kosovo, he'd gone into his mother's wardrobe, opened the doors, and pulled open all the drawers, where he'd found gold and silver jewelry from the time when his mother had married his father. There were only a few pieces left, because in recent months people had been forced to sell any gold they had, though the bride is supposed to keep the wedding gifts received from the groom's family until the day she dies.

Agim had draped the jewelry around his wrists and neck and slipped the oversized rings onto his fingers. I was just fooling around, I wanted to imagine myself in a different place from this, said Agim, and I completely understood him because it felt as though nobody wanted to live in Albania anymore; I might have done the same thing myself.

Because Agim had thought he was at home by himself, he'd taken a red dress out of the wardrobe, pulled it on, and stood in front of the mirror admiring himself. *I looked completely different, Bujar, it was incredible,* he said, *especially when I put on my mother's red shoes too.* Then all of a sudden his mother appeared in the doorway. Without saying a word she tore the dress over Agim's head, snatched the shoes, clothes, and jewelry, and put everything back in its place.

That evening Agim's mother told his father about what had happened, told him there was something truly wrong with the boy because he seemed to think he was a girl, and right there and then Agim's father picked up his belt as though it were a club and shouted for his son. Agim knew to take off his shirt and kneel down in front of his father. *It didn't hurt at all,* he assured me, though when he showed me his scarred back I knew he was lying, because the skin was like that of a roasted chicken.

"I'm going to get out of here," he said as he pulled down his shirt, puffed out his chest, and held his breath. "And I want you to come with me," he continued, giving his shirt a tug at the back, gritting his teeth.

I wanted to strangle Agim's parents, lop off their noses with a pair of scissors, saw off their ears, stuff their mouths full of sand and glue their nostrils shut.

And where would we go? I asked him, and Agim replied that we could go wherever we wanted, *Anywhere would be better than this, I'd rather die than live here another second,* he said decisively. *Either way, I'm going,* he said. *Everyone's going—don't you listen to the news?* he asked, and I didn't doubt for a single moment that he meant it, that he really would leave.

THE SWEPT CITY

The more time passed, the more it became clear that my mother had given up—on me, on Ana, on life itself. Agim's father essentially kept us alive; we ate their leftovers, and my mother didn't seem to think there was anything wrong with it, anything to be ashamed of. *I don't know what I can do,* she said, *everyone has died, your father, my parents, I can barely take care of myself. Don't look at me, and don't ask me for anything, do as you please,* she told me and Ana and retreated into her room to weep, to wait for Agim's mother to knock on the door and bring us some of the food she'd prepared. And that is what Ana and I did: we came and went as we pleased.

I wandered around the city center like most children my age and some even younger. Tirana was chaotic; there were protests everywhere, nonstop. I tried to sell our belongings to strangers in the street, our crockery, my father's old clothes and shoes, his used razor blades with dried skin cells on the surface that still smelled of him, his old hats whose inside rims were faded with ingrained grease and dandruff. But nobody was interested in buying them because everybody was in the same situation, everybody was trying to sell things that were barely usable and that nobody needed. I begged shopkeepers and traders at the bazaar for water and something to eat, anything I could put in my mouth. Sometimes I was thrown a chunk of stale bread and sometimes a small cup of mashed beans or a slice of onion pie to go with it, and when Agim's father told my mother he'd seen me on the street holding out my hands and heard me begging strangers for a crust of bread, my mother didn't care, or at least it wasn't enough to bring her back from the brink. I think she simply wanted to die, because she probably knew that it would happen anyway. If we didn't do anything about it, sooner or later we'd all starve to death.

On the last day of March, after dozens of marches and protests, the Democratic Party of Albania won the parliamentary election. Albania was declared a secular state and everyone was guaranteed basic human rights, including the freedom of religion. On that day nobody was hungry because the last coins in people's pockets had turned into packs of cigarettes and bottles of cognac.

Agim and I went to Skanderbeg Square, where people had gathered in great, bustling crowds like scattered shoals of fish. In one of these clusters, a group of elderly men in lines were dancing a *shota,* in a second group a gaggle of shy little girls cast furtive glances at a third group where young men had gathered around a cassette player spewing at full blast a song that Agim recognized. The song's name was "Like a Prayer," performed by someone called Madonna, and the boys were singing along: *"I think I'm falling from the sky."*

"That's *si një lutje* in Albanian. It's a metaphor," Agim explained, stopping for a moment to listen and look at the men, showing particular interest in one of them, a youngish boy with cropped hair and smooth cheeks. "But I don't understand why someone like Madonna needs to pray," he continued. "Do you?"

"No," I replied.

"I mean, what does Madonna need that she has to pray for? What's she praying for in that song? What the fuck is she praying for?"

I wasn't sure what I believed in, but I knew Agim didn't believe in anything because his father didn't believe in anything either. My own father was a Muslim and my mother a Christian, but they never spoke to me about their faith in anything other than vague terms, saying things like God created the world and all the animals, he gave man free will, which has led to all the evil in the world, or to say that everything people say and do is written down in God's book and read out on the day of judgment, or that there is no point spending all your time thinking about whether God exists because God is great and God is everywhere and God already knows about every last thought of every living person.

Hoxha considered all religions to be dangerous. Though churches and mosques had existed for centuries, though they were everywhere and sometimes even right next to one another throughout Albania, and though people had always believed in something greater than themselves, Hoxha decided to close all the mosques and churches, and nobody said anything about it and instead got used to never mentioning God—because if they didn't get used to it, a harsh and cruel fate awaited them.

"Everything here is stupid," said Agim, probably thinking of all the people he'd seen in magazines and on television, people who lived abroad and for whom anything was possible, and if it wasn't they would fight for their rights and their very existence until they won. "What about us?" asked Agim and wondered how immigrants coming to Europe from Africa managed to get themselves an education and turn into successful doctors and lawyers.

"Then they dress up in fancy clothes and pose in front of the cameras and flashing lights and smile as though nobody else has sacrificed anything for their achievements, as if thousands of people haven't given their lives to secure their freedom," he said.

"Right," I replied.

"That bitch should come here and see whether she really needs to pray or not," said Agim, pausing for a moment. "My father said Hoxha was right about one thing, and that's the fact that there's no God," he said in a single breath, and once the boy he'd been watching disappeared into the crowds he turned to me and looked like he was waiting for a response.

"Don't say that," I implored him, because it felt as though he'd said something that you should never say under any circumstances. "You can't possibly know that."

"Can't I?" he snapped, staring at me, his eyes now almost threatening. "Does it look to you as though God exists?"

When I didn't answer him instantly, he started bombarding me with questions, as though furiously trying to prove he was right.

"Where was God when your father died?" he asked. "Where was he when a man killed that young university student for the sake of a wristwatch? Or where was God when the Serbs went into Bosnia to kill all those people, to rape those wives and daughters?"

"Shut your mouth," I said, shoving him with both hands as far as I could before stomping off in the opposite direction.

"Idiot," I heard him call behind my back, then beneath the sound of the sand grinding under my feet I heard his delicate feline steps, heard how he almost glided in my footsteps, how he wanted to apologize but settled for walking behind me like my confidant.

Then came April, and everybody had wasted the little money they had left and a thin layer of springtime dust settled over the cigarette ends and empty bottles littering the streets, everything was as it had been, the government's promises proved as empty as the ghostlike, desolate boulevards around Skanderbeg Square, where even the statue of Enver Hoxha had been toppled during the riots, and with that all those years were erased, forgotten, nobody had ever witnessed them, God did not exist and neither did Hoxha, and the people's prayers were nothing but a meaningless muttering inside their heads.

———————

On the second Friday of May, Ana disappeared. As she left for school and closed the door behind her, I didn't know it would be the last time I saw her.

My sister and I had never been especially close. She was a few years older than me; she had her own friends, her own status. According to the laws in the *Kanun* she would get married and move into her husband's home, and I would bring my future wife to live in our home, the room I shared with Ana would become a room for me and my wife, and our children would sleep in the living room until my parents died and freed up another room for them, and so it would continue from one generation to the next until the house eventually fell down and a new one was built in its place.

Ana would begin a new life elsewhere, she would be brought into her husband's family and she would look after someone else's parents instead of her own, and gradually she would forget where she had come from and start to call another place her home. She never became attached to my parents; perhaps it was because she knew she would eventually join another family, because she was only too aware of a system that had lasted for thousands of years, of a pattern that would repeat itself with her too, and of a fate that she could not avoid.

The day after she went missing I knocked on my mother's bedroom door. Without waiting for an answer I said that Ana hadn't come home that night. I heard my mother climb out of bed, walk across the room, and pull the curtains shut. The strip of light beneath her door turned a shade darker.

I couldn't concentrate on anything but my own helplessness, and I waited until noon, from noon to afternoon, from afternoon to evening, imagining what kinds of clothes Ana had put on that morning, a pair of straight black trousers and a red, long-sleeved blouse, a thin white windbreaker, clothes that didn't attract any undue attention and that clearly indicated that the person wearing them didn't have any belongings whatsoever.

I imagined her walking along the highway, on her right the steep mountains, their slopes wrinkly like a flabby stomach, on her left the undulating meadows, and behind them the woods aching with thirst. She was walking forward with determination, the low-rise white houses and the fields around them disappearing behind her.

In my mind a small white spot appears out of the thick dust.

It grows and starts to shimmer against the blue blaze of the sky, and eventually Ana notices it is a van. She flicks her hair behind her ear, clears her throat, and starts to fasten the zipper on her jacket. She suddenly feels cold.

Before long the van is close to her. Hands with lots of rings and expensive-looking watches dangle from the open windows. Ana stops and sees two men with short-cropped hair and dark sunglasses sitting inside.

The men step out and stand, silently staring at her slender body and thick curls. One of the men pulls a pack of cigarettes out of his jacket pocket and lights up, all the while glancing around at the deserted landscape, the mountains that now seem to be looking at them as they rise up into the clouds.

"*Qiko,*" one of the men begins in a chummy voice, looking over at his friend, whose mouth is twisted into a mischievous, smoky smile.

"I don't want any trouble," says Ana, her voice confident as she pushes her hands into her pockets and takes a step forward.

One of the men throws his cigarette to the ground and steps closer to Ana, bends down to meet her eyes, and presses her chin to one side with his finger. When the man begins running his hands through her curls, Ana turns her head as though to defy him.

The other man grabs hold of her with both hands, while the first lights another cigarette. Then everything happens very quickly. Ana gasps for breath in order to scream louder, she kicks and struggles, and the men laugh at her attempts to resist as they touch her breasts and groin and give her sloppy, wet kisses.

And her screams. They are hollow and carry all the way up into the mountains and far beyond, and before long her voice turns into a wolf's howl. It is the most shattered voice I have ever heard.

Once the men have bundled Ana into the back of the van, they drive away. For a while the sounds of banging and shouting can be heard filtered through the steel walls, only to be drowned out in the terror of gravel crunching beneath the tires and dust floating in the air. And thus all traces, all sounds of Ana, disappear.

I went into my mother's room. She was sprawled on the bed like a torn bag of flour. I pulled the blankets from around her and told her to get up. Go away, she said, then began weeping inconsolably, and a moment later her hands rose up to her face, her knees pressed against her chest, and her back shuddered in time with the air escaping from her lungs.

I ran out to the balcony and vomited over the railing and into the garden, the half-digested chunks of bread hitting the grass like the lazy clapping of sweaty hands. I went back inside, listened to the murmur of my mother's breath in the room, then went outside again, opened the door of the neighboring apartment, walked into Agim's room, and told him we were leaving, *I want to get out of here,* and Agim grabbed my neck with his right hand, wrapped his left arm around my waist, and pressed his forehead against mine.

"Let's go," he said, smiling, then kissed me on the mouth.

I pushed him back, wiped a thumb across my lips, where I could still taste the cherry tang of his breath, and pulled his arms from my neck and waist.

"Let's go."

II

At first I felt myself, so to speak, like a guest in the world of convicts—not just me, but all of us—I believe because of the understandably deceptive tendencies of human nature.

IMRE KERTÉSZ, *Fateless*
(trans. Christopher C. Wilson and Katharina M. Wilson)

1 THE EAGLE

'm standing on a mountainside in a pair of high heels, a set of white wings growing from my back, and I imagine this is what it must be like to be dead, as my shoulder blades snap open, my skin rips as though a filleting knife has been drawn along it, as the moist, dirty covering of feathers pushes forth from my back like a newly born, shapeless foal. Then, little by little, I start to feel a stinging in my new wings, like the sensation as blood begins to flow through numbed limbs, and my wings open up around me like a valiant suit of armor, as though there has never been a time when I'd lived without them, as though they had finally been set free to fulfill their purpose. I am about to leap into flight, from the mountainside and out across the orange sky, when my head shatters into a million grains of sand and drains over my shoulders, and a flower begins to sprout at the top of my spine forming a head, then another, like two rosebuds, four snow-white eyes, two mouths, and two long tongues with which I feel the heaving of the damp earth and the scorching heat of the sun.

There is a powerful sound, a deep hum like that caused by a sudden gust of wind or a small shock wave, and with that I rise into the air, my wings flapping at my sides, and I am flying. One of my shoes falls down to the mountain far beneath me where a familiar-looking boy is standing. The boy looks just like me, and he grabs the high heel with both hands, and after examining it for a moment decides to try it on, and I look at the boy from above, watch how he stands up, the shoe on one foot, then topples over and starts rolling down the mountainside, how he shouts as he hits the stones and branches strewn across the terrain, how he rolls all the way to the bottom, and how he eventually strikes his head against a boulder and dies wearing the high heel, in a land where no one will ever step foot.

As I open my eyes, my field of vision is flooded with bright, searing light. I hear the beeping of hospital equipment and loud conversation that I try to latch on to but that I'm too groggy to understand, and when I notice that my right leg is wrapped in a plaster cast and propped up on a bar hanging from the ceiling, I realize I've been dreaming. Swallowing hurts, my joints ache, for all my misery I cannot formulate a single thought, cannot move or call out to anyone, and I begin to cry, though for some reason I am convinced that my body is no longer able to produce tears. I lie still, and to me it feels like years before anyone approaches the bed.

Are you okay? someone eventually asks, and I notice that the stocky, jolly-looking woman standing at the end of the bed has taken hold of my ankle. *No,* I answer, then she disappears from the room and returns with two pills and a glass of water. She presses the pills into my mouth and lifts the glass up to my lips, *Well done,* she says, holding up her small, thick, penis-shaped thumb once I've managed to swallow the pills. I fall asleep, wake up, fall asleep, wake up, and after a while I begin to feel slightly better.

I've heard people say that you see the events of your life in the moments before death, but as I try to remember the seconds before impact I can't recall a single image, a single moment that I'd like to relive, a single person who might grieve for me.

I spend weeks in the hospital. At some point I am transferred to another ward, where I quickly realize that the patients are either mad or well on their way to losing their minds. My personal belongings are confiscated and I am locked in a room with only a bed and a desk. The ward is a depressing sight: plastic chairs, plastic tables, plastic cutlery, all surfaces painted in white and ascetic pastel shades.

The other patients on the ward seem confused and their speech is like porridge; they might suddenly burst into tears in the middle of a meal or shout out someone's name during the night; some of them avoid eye contact while others stare at you constantly. Many of them stay in their own rooms, just like me, reading books; some watch television in the common areas. I try not to make too much contact with anyone or raise my voice; I don't want to get into an altercation with anyone because the staff doesn't think twice about pumping us full of sedatives. The smallest mistake, contradicting or disobeying one of the staff, infuriates the nurses, then they march up to me, carry me to my room, and strap me into a straitjacket, though I don't see any point in trying to resist a group of people like that, and sometimes I lie still from sunrise to sunset, unable to move.

You are a very lucky . . . person, the nurses say when they are in the mood for talking, which is mostly just before lunch is served. *You almost died, but now you have another chance,* they add, and my doctor asks me about my homeland, my friends and parents, and I respond by saying I no longer have friends or parents, even though it's not strictly true, and that I cannot and don't want to return to my homeland.

"How do you feel now?" the doctor asks after a few visits, once he thinks he's got some clarity on what has happened in my past.

I sit opposite him in a large leather chair and think about all the things I could tell him about what it feels like to be me, that it feels like everything and nothing, like a slit throat, shoulders stiffened with cramping muscles, the pounding of my heart when I place my left ear against the pillow, almost as though I can't find my own pulse, as though I'm a mere cameo in my own story, as though I'm in a constant struggle with myself whenever I have to move from one place to the next or talk to other people. And that sensation is always present; there isn't a day that goes by when I don't think about it, about how inevitable it is that all life will eventually end. It is everywhere, in the pauses in my speech, between the words in the books I read—it is wherever I experience life, for wherever there is life there is the promise that at some point that life will cease to exist.

And I could tell him how many times I've thought about suicide, how many times I've thought about throwing myself in front of a train when I'm waiting for the subway, how many times I've climbed up onto the window ledge and thought about jumping off. I could tell him about all the lies, how I've sold myself to make a little extra cash, I could tell him that and he would probably believe me, he would believe I've had sex for money, sex with other men and old women.

"Not as bad as before," I reply, and by avoiding his eyes I give him just enough space to imagine that I'm thinking about my life and the events in my homeland, because I believe that by answering his questions I will make progress, he will check all the right boxes and will soon let me leave, and I won't have to be here any longer.

I was sad, I say after a moment. *I'm not happy here, that's the reason,* I continue, because I know that his questions are leading up to this. He wants to know why I wanted to kill myself by jumping in front of a van.

Then I start complaining. I'm twenty-two years old and unemployed, I begin. I'm studying independently and all the while trying to find a job. It's not easy here, I add, allowing a few tears to trickle down my cheeks. I've wandered around hundreds of cafés and restaurants and laundromats and asked for work, often right in front of the customers, and time and time again I've been dismissed out of hand, and in every single place the customers listen, curious, and when I eventually have to leave the establishment like an unwanted intruder what upsets me most is not that I yet again haven't been given a job but that all those people bore witness to my failure. Nobody deserves to be humiliated like that.

"Do you know how humiliating it is when you can't even get the things you don't want? You're a doctor, so you probably don't know," I say, and he swallows, lowers his eyes to his clasped hands.

People don't consider special—in any positive sense of the word—those who are too different from themselves, I say, and he raises his gaze to me once again. *That's the way it is, here and everywhere else,* if your native language sounds a bit too strange or you look like you've come from too far away, it's no longer special; it's strange, like a wild buffalo standing in the middle of a market square. And an immigrant like me, a foreign intruder who speaks a different language, should know and be constantly aware of the fact that I shouldn't strive toward the same goals and values as the Italians, for in their eyes I don't deserve them because my ancestors didn't fight for them. *A white wog, a gypsy, a Muslim,* that's what they call me when they hear where I come from, though I look exactly the same as them.

"Or do you disagree?" I ask, as the doctor doesn't answer for a moment. "What would you do if you were me? If you looked like this? If you looked this awful?"

He gives me a compassionate look, and with his encouragement I continue. *Things didn't go the way I'd hoped, but now I understand,* I say, staring past him, gazing at the paintings on the wall behind him, one of which shows the entirety of the Colosseum, a paean to the city's delusions of grandeur.

"What do you understand?" he asks, drawing my attention back to his eyes.

"You can never give up. As Nurse Maya says, life is a gift, and I've been given a second chance," I say, and it seems as though the doctor is trying to stop something approaching a smile of satisfaction from spreading across his face.

The following week he says that I can go home, but on the condition that I promise to visit his office once a week and attend meetings of a support group. He hands me a list of different groups and meetings across Rome, circles the one intended for me, and asks whether I promise to do exactly as he says.

I promise, absolutely, I reply, then return to my room and begin packing. A nurse I have loathed fetches my things and wishes me good luck. *This isn't such a terrible place after all, now, is it,* she says as I am about to leave.

On the way home I try to think of ways of killing myself, ways that would be surer to succeed, but for some reason I find myself thinking about my father and that transient moment years ago when I felt as though I belonged somewhere.

Back then I was curious and carefree, only a child, and I wanted to ask my father why the Albanian word for "Albanian" is *shqipëtar,* the son of the eagle, and why Albania was called *Shqipëria,* the land of the eagle, and why there was a two-headed eagle on the Albanian flag. My father sat cross-legged on a mattress folded on the floor and stirred his tea, and upon hearing my question he tucked his shins more tightly beneath his thighs, clasped his hands together and popped the knuckles in his fingers, tapped the mattress next to him, downed his tea in a single gulp, and asked my mother to refill his glass.

"All this happened thousands of years ago," he said once I'd sat down, and I listened very carefully because I could sense how much my father wanted to tell me this story.

The story was about a little boy, who one day was hunting in the mountains with his bow and arrow, when all of a sudden he saw a great eagle soaring above him with a fully grown sand viper dangling from its beak. The eagle had a white head and a crimson beak like a rusty hook, and it flew so fast that its wings seemed to cut through the sky. It landed on a craggy outcrop and the nest it had built of branches and twigs, dropped the snake into the nest, and flew off again. The boy climbed up the steep mountainside to the ledge and saw a young eaglet playing with the dead snake at the bottom of the nest, pecking and clawing at its scaly skin, its eyes and mouth, shamelessly flicking its lifeless body over and over.

But the snake hadn't died after all, and in the seconds that followed it suddenly stiffened as though from an electric shock. Its body stretched so that it was many times bigger than the eaglet. The zigzagging lines across its skin were covered in soil and dust but its sharp teeth gleamed, dripping with a hunger for blood and flesh, and in those same few seconds the boy grabbed his bow, positioned an arrow, and fired it, managing to pierce the snake's head just before its fangs could sink into the eaglet's back.

Then the boy picked up the eaglet, which was whimpering with fear, and took it with him. A moment later he heard the sound of the eagle's massive wings beating behind him like wind through a stormy forest.

"Why have you taken my child?" asked the eagle, weeping, as it landed on a knoll in the woods and dried its eyes on its wings.

"Your child is my child now," said the boy, and turned his back to the eagle. "I saved him from the snake, which you didn't manage to kill, so I can take better care of him." He carried on walking in the opposite direction, certain that now he could become a better father to the eaglet.

The boy heard the sound of the eagle taking flight behind him, and a moment later it landed on a tree stump in front of him. The boy took out his bow and gripped the vane of an arrow in the quiver hanging on his belt.

"Let's make a deal," the eagle began, solemnly spreading out its wings. "Give back my child and you shall have everything I own, my ability to fly, and the power of my vision. You will become invincible, and from then on you shall bear my name."

The boy agreed to this and handed back the eaglet, which as he grew older remained faithful to him and followed him everywhere he went, keeping an eye on him and watching his back. The boy grew into a man, and with his bow on one shoulder and the eagle on the other, he truly was invincible, just as the eagle had said, and after countless victorious battles the boy was eventually made king and given the name *Shqipëtar*, the son of the eagle.

I arrive home, manage to have a shower, and lie down on my bed. It is August and dust hangs suspended in the columns of sunlight streaming through the curtains, and for a moment it feels as though I might never get up again, as though a heavy tin plate is weighing down on me, bolted to the edges of the bed with me trapped inside like a bug in a cocoon. I think of the last few months, the time before that, the hopelessness I felt here and in Albania, the sense of boredom, the lack of fulfillment, like a piece of food lodged in my throat, and the incessant guilt that grips my heart like a strong man's hand.

Someone once asked me what death feels like. I asked him not to think about things like that, because we were both so very young back then, beautiful even, and the world was waiting to take us in its arms. Later I replied that it always feels bad when life comes to an end, because I've seen a dead person and heard many stories about the dead. I wouldn't answer like that now. Now I'd say that death is just a word, the feeling that you no longer fit in your own name, your external form, like having someone else's face drawn across your own.

To die and to be dead are two very different things, I'd explain. People can be dead in a variety of ways. Being dead is to go into hiding, to stop your own speech, not to remember to eat or say hello to your neighbors. It is not noticing the red lights, not experiencing thirst or hunger, the feeling that you want to die but that doing it in front of other people would be too shameful, though you don't have the nerve to do it out of sight, and so death is in fact the act of staying alive, waiting for death rather than it actually happening, being stuck between the two.

So I start thinking about the end of the world, the moment when it finally comes, when the sun doesn't rise across the sky and the planet stops turning or splits in two. I take great comfort in the fact that this will happen before long: the heart of every human and every creature will stop, and everything that has been created on earth, everything that is left, every letter that has ever been written and every story and nation will all be destroyed. I tell myself this, and go look at myself in the mirror; *I am ugly,* I say, *I am alone. I am so, so ugly,* I say and take my clothes off. *I am pretty,* I say then, *so beautiful,* and at that I find the strength to stand up and start again from the beginning, invincible.

2 A MAN'S LIFE

I remember the merciless sun in Tirana, the long summers, the old men with faces corroded by the spittle of the light, and I remember the litter on the streets and piled up at the edges of houses, children playing among the rubbish, women burning trash in the streets, I remember the black, heavy reek of melting plastic, the metallic stench of the sewers like the air inside a damp, rusted container. I remember the sense of nausea upon grabbing my crotch as girls walked past, because that's what my friends did, the anxiety when I didn't cry though I wanted to, because I knew that men weren't supposed to cry, and I remember the dizziness when my parents began talking to me about marriage and continuing the family line. I remember everything, as though it all happened barely a moment ago, and now I know that the farther away from it I have come, the more content I am and the more rarely I think about where it all began.

My mother once said that people think with their brains but

feel with their hearts. She was crouched on the bathroom floor washing tea glasses that were so delicate she had to clean them with her bare hands. *You'll feel it when you fall in love,* she said with her back to me as she submerged a foam-covered glass in the dishwater. *Your heart will feel it, and after that nothing else will matter. When you meet the right woman, you'll notice that you won't think with your head. Then you'll marry her, you'll have children together and look after us,* she said almost in passing, as though she knew precisely what my future would hold.

I have shown her words to be a lie, for throughout my childhood I hated myself with all my heart and mind, and I don't think I ever really loved anyone. I hated how obsessed I became with studying, how I walked, the sound of my voice, the smell of my sweat, and the color of my urine, hated how I starved myself, hated the binges this self-imposed regime brought about, and how woefully I would weep after bingeing. I wanted to be like the people I'd seen on television, wanted to look like people in the West with clean skin and neat clothes with no clumps of fluff, no signs of wear and tear. I wanted to look like a movie star, I wanted skin without any imperfections, without a single furrow etched by worry and the sun's rays.

I hated the things I could never become and what I therefore wished on those close to me. I wished a war would break out, wished my homeland would be attacked, wished that someone would drop an atomic bomb in the middle of Tirana, killing every last inhabitant. I wished a volcano would erupt, engulfing everything in lava. I wished my family would die, my friends too, everybody I knew, because only that way could they never follow me wherever I went.

I was ashamed of my family, especially my mother, who couldn't read or write and who didn't seem bothered by that fact. I was ashamed of my sister and the inability of my aggressive father to deal with his emotions in any other way but through violence. Perhaps this was the reason it was so easy to wish a dreadful fate upon them. In the end, their continued existence was immaterial to me, I wasn't that interested in them, and I didn't consider them special in any way. They simply existed; the fact was they lived in the same apartment and made sure there was always something to eat. They were on the periphery of my life, like music you can't hear properly over the noise of the traffic.

I couldn't stand the way people spoke about the past, Albania and the Albanians, as though there was something in our history that our future could never equal, as though there was something great and all-encompassing in our nationhood, as though Hoxha was the most important figure in our history, as though it was a privilege to have lived in that world, in the greatest lie known to man. I couldn't stand the way people talked about love and marriage, of a whole life planned out in advance: a chosen wife and a chosen husband, at least one son, the gleam of honor always at the back of the mind, wrapped around a person like a set of clothes.

I was nine years old when Hoxha died. The most visible difference from the previous day was that women were weeping in the streets and some of the men were walking around in celebratory groups, others arm in arm as though they were keeping one another upright; they had taken off their hats, holding them in their hands like bricks, and dragged their feet, ghostlike. I could almost make out the grief in their gait, some furious, some overjoyed, and I was afraid; everything felt, tasted, sounded so clear, there was a feeling that something irrevocable had happened, the sense that the whole city was attending a wake, and it felt as though the earth shuddered beneath my feet, and I imagined that deep under the streets lay the heart of the city, an enormous, palpitating heart pumping to an arrhythmic beat of its own and with all the constituent parts, its chambers and blood vessels the twisting sewer system, winding streets and alleys, the mountains surrounding the city like lungs around the heart.

After Hoxha's death, many people, my parents included, believed they were finally free. We bought a new television, a new refrigerator, then another new television, and before long my father wanted new furniture too. My father began praying five times a day, and my parents started talking about God. Suddenly the entire world that had been built, the world in which he and my mother had lived happily, no longer existed. In its place was a new life, a new tomorrow where heavy rainfall had washed away the past.

When I first arrived in Italy, I looked for a police station and told the authorities that I belonged to a sexual minority and that for this reason I could not return to my homeland. *They beat me,* I said. *I'm homosexual, it's very hard and I'm very scared,* I continued, because I knew this was my ticket into the country. The woman dealing with my case looked at me, and I guess she used those few seconds to imagine what it would be like if she fell in love with another woman and wanted to stand next to her beloved, the way she should, but couldn't because she knew that a large crowd of people would beat her to within an inch of her life.

I'll kill myself if I have to go back there. Albania is no place for me, I continued solemnly, after which she doubtless thought about all the stories the Albanians trying to get into the country told about their past. They were prepared to say anything to secure a residence permit and stay in the country, anything at all except the one thing I had just told her. *I'll do what I can,* she said, looking at me with compassion.

A few months later I was granted political asylum, then a few years after that I was awarded the permanent right to remain and an alien's passport. After that I moved to Rome and decided to forget everything that had happened to me, I erased my name from my memory, forgot my former home and deceased relatives, people who once walked by my side but who eventually fell by the way. I forsook my hopes and dreams, for there was nothing good about my past, there was nothing in the past to which I wished to return or that I wanted to tell people about, and nothing in my past had helped me get where I wanted to be.

I decided to create new hopes and dreams, find people who would become a part of me, and who with time would become my new family. I decided to take hold of each and every day, every moment, as though it were a unique opportunity, and I repeated to myself that in this country every day is a new chance to be a new person, to be exactly the kind of person I'd always wanted, because I had blindly believed that one day, before long, everything would take a turn for the better, the way books and movies teach us about life, and I would step into the spotlight, I would be seen. I believed that at some point this simply must happen, because there was nowhere I could return to. I no longer had a homeland.

But how can you go about starting over, working in a language you don't understand? What is the best first step? How can you establish a relationship with someone if you want to deny your past, your nationality, if you don't want to tell anyone anything about yourself, if what you most want to do is forget where you've come from, wipe your past away like a smudge of dirt from a shoe? In a situation like that, what choices do you have?

3 UGLY / BEAUTIFUL

My new life begins in Germany. I find myself living in Wedding in northwest Berlin, an area popular with foreigners and one of the poorest parts of the city.

I spend the first few weeks taking in the sights: I admire the tall Television Tower in Alexanderplatz and wonder how it was ever put up at all, I visit the site of the Berlin Wall and try to make sense of the pictures and messages in different languages daubed across the remaining chunks.

The people here are different from the Italians; they leave one another in peace and don't stick their noses into one another's business, don't care about one another's families or what other people say. My neighbors here don't ask me where I'm from, what kind of food people eat in my homeland, or what the people are like there, how far away my homeland is or whether there are even any flights that go there, what things the people there believe or whether women have the vote.

Germans are more intelligent and more cultured than the Italians. They are interested in where I am right now and where I'm going, and they tell you the same about themselves. My days are filled with people who start conversations though they know our paths will never cross again, elderly tourists whose eyes bulge in museum exhibitions depicting historical events one more gruesome than the other, and artists standing in squares and in front of buildings in their underwear.

I sign up for a creative-writing class. I've never written anything before, but I don't let that hold me back because I know I can tell a story or at least come up with something that might interest other people.

We meet once a week in a school classroom in Prenzlauer Berg, and when I arrive slightly late for the first session I apologize and hurriedly head for a seat in the middle of the classroom. I tug at my clothes and run my fingers through my long, loose hair, set myself on the chair, and lay out my things on the desk. I can feel my perfume spreading through the room and sense the other students watching me as though they know from my movements and the way I look exactly what I'm like and what category I belong to.

The suffocating conversation they must be having in their minds is part of the reason why I don't enjoy their company and why I'd much rather be alone. They speak of people's sexuality, their gender and nationality, as though they were things that never change, and their newspapers preface public discussion by making an individual the face and voice of a community, and nobody seems to care about how damaging this can be. *Schoolgirls enjoy reading adventure books too. In the construction industry there is one woman for every twenty men. Homosexuality is not a disease. Disabled children enjoy long walks in the woods.*

The teacher is a woman in her fifties who has published several thrillers and children's books that have been translated into other languages. She begins by introducing herself and her books and talks about her mysterious protagonist, a homosexual detective and his prejudiced partner. She speaks about herself for a long time, as though she wants to underline her own significance and contribution to global culture. *All writing stems from deep within. You can't tell a story if you're not being genuine. Always remember you're telling the reader a story and not what your protagonist is thinking at any given moment; the reader isn't interested in that. Always tell everything through events,* she says, as though she's finally remembered her job is to teach us the art of writing.

But, she says eventually, *perhaps it's time for the eight of you to introduce yourselves, tell us why you're here and what you want to write about.* The teacher crosses her right leg over her left and asks the elderly lady on the left-hand side of the front row to get the ball rolling.

"My name is Ann," the woman begins in a booming voice, then glances down at her clenched hands. She looks pale, as though she regrets her presence and the words she is about to say next. "My husband . . ." She pauses. "He filed for divorce and went off with another woman. We'd been married for over forty years, and I don't know how I can live without him," she continues, and lowers her arms to her sides. "That's what I want to write about, about being abandoned."

"Thank you," the teacher replies, placing a forefinger on her glasses and pressing them farther up the bridge of her nose.

Sitting next to Ann is the only man in the group. He introduces himself as Anton. He looks wealthy, the kind of man who people notice whenever he appears. His skin is bright and smooth, his nails gleaming and well looked after, his hair thick and impressive, his eyes blue.

He explains that his sixteen-year-old daughter has died—that she jumped from the fifth floor to the asphalt below, he adds like a seasoned liar—and I follow his movements, the stiffness of his neck, the way he scratches his thumb against his forefinger, and I listen to him, entranced. Then he asks why such a young person would want to miss out on the life ahead of her and explains that he wants to write a book about his daughter, a memoir of sorts.

"Sometimes I'm so sad that I wonder whether it's possible to die of grief," he muses, and presses his fingers against his eyes, and I am amazed at how openly the participants talk about their lives. "Parents should never have to bury their children. Life is so boring without her. That's why I want to write," the man says.

The teacher first blows her nose, then thanks him, then asks the next participant to introduce herself, and though the inevitable approach of my own turn cakes my throat in phlegm, I hear nothing of the following speakers, because something about the man's words has broken my concentration.

No, I feel like saying, you cannot die of grief because grief is what I know, but I believe you can die of boredom, because grief—the loss of the desire to act—is nothing compared to the lack of anything to do. That is what brings a person to ruin.

When there is nothing to do, when you've tasted every food there is, when you've experienced life alone and life with someone else, when you can no longer find music you enjoy, when you no longer take satisfaction in expensive evenings at a restaurant, the most famous attractions in the world, or the most revered works of art, when you are simply no longer interested in news about parents who travel on foot to the other side of the planet to secure their children's future, when you are no longer moved at the sight of two men who love each other being flogged in public in the middle of the afternoon, when you have no job and nothing is pending or around the corner and when you have no inclination to start anything, when you have nowhere to go at a certain time each morning and nobody with whom to fall asleep in the evenings, life must indeed feel deathly boring; then it probably makes no difference whatsoever whether you're alive or not.

I could write about that too, I think, and the man could write about it, he could get there before me, have his book published and become famous.

Excuse me, says the teacher.

A moment later I realize I'm hearing her voice for the second time, the leaves in the courtyard of the old school look like dead fish, and the rocks rise up in the distance like abandoned homes.

My name is Ariana, I begin, *I'm twenty-three and I come from Bosnia. Some months ago I tried to kill myself by jumping in front of a van in Rome, but I feel much better now.* The words flow from my mouth, and I notice I'm afraid that I don't stand out from the crowd enough.

The man turns to look at me, everybody turns to look at me, and suddenly it seems as though my story is the freshest and most fascinating, my misery and despair are something to really draw upon. *I am an exchange student, I study medicine at Humboldt University, and I don't know what I'd like to write about yet, perhaps about that, my experiences in Germany, perhaps about nationality and identity.*

I hear the man swallow, then he raises a hand to his shoulder and starts scratching himself. The teacher clears her throat, and again her glasses have slipped down her nose; she peers at me with pity in her eyes, and I bathe in their gazes like in the Jacuzzi of a five-star hotel until it is the next participant's turn to speak.

For the second session we each write a few pages about our life and thoughts. The others' texts are barely collections of disparate notes. Their writing tries to explore themes of loss and grief, or how life changes after having children, or how we are creating a future controlled by telephones and the internet: superficial things that anybody could write down. Badly written observations in which the writers essentially contemplate aloud, describe inconsequential matters with disconnected aphorisms copied from other books and thrown in for good measure.

My own text, however, is a story that I describe to the other participants as the tale of my own life that I've been honing all week. The protagonist is me, I explain, an ugly thing who spends her entire life trying to escape her terrible ugliness, only to find her abhorrent self again and again.

Once upon a time there was Ugly.

Ugly was born in Sarajevo to poor parents who gave their ugly child a beautiful child's name. Ugly was soon joined by a somewhat ugly sister, and she attended a school for ugly children, where she was by far the ugliest child of all. Ugly wore the same clothes every day because the family had no money, she constantly chewed her fingernails out of hunger, and she sat awkwardly in places where one was supposed to sit with a straight back because Ugly lacked both good posture and a sense of situation, and the only thing remotely exceptional about Ugly was her arresting ugliness. And Ugly knew this, because she was called ugly every day, whether it was because of her yellowed, crooked teeth or her asymmetrical face and shapeless lips, which looked like two deflated life preservers, as her teacher had once said.

War broke out when Ugly was a teenager, and that changed everything. Ugly's father was killed by a Serb bullet in Herzegovina. Ugly, Ugly's sister, and Ugly's mother managed to flee the war. They started a new life in another country, but it wasn't as easy as all that. Ugly noticed that in the new country she was even uglier, even more worthless. Nobody so much as glanced in her direction, nobody answered her greetings, though for their benefit she learned to speak another language and dress a different way. Time and time again Ugly found herself in cafés watching other people, people who lowered their heads or started laughing out loud when they noticed her ugly, repellent grin and her expression in which her crazed eyes were different sizes and her rows of teeth looked like a pocked, dusty road.

And so Ugly and her family decided to return home. It's best for them and us, they tried to convince one another, and again they began building up their lives from scratch. The war had ended, but it had changed the country. The people, even the buildings, weren't the same, her homeland had been destroyed, ruined, and it made her angry that she could no longer be proud of her country. She was angry at the men who had died in the conflict, men who had become war heroes, the history of Sarajevo, and the ugliness of the city. Her homeland was ugly, *every bit as ugly as herself. And so Ugly buried her ugly face deep inside hoods, hats, and scarves, and when she crossed the road she no longer bothered looking in either direction.*

When Ugly had had enough of suffering, she decided to become a doctor. After years of diligent study Ugly learned that she had been accepted to the department of medicine at the University of Sarajevo. From now on she would be able to take better care of her widowed mother. But what Ugly did not know was that even success could not rescue her from ugliness. She studied and studied and tried to push the ugliness farther from her thoughts, but in the early hours of the morning she stood in front of the full-length mirror and looked at herself and wept, wept at how the ugliness had settled in her past: her only memories of childhood, youth, and adulthood were of her ugliness, and it was only through other people's pity at her ugliness that she had anything to do with the outside world.

In this way Ugly lived her life. She grew older and her mother died, and then her sister, and soon afterward Ugly died too. She was zipped into the darkness of a body bag, and nobody had to tolerate her horrid face ever again.

After class there is a little time left for conversation, and just as I'd guessed, the man comes up to me straightaway. I have prepared for our encounter by dressing in attractive colors, a tight blood-red top and a yellow silken scarf wrapped around my shoulders. He liked my story a lot, he says, and hopes he'll see me again next week.

"I'm not sure this class is for me," I reply timidly.

"Would you like to have a drink with me?" asks the man. "There's a nice little café nearby."

"Why not," I say, flicking my bangs from my eyes.

The man takes the trench coat hanging over my arm and helps it over my shoulders. He thanks the teacher as he walks out of the classroom, pulling me along beside him like a bicycle.

In the café we sit opposite each other. Our conversation seems promising, with only a few quiet pauses, those too filled with long, meaningful glances, secretive smiles, and the furtive touching of hands. The man tells me a lot about himself, as though he's talking about his best friend. He has a master's degree from the university, progressed on his career path to a midlevel position at an information technology company, a job that has taken him from Paris to Berlin.

"Boring," he says to round off his monologue and clasps his veiny hands on the table.

Then the man gives me an encouraging look; it seems he wants me to share something about myself too. And so I begin to speak. I tell him about the country I've said I come from, its people, who love God and cars, a world in which the Serbs made it impossible to live, about things I knew about Bosnian history, the massacre at Srebrenica, the gang rapes and mass executions, about Yugoslavia and Tito. I tell him I feel embarrassed at sharing what happened in Rome with everyone in the group, because I'm about to graduate and become a doctor, I should know better. That's just it, says the man; dark thoughts and acts don't reflect a person's background, they're not in any way dependent on a person's position.

You're right, I say, and then words begin to flow uncontrollably from my mouth and I explain that I moved to Rome for love. *My Italian husband and I were so in love that sometimes I am still astonished that we don't see each other anymore, that he is gone, how incredible it is that all the love I felt for him and that I thought would last*

forever is now a love between him and someone else. That's why I did it,
I guess, because I had nothing left.

"I'm very sorry," the man says and places his hand next to
my own, his cold fingers licking the back of my hand.

I can see that the man likes me a lot, likes the story I had
written about my life—and everything I've told him about
myself he seems to like even more, as he looks me in the eyes so
intensely that for a moment it feels as though he can see right
through me and doesn't believe a word of it.

"I'm sorry too," I reply and move my hand to my lap. My
thighs are as moist and rough as a shark's skin.

"I really liked your story," he says, and takes a sip of his
drink. "But you shouldn't think of yourself like that."

"What do you mean?"

"You are a beautiful woman," says the man, and I thank
him while at the same time curling up, my slender shoulders
retreating and shading my chest. "A very beautiful woman,"
he repeats, looking around as the table next to us erupts in a
volley of laughter.

The man begins to drink and starts telling me his opinions of
the movies he's seen, the books he's read, and his voice grows
louder with every serving of alcohol he consumes. He orders
drinks for me at the same rate as he knocks back his own, and
before long we are caressing each other beneath the table, our
sense of touch is dulled, and a soulless film rises across our eyes.

The man invites me to his place, and I say yes. We take a taxi
to his apartment in Friedrichshain. He takes off his shoes and
my coat in the hallway; his dark-grey socks are damp around
the toes. The man pulls me into the bedroom, where he strips
off the rest of his clothes.

He kisses my shoulder and neck, runs his tongue along my

clavicle, paws my nonexistent breasts, my thighs and butt, presses his body against mine, and begins to pull off my shorts. I ask him to switch the lights off. He agrees, then almost glides back next to me. The smell of his feet and groin catches my nostrils, and I can feel myself becoming agitated as a moment later the man has taken off his underpants and my bra.

He pushes me down on the bed, jumps on top of me, and presses his hand into my panties, and there's no time to steer his hands elsewhere before he feels the form of my groin against his hand.

At this he freezes, as though he's heard a life-threatening sound behind him.

"What's this?"

"I'm sorry," I say and turn my head.

"What the fuck is this?" he asks tersely. He jumps up to switch on the lights, then returns to the bed, grabs my panties, and yanks them off.

I close my eyes tight, pull my knees up to my chest, and press both hands down to cover my groin. I can feel the flames from the ceiling lights on my body and the man's gaze burning into my every pore. *Please, don't look at me. I'm really sorry,* I say, and I begin reaching for the clothes the man has cast across the floor.

The man doesn't respond. Instead he grabs me by the ankle and pulls me off the bed like a dirty sheet.

Fuck, he says, and kicks me in the ribs.

Go to hell, he shouts after he's gathered the sheets into a ball in the middle of the bed and kicks me again so that the clothes I have managed to grab fall to the floor.

Get the fuck out of here, he repeats, shoving me with his hands, and I no longer know what to think or do or say, because I realize that any word, any action, will only fuel his anger, and because of that I can barely move the way I want to, my limbs will not obey my instinct to run headlong out of the apartment.

Before I can gather my clothes, the man grabs my hair with both hands and pulls me into the living room, pressing my face and body hard against the wall as he reaches for the peppermill on the dining table.

Let me go. Please let me go. I beg him to stop between my whimpers, and as I try with all my strength to twist away from his hands, he tightens his grip; his elbow feels like a knife sunk into the middle of my back and his hands are like giant clamps pulling my skin in opposite directions.

Shut the fuck up, he shouts into my ear and spits on my cheek. His saliva smells of stale alcohol and used dental floss.

He tightens his hold on me even more and tries to thrust the peppermill inside me, and I start screaming my heart out, then the man finally stops and I grab the peppermill and throw it against the opposite wall and carry on screaming at the top of my lungs and take hold of his furniture and hurl it across the room and rage through his apartment. I shove the television to the floor, pull the books from their shelves and smash a guitar propped in the corner of the room and finally pick up a knife I find in the kitchen drawer and brandish it at him, his face stony and lifeless as he stands among his scattered belongings like a child, and the man says nothing and I say nothing, as I rapidly collect my clothes and pull them on even more quickly, all the while ready to slash his throat, ready to strike the knife into his groin, and once I've slammed his front door shut I run down from the third floor and hide the knife in my bag, and I feel an almost unbearable urge to cry, but I simply run and run and run.

·   ·   ·

I return to my apartment and take off my clothes, wash the smell of the man from my mouth, rinse his punches from my face, and wonder whether I should report the incident to the police. It would be easy, I could simply walk into the nearest police station, I had the man's details and proof that I had been with him, there are bruises on my skin. It would be only right to punish him for his actions, I think, and for a moment I can almost lick the fruit of my own determination.

But then I realize they would have to interview witnesses and I'd have to tell the authorities everything in detail, show them identification and paperwork, documents that aren't even my documents but that I carry around like excess fat, and I'd have to justify myself, explain myself, spell out the fact that I'm under no obligation to reveal my gender to anybody, that what people think they know about me isn't my responsibility but their own construction, their own assumption.

And besides, the man would probably be given the benefit of the doubt, he presumably has a spotless record and he comes from a decent background, and I am something completely different, I have spent nights in jail cells and been given countless fines. Nobody would believe the protagonist in my story. They would say I unfairly led the man into a trap by pretending certain things were exactly as they seemed, and that to do something like that I must surely be deranged by all the misery, the thirst for love pent up inside me. They'd think I was the monster, and not him.

So I decide to forget all about him and the creative-writing class and to do something else. I sleep badly at night and wake up early in the mornings and try to think what that something might be, but I can't think of anything except getting a job until I work out what I want to do next.

I land a job at a Turkish restaurant a stone's throw from my apartment. I walk in dressed in neat but baggy men's clothing, say *Salaam aleikum* and tell them I'm a Bosnian Muslim in need of work. The restaurant owner, a man with thick stubble and a benevolent face, invites me into the back, and the following day I find myself unloading deliveries, washing dishes, and chopping vegetables; I go where I'm needed, and for the first time in a long while I feel as though I have a reason to wake up in the morning.

The flow of the service, the taste of the food, and the customers' overall enjoyment all depend on my presence, and it becomes increasingly important to me to wake up early and garner praise from my boss. I deliberately keep a distance from the other members of the staff, men who all look the same and who work with me from morning till night, and only speak to them when they need something from me. Otherwise I listen to music on a set of headphones, and after a while, thankfully, they stop trying to get to know me.

Soon, however, my life seems at a standstill; it is cheerless and predictable. It's impossible to find what you're looking for in the back of a kebab restaurant, I think, and so after six months I give notice to my landlord and quit my job, pack up only the bare essentials, and carry my few pieces of furniture down to Müllerstraße for passersby to take away.

4 LOVE

I leave for Madrid, and one day I am sitting at a café on Calle Gran Vía, a busy shopping street, when a woman who soon introduces herself as Rosa asks what book I'm reading. Rosa says she's never heard of the book, so I explain it's a story about a Cuban fisherman who hasn't caught a fish in eighty-four days; he takes his boat far out to sea, and eventually a large marlin bites on his hook, but because the protagonist, Santiago by name, cannot haul it into the boat by himself, he decides to exhaust the fish to death instead. However, the fish takes three whole days to die, I explain, and so Santiago, who by this point is hungry, thirsty, and covered in bruises, decides to drag the fish to shore, only to realize that the sharks have eaten it on the way. I've read this novel before, I say as I go along, and so I'm able to tell her how the story ends. Rosa smiles and says she rarely reads books, picks up her paper cup full of coffee, and takes a small sip.

And so we meet each other, on a day when both of us woke

ing it would be a day like any other. I fall in love with
uppose it's love, because she is tall, slender, dark haired,
and er face is beautiful and symmetrical, and she wears every
item of clothing as though it were worth thousands. She looks
exactly the way I might want to look, curly hair and deep-
green eyes.

Rosa works in a bakery and starts every day by eating pastries. *I love my life and I love you, love that you are in my life, and I
love sweet things,* says Rosa as we walk hand in hand through
the streets of downtown Madrid, a city that looks almost like
a mushroom forest, and so I say to her, *I love you too, I love you
too, baby,* and she doesn't loosen her grip though the sun beats
down on our bare arms so mercilessly that our palms are sticky
with sweat.

Rosa kisses me vigorously in museums and restaurants and in
the street, then she asks to visit my homeland and meet my family, but *There's nothing in Italy,* I tell her, *let's stay in your homeland
because I don't have a family anymore, they all died when I was young,
in a fire,* and for a moment Rosa weeps against my shoulder, says
she's terribly sorry to hear that, and I ask that we never bring
up the matter again.

I move into her apartment, which smells of clean clothes and
freshly baked pastries. With the help of her brother I land a job
at a bus company driving tourists from Madrid to Valencia and
back, and I even manage to learn some Spanish. I become used
to living with her, to the Spanish sunshine, to eating at the same
time as the locals, and I don't even mind having sex with Rosa.
What's more, I clearly impress her parents and siblings because
I say I am prepared to move to another country for my love,
even though I'm the man in the relationship. *Because we love our
sister,* Rosa's brothers explain, shaking my hand and inviting me
to their homes to taste some wine.

For a while everything is bright and buoyant, carefree, *We are together now and we will be together forever,* I find myself thinking, she brings more meaning to my life than anyone in a very long time, she brings order, rhythm to my everyday.

"I want to have a baby," Rosa says one morning as we're sitting in the park having a picnic she's put together. It's going to be another scorching day and we're sitting in the shade. I see a little boy, thrilled upon finding a coin in the street; farther off an elderly woman is gesticulating at a market vendor, but a moment later starts smiling again, the vendor hands her a loaf of bread wrapped in newspaper, the woman gently places it in her handbag and continues on her way.

"Really?"

"Yes, I've been thinking about it for a while now. You'll make a great father," she says as she picks up a strawberry from a box in front of us. "You'd be so gentle. And I want to start a family."

"I love you," I tell her. "I'd like to have a baby too—just imagine how beautiful it would be."

She crawls into my lap, the strawberry still in her fingers, then replaces it in the box.

"I'm so happy," she says and wraps her arms around me.

"Me too," I reply, stroking her slender arms, and I think that one day I will learn to love her the way she loves me, because I feel so much passion from her as she sits up from my lap and turns her head toward me. I notice how much passion there is within her, in her timid eyes, in the way she touches my face, when she brushes her bangs to one side and says *See you later* and kisses me, I can feel it in her lips, and I know that she's thinking about how she'll get through the day without her beloved as she reluctantly begins walking away from me, turns her head, and blows a kiss in my direction.

When one Saturday evening Rosa comes home earlier than expected and finds me dressed in her clothing, she is not nearly as shocked as I am but smiles as if she'd walked in to find me covered from head to toe in flour. She wants me to try on her scarves and cocktail dresses, and I do as I'm told, my cheeks burning, and by now she is laughing so hard that she almost chokes, propping herself on her knees and rubbing her chest.

Don't laugh at me, I snap at her, and I feel a tingling in my palms, an urge to punch her. *You look so ugly as a woman,* she says, *your massive nose and angular chin aren't very . . . pretty,* she adds, and she seems thrilled as she suggests she do my makeup too. *But first you have to walk,* she says as she pulls out her cosmetics. *Walk, come on, just walk, I want to take a picture, my brothers are going to burst with laughter,* says Rosa, and I'm not sure whether my next movement is because of Rosa's hysterics or because she won't obey me, her boyfriend, who has specifically asked his girlfriend not to laugh, or because I know I can look every bit as much of a woman as she does if I want to, but I build up as much momentum as I can, punch Rosa in the stomach with both fists, so hard that the back of her head smashes the glass in a painting hanging on the wall and blood starts trickling from her head.

You're crazy, Rosa stammers as the initial shock dies down. I pull Rosa's clothes off me and put on my own. She calls her brother. *You pig,* he whispers as he helps Rosa out of the apartment. *I'll fucking kill you.*

Two weeks later Rosa calls me. *You can pay my medical bills. You owe me that. You're sick, really sick,* she says in a single breath. *Now I know how sick you really are, admit it, you're one of those trannies.*

So she disappears from my life and our love is snuffed out in a single moment, a single unhappy chain of events, and she turns from a living person into a series of images in my mind, a story, a character I can pull out like a playing card whenever I want to talk about her, turn her on and off like a television channel.

In Albania there are many different versions and variations of the legend of Doruntina, Konstandini, and their family. The beautiful Doruntina is the only daughter of thirteen children in a fatherless family living deep in the countryside. One day she encounters a foreign prince as he passes Doruntina's village. The prince falls in love with the young, vivacious Doruntina and wishes to take her hand in matrimony, but only Konstandini, the youngest of Doruntina's twelve brothers, is in favor of the marriage. Nobody else in the family wants to wed Doruntina so far afield because the family has experienced great hardship, the plight of poverty, and the tragic death of the family's father.

And so it was that Konstandini, who wishes his sister to be happy with her betrothed, promises their mother, who disapproves of the marriage, that he will fetch Doruntina and bring her home whenever their mother starts to long for her only daughter. Eventually the whole family agrees to this, and Doruntina is married to the foreign prince with much pomp and ceremony. It is said that never in the whole of Albania was there a celebration the like of the marriage between Doruntina and the foreign prince.

Soon after the wedding, a war breaks out and all the family's sons die one after the other, from the eldest to the youngest just like in a poem, from cannonballs, swords, beneath collapsing buildings, in torture chambers and fires, until the only member of the family left is the mother, now living alone in the house, longing for her daughter, and whose incessant weeping can be heard throughout the village at night. In a terrible fit of anguish the mother curses Konstandini's soul, for it was he who gave her a promise he could not keep.

The curse awakens Konstandini from the dead. He climbs on his steed and rides through the black night from one side of the earth to the other and finds his sister, dressed in white and blissfully unaware of her brothers' fate. And so they set off together, and during the journey back Doruntina asks her brother about their mother, how she is faring, about all her brothers and the villagers, whether the land has provided for the winter. Konstandini, however, does not answer a single question but simply urges his steed onward, and as she shivers on the back of the horse Doruntina's white dress turns the same color as the dry earth and the dust that cover Konstandini and his mighty steed.

However, the most chilling part of the story is its final scene, the moment at which Konstandini helps Doruntina from the horse's back at the edge of the village and returns to his own grave, leaving Doruntina, covered from head to toe in dirt, to walk up to her mother. At first mother and daughter embrace each other for a long time, and then her mother asks, *Why are your clothes so dirty, Doruntina, your dress covered in dust, your boots so muddy? How did you find your way here, Doruntina? Who brought you back to me?* Her mother speaks in amazement, and Doruntina looks at her mother, bewildered. *Your brothers are dead,* her mother explains before Doruntina can answer. *They all fell in the war.* And with that Doruntina runs straight back to the front door and gazes out into the night to see her brother again, but he has already gone, and the hollow neighing of a black horse is the only sound that carries over the darkness.

When the story ends, the reader will understand the essence of the Albanian spirit: that a mother's grief has the power to waken a child from the dead and that the Albanians will rise from their graves to keep their promises.

The first time I heard this story, the black horse and all that violence frightened me, but when I heard it a second time, in a version in which Konstandini was dressed in white, it didn't scare me as much and I liked it all the more. But when I heard a version in which instead of twelve there were only nine brothers, and a version in which instead of living in the village the family lived in the middle of a city, I realized that the small details had no meaning, that every person told the story in a unique way, arbitrarily adding elements that pleased them the most.

For storytellers, the skeleton of the story was the most important part, the noble message about humanity, but for me the most unforgettable part of the story was its myriad details, the sound of the horse, the colors, the dust on Konstandini's metallic armor, the pitch-dark moonless night, and the lonely old widow's house with one light flickering in the window, a mother's face knotted with grief as she weeps for her daughter, and a man risen from the dead only to return to the bosom of the earth.

5 THIRST

In New York, man is a bird, man is a crane, he is the steam rising from the sewers, he drives a yellow cab, he bears a mustache or a turban or stands on the street with a watermelon in his hand, he is a Mongolian monk or a samurai, man is a revolving door and a wide highway, man is a one-dollar lunch, the sound of the subway as it brakes at the station, man is a homeless person who pulls down his pants and shits in the middle of the eternal neon daylight in Times Square, man is a man who walks past the homeless person shitting in the middle of Times Square without paying him the slightest attention, the one who shouts at the homeless person, the one who takes the homeless person away, the one who washes away the homeless person's shit. Man is in a hurry and has no time for other people.

Though there are people all around, vast numbers of people, I am lonelier than ever, and I don't know where I am going or where I'm coming from. I walk around carrying a cup of take-out coffee, I exchange pleasantries with the waiters and other people standing in line, but as I walk from one place to another I never look anybody in the eye. I saunter up and down Manhattan on foot, cheap Chinese-owned nail salons on one side of the street and one of the most expensive eateries in the city on the other; I pass South American workmen who call out after me and blow kisses in my direction, I pass Asian businessmen talking incessantly on their cell phones, African American teenage boys, groups of whom barge onto the subway with a portable ghetto blaster and begin dancing on the seats. Everybody here seems to be among their own kind.

Everything is gigantic—the cars, the doors, the coffee cups and furniture, the counters and trash cans—and the buildings are so tall and huge that the sun never shines on both sides of the street at once. People too are large, hairy and heavyset, everything about them is significantly larger: they have bigger thighs and wider faces, bulkier legs and hands, and my eye constantly lights on men's rotund bellies, hanging over their belts.

The ads on the subway walls ask, Have you injured yourself? Have you fallen over in a store or near your apartment? Has your phone operator or insurance or electric company overcharged you? Anybody can call the free customer service number on the ad and tell the representative about any kind of incident that has caused any level of suffering. Based on the calls they receive, the legal company chooses which customers it wishes to represent, then individuals or companies or housing associations are served with the most outlandish accusations and sued for even more outlandish sums of money, from which the legal company takes its own cut. Many people try to solve their problems through the courts, and when people argue they threaten each other with lawyers.

"The United States spits on the very people that have built its countless skyscrapers and bows down to those with money," someone shouts as I walk from the corner of Central Park and down Fifth Avenue, and as I look at the grand, refined façade of the Plaza Hotel and the people walking through the square across the street and pushing everything they own in a shopping cart, I realize that clichés are born for a reason, that it's true what they say, you are nothing without money here. Without money there is no access to education or health care, and if you look like you don't have money you won't get service either. Even those with no papers will survive in this city longer than those without money, because at least you can hide the fact that you don't have the right documentation. Poverty weighs far more than a United States Social Security card.

I decide to stay in the country illegally. I find a cheap room in an apartment in the Bronx, near Yankee Stadium. The other room is occupied by a Finnish woman called Maria. She is tall and thin, and you can tell she must have been very beautiful when she was younger. She tells me she moved to the area decades ago with her husband, whom she'd met on holiday in Miami. After a decade together they got divorced and Maria decided to stay because she was used to the city and had built a life for herself.

She is kind to me, I can come and go whenever and however I please, and she speaks warmly of her former husband, her catering company and American friends, and her family in Finland. *Finland is a lovely country,* she says. *Four real seasons, all that forest and thousands of lakes and rivers, it's so beautiful there.* Maria takes books from the shelf and shows me some photographs of bright blue, pristine lakes, islands that look like scabs on the surface of the water, forests that seem to go on forever, small, charming wooden cottages dotting the green landscape like billiard balls. Finland looks beautiful, so unique and unreal, and when Maria tells me she plans to move back when she retires, I start to envy her.

We're eating breakfast at the kitchen table. I smile. If only I could think of my home country the way you do, I say, but I can't stand Spain, that's why I came here, because I couldn't bear it, I felt like I was going to suffocate in Madrid, literally. I wanted my dreams to come true and I thought that here I might be able to achieve something.

"Like what?" Maria asks.

"I don't know yet. I could be an artist, someone famous," I reply. "But there was nothing for me in Spain. I don't think anyone's dreams could come true in a place like that."

Maria gives a curt smile and places her massive coffee cup on the table. "Everybody here wants to be an actor or a singer," she says. "Everybody wants to be famous. Everybody."

"I've acted all across Europe," I quickly say then, spooning my breakfast from the bottom of the bowl, slices of apple mixed with natural yogurt. "I've been in lots of movies, but they were all minor productions; in Europe people do things on a much smaller scale." I look at her expression: her eyes are open and her pouting lips press along the edge of the coffee cup like gills.

"What kind of roles have you done?" she asks as she places her cup back on the table and wipes her upper lip on her wrist.

I explain that in a Spanish movie I played a man who wanted to be a woman, and that I also starred in an Italian movie about life after an unsuccessful suicide attempt.

"Really?" she says as I push the spoon into my mouth. *Yes,* I say. *I can play all kinds of roles, you'll see,* I continue, smiling proudly. *There's nobody else like me,* I add and walk out of the kitchen.

Maria's apartment is old and in bad condition, but it's cheap. The walls are a bit lopsided and there are large black stains on the bathroom ceiling. Cockroaches scurry out of the drain in the sink and the cracks between the floorboards if you leave food or water out. The floors creak and the sounds of arguments, children and women shouting, people arguing about money, heels pummeling the floor above, can constantly be heard from the other apartments, and in the evenings I can hear the scratching of mice and rats between the walls. The insulation in the windows is faulty and I have to stuff the gaps with cardboard and plastic bags. Almost everyone in the Bronx is African American or Latino, Maria warns me. *So you've got to be pretty careful around here,* she says, giving me motherly advice and explaining that only ten years ago you could see badly injured or even dead people lying in the streets.

Nobody cared about them because they were Latinos and blacks, and people thought violence was somehow characteristic of them, Maria says, *but things are getting better all the time.*

We visit a place in the heart of the Bronx popular among Italians and Albanians: the real Little Italy, they call it. It's essentially just one street lined with Italian restaurants and kiosks owned by Albanians, and I pretend not to understand anything coming from the mouths of the kiosk traders and people walking on the street, though of course their speech is the focus of my attention: how distant and foreign my mother tongue sounds, as though it had been mixed with the stresses and cadences of another language, as though it could no longer be used to discuss the world from which it had once come.

We visit restaurants together, catch movies together, as far away as the Jersey Gardens mall in New Jersey. Maria talks at length about the city around us as if immensely proud of everything in it.

She teaches me how to tip in restaurants and taxis, gives me advice on which detergents and medicines are the best, and even how to walk along the street. *You can't stop, especially not in the middle of the sidewalk, and you always have to walk on the right-hand side, quickly, because the people behind you might be in a hurry, and in cafés you need to know what you're going to order before it's your turn because nobody has the time to wait for you to make up your mind at the counter. Here you have to be brisk and respect other people by not wasting their time,* she explains. Maria finds something to say about everything, something it would be useful for me to know, and she talks to me as though she were my mother and I were her teenage son, as though I were dependent on her. I go out in search of work, ask around the local establishments, and it doesn't take long for me to get lucky. I get a job as a host at a nearby restaurant, where it's my job to greet customers and show them to their tables, and to check throughout the evening that the staff are taking good care of them. *I want you to smile when customers step inside,* my boss Juan explains, and in the course of my interview he doesn't bother asking me anything else except when I can start. *With you standing by the door smiling that white smile of yours, the customers will come flooding in.* He seems so excited that he almost forgets to mention that I'll get paid in cash every other week.

When I'm out clothes shopping, I immediately get handed a bag when I step inside, but the African American girls walking in front of me don't get as much as a hello. I am allowed to use the bathroom in cafés and restaurants for free. At the corner shops, the clerks pack my shopping into bags but don't do that for customers who look the same as them, and when I'm standing in line at a nightclub, the security guard calls me over. *Step right in, honey,* he says.

I start wearing clothes that show off my slender body, I saunter into small markets and kiosks and fill my handbag with food and cosmetics and walk right out because I know nobody is following me, nobody is watching what I get up to.

Gender and sexuality don't matter here, anybody can be a man or a woman, gay, lesbian, asexual, male couples, female couples, anyone can walk hand in hand, a man and a robot, a woman and a soft toy, nobody is interested. On the other hand, everybody pays attention to race: white, Asian, black, Indian, Latino, mulatto, white Latino, white black, white Asian. It's as though there's a certain pecking order in the city with rich white people at the top, then rich Asians, and all the dark-skinned people right at the bottom of the pile. Nobody seems to care about homeless people; they sit on busy streets or at the entrances to subway stations with cardboard signs in their hands reading I NEED MONEY FOR FOOD or GOD LOVES YOU.

"There's so much racism here," I say to Maria when we're in the downstairs laundry room at the same time. The machines only work with quarters and you can't leave your clothes unattended or the other residents might steal them.

"I mean . . . ," I stammer as I notice how focused she is on separating her clothes into different machines, as though nothing could possibly disrupt her concentration. "Life is so much harsher and more difficult here than it is in Europe. Especially for African Americans. Would you want to live here if you were black?"

"What do you mean?" she asks, glancing up at me and the large plastic bag from which I start separating my clothes into different machines, almost mimicking her movements.

"Can you imagine life as a black person?" I ask. "I mean, if people started following you around in the store, how would that make you feel, or would you even realize it's because of the color of your skin or because you come from somewhere else? Or could you imagine that because of the color of your skin nobody would ever stop you in the street and ask you for directions or that there would be no point in ever asking to borrow somebody's phone, even in an emergency?" I add before she has a chance to respond.

"I don't believe any white person can imagine what life is like for black people," Maria replies.

She closes the washing machine doors and begins adding laundry detergent with a small measuring cup.

"Is it like this in Finland?"

"I don't know," she says, pressing the start button and sitting down on the bench opposite the row of machines. "When I left there was nobody there except Finnish people, and I was living in Helsinki, the capital."

"Really?"

"If you want to live in a bubble, shut yourself off from the world and the difficulties most people experience, it's probably a good place to live," she says haughtily, almost disdainfully.

Then we stare at the washing machines, watch the way they toss the clothes around, as soapsuds gather on the surface of the glass like spittle around an old man's lips, and when Maria closes her eyes for a moment, I imagine her continuing the conversation about how backward Finland is, though to me it doesn't sound like a bad place at all.

Soon I'm working more than eighty hours a week to try to build up some savings. I take on a second job, a third job. In the mornings I work as a cleaner at an illegal clothes factory in Queens, in the evenings I'm either working as a host at the restaurant or washing dishes in the basement of a Spanish wine bar. Every day I travel from the Bronx to Queens and back again on the subway, where lots of my fellow travelers sleep, and I imagine that these subway journeys are probably the only opportunities they get to rest.

After six months I start sleeping on the subway too. I realize that New York City kills off the dreams and aspirations of new arrivals by drowning them in endless everyday problems, by incessantly grabbing money from people for anything and everything, and that the city doesn't leave people time to do anything except earn money or think about earning money, and everybody is up to their neck in debt.

Every now and then the city extends a little finger to new-comers: newspapers and television talk shows run stories about people whose dreams have come true. It's as though the city wants to make sure that the constant flow of people never ends. Your dreams will come true one day, sooner or later you'll be an international superstar, an actor, a musician, or a writer, in this city and no other—that's the underlying message—because everything you need is right here, as long as you try hard enough, as long as you work relentlessly, as long as you never give up, one day you'll reach the top of the tallest sky-scraper, the summit of the greatest mountain, the most breath-taking view in the world.

And I realize that the light of these images blinds me too;

they are the last things I think about in the evening, the first things I think about in the morning, and the belief that one day the winning lottery ticket will be mine keeps me going. The eighteen-hour days and the continual exhaustion will be worth it, eventually it will all pay off.

But those news and talk shows don't tell the whole story, because nobody wants to watch the worst scenes, to be reminded of the despair, the anguish, the pain: a grown woman devouring four pints of ice cream, then kneeling in front of the toilet and stuffing her fingers down her throat, and once she's thrown up all she can she twiddles her finger in the vomit floating in the bowl then back into her mouth because she's worried there might be something left in her stomach. Nobody wants to see images of homeless people picking up cigarette butts that businessmen throw on the street, of children working in factories or whose parents beat them up on the subway on the way home in the middle of the night, of babies who have been with their working parents all day now sleeping in their arms, of infected feet, of skin that's been eaten away by the cold. Nobody wants to hear about people wasting away on death row, praying in solitary confinement, about an old man dying alone in his home and being found only when a neighbor notices the smell, and nobody wants to watch as the thousands of people with more money than they could ever spend won't give a homeless man a dime or even glance down at the text written on his square of cardboard.

The world wants to see an image of someone smiling with success, radiating contentment, a person behind whom the world is at its most beautiful, a person who has remained untouched by the icy fingers of bitterness. The world wants to hear about this person, a victor who has demolished all walls in his path, about a stay-at-home mom who has lost a hundred and thirty pounds, about an illegal immigrant who has graduated from medical school, about the homeless who have pulled themselves up by their bootstraps and gotten a job and a place to live. This is what makes people open their newspapers, what makes us give it one more shot, again and again, makes us scream louder and want more and more and more, so that one day we might see it—the peak, the whole world the size of a marble in the palm of a hand, the face of God himself—before it's time to start all over again.

6 SAMMY AND THE DRAGON

Then I meet Sammy. It's winter, and Sammy is standing at the entrance to the subway station at the corner of Fourteenth Street and Eighth Avenue, shivering because his coat zipper is broken and he hasn't got any gloves. He's dyed his black curls a golden yellow, and he's handing out flyers to passersby. He's got a gig that night at a local piano bar, where he works in drag for tips. His dark face is as beautiful as that of a young boy, though he is twenty-eight. *Welcome to my freak show, gorgeous,* he says, handing me a flyer with a photograph of him in a wig printed on cheap paper. *Can I buy you a coffee?* I ask, and to my surprise Sammy agrees. *Thank god. I thought I'd freeze to death,* he sighs as we step inside the café opposite the subway station.

Sammy tells me a great deal about his life. He was born in Connecticut, and after his mother fell ill and his father descended into alcoholism he had to fend for himself from the age of eighteen. *I don't know, and I couldn't care less,* he says when

I ask where his father is now. Sammy earns a living working in two different cafés in Brooklyn and every now and then doing drag shows in a bar. In and around Chelsea and Hell's Kitchen he's better known as Sandy Ho. It means an older woman who is volatile and short-tempered because there's sand in her pussy, Sammy explains, someone who's difficult and annoying as fuck, a real turn-off who'll go home with any guy who buys her a drink.

But I hate being here, I hate this city so much, god how I hate every-thing about this place, he says, and I nod. I tell him it seems as if everybody born in New York City wants to get as far away from New York as possible, and everybody who has moved to New York from elsewhere becomes embittered sooner or later. *Honey, no,* Sammy interrupts me, placing his forefinger firmly on top of my coffee cup. *It's not the city, it's the world. If you can't find what you're looking for here, you won't find it anywhere else. Come to the show this evening and you'll see,* he adds so firmly that for a moment I didn't dare ask him anything else. I like him a lot; he's at once unconditional and timid, like a teenage boy who after behaving boastfully to his friends starts stammering when he has to give a talk in front of the class.

Sandy Ho's gig is in a typical New York bar in Chelsea, in a rectangular space with warm light that is merciful on the skin and with ripped, shirtless bartenders. At the back of the bar is a space that is pitch-dark, with cubicles in which the customers can have sex with each other.

I arrive an hour ahead of time: the tables are almost all empty and the bartender tells me Sandy Ho is backstage getting ready. I feel excited and impatient as I wait for her, and when Sandy

Ho finally appears she looks even more artificial than earlier in the day. Her makeup is striking, dramatic eyes highlighted in shades of green, and her face looks as though she has stuck her head in a vat of glitter. She is wearing a pair of PVC boots with the tallest heels I've ever seen and a skintight black sequin dress that reaches halfway down her thighs, and her huge white afro makes her look taller still.

I can't take my eyes off her; I've never seen anything like her, I think as I sit at the bar trying to break the ice cubes in my drink with a straw, never seen anything as beautiful as her long, muscular legs in knee-high boots and her slender shoulders and bare, angular clavicles, and the glass I'm holding almost breaks in my grip—that's how much I want to scrape the mask from her face and take her clothes.

Ho, ho, ho, Sandy begins. *Welcome, bitches,* she continues into the microphone, utterly self-assured. *And yes, this wig is genuine fucking polar bear,* says Sandy, and when everybody in the room begins to laugh, she shouts.

"Shut up!"

During her show, Sandy Ho performs countless famous songs, Cher, Céline Dion, and Shania Twain. As the original versions play in the background Sandy moves her lips and imitates the gestures and expressions of her chosen artists. Amid the lip-syncing she tells sarcastic jokes and ridicules the artists and their lives, as though she knows them as well as her best friends. She is magnificent, and somehow that disturbs me.

At the end of the show, Sandy Ho fetches a large glass bowl from the bar, and her face looks almost colorless when she returns to the stage to inform the audience that, as they know, the polar bear has to get back to the North Pole—Queens, that is—so please be generous.

I follow the bowl around the room. People react slowly though the bowl is quick to approach them; they let out quiet comments, *I've only got a twenty* or *Oh, the bowl is gone already.* I look at the dollar bills reluctantly left at the bottom, and once the bowl has done a full circle around the room, now gripped in an air of awkwardness, one of the bartenders fetches it and stashes it behind the bar. *Thank you!* Sandy shouts, disappearing backstage.

An hour later Sammy reappears, sits down on the stool next to me, and orders a rum and Coke. He looks completely different, crushed. Most people who had seen the show probably wouldn't recognize him. *Fuck,* he says once the drink is placed in front of him. *Fifty-three dollars. And I was wearing at least twenty bucks' worth of makeup.* I express my sympathy and say I'd be glad to pay for his drink. *You're sweet,* Sammy says, and smiles.

I praise him, saying he's one of the most beautiful women I've ever seen. *You're an amazing, luminous performer.* Sammy thanks me and takes a large sip of his drink. *The only thing I wondered about,* I continue, *is why do you go so over the top when you're playing a woman, when you could dress and make yourself up far more subtly? Then nobody would know you're a man,* I say, picking up my glass of wine.

"You think I do this because I want to be a woman?" he asks, and then takes a deep breath. "No, no. I'm not transsexual or just a guy in a dress. Drag is different, it's art, one of the most complicated forms of self-expression, it's total commitment, role-play that requires intelligence, an aesthetic eye, and the ability to put yourself out there. It's far more than being born a man and showing up somewhere dressed as a woman. Drag is the royalty of gender, it's being above gender by performing all genders at once," Sammy declares, and midway through his monologue I realize that he has misunderstood me, because it seems as though he's said these exact words thousands of times before to people who know nothing about drag.

"I've got to be heading home," he says after downing the remainder of his rum and Coke.

"Don't go yet," I say. "I'm sorry."

"No sweat, it's not that serious. But it's a long way out to my place in Queens and I've got an early start," he says, and he is about to slip down from the barstool when I grab his arm.

"You can spend the night at my place," I say, not caring that I haven't corrected what I'd just said by asking whether it wouldn't be better if we could all live as though gender didn't exist. Instead of being a man or a woman, wouldn't it be better to concentrate on being unique?

Sammy laughs. *Okay, stranger. Let's do this.*

Sitting in the back of the cab as we head north along Twelfth Avenue, Sammy puts his hand on my thigh and comments on everything around us, the large piers and the *Intrepid* landing pad that serves as a sea, air, and space museum, the lights of New Jersey across the Hudson River, the millions of people crammed into such a small area, so many crushed dreams in only a few square miles, he sighs, so many deflated souls. *The world is such a shitty place.*

We arrive at my place at three in the morning. I show him my room and ask him to keep in mind that my landlady is asleep. I go into the kitchen, spread Sammy two slices of bread with butter, and pour some orange juice into a tall tumbler. Sammy sits in his underwear on the edge of my bed and gratefully takes the plate as I hand it to him. He eats the bread quickly and finishes the juice in only a few gulps, then places the dishes on the floor. He is like a small doll made of glass, and as he lies down next to me and slides his left leg around my own, as he says *It's so cold in here* and rests gazing out at the darkness beyond the windowpane, and as he breathes so deep that the excess air pushes its way out of his body in a momentary shiver, I ask him if I might try on his costume sometime, to which he says simply *Maybe sometime, stranger,* then raises his head and kisses me on the cheek.

When I wake to the sound of my alarm clock, Sammy is gone. I sniff the sheets for a moment, as they still bear the smell of his musky skin, and when I notice that my drawers are open I realize that Sammy has found my savings and taken everything with him. Then I get out of bed, brush my teeth, dress, ride the subway, go to work, come home again, undress, ride the subway, and everything around me is once again frozen, the entire city and its stony heart.

I tell Maria I'm leaving. *Where?* she asks, a note of irritation in her voice, and at first I imagine it must be because it will be tough for her to find another reliable tenant. *I don't know,* I answer. *Something happened, I've got to go, I can't stay here any longer,* I say, and at this she bursts into tears.

Please don't leave, she begs me, and it dawns on me that not a single person has visited the apartment since I moved in. *You're like a child to me,* she continues, pulling a tissue out of her pocket and wiping her teary eyes. *I don't want you to go,* and I pity her so much that I want to say *All right then, I'll stay,* but instead I tell her that coming here was a mistake, *I'm so fucking stupid, I wish I'd never come here, I wish I didn't exist at all,* and the words come from somewhere so deep within me that I turn my back, walk out of the room, and slam the door.

I sit on my bed for several hours and sob. I try to think about what to do next, where to go, but for a long while not a single thought crosses my mind.

Eventually my eye catches on the spine of a book that Maria gave me, a book about Finland.

―――――――

When I was a child I heard a story about a girl who became a boy. It was crazy and impossible, like all my father's stories, but of all the stories I ever heard this was the most random, the most raucous, for in it there were flying dragons and flashing swords, the girl wore men's clothing, and animals could speak to humans and humans to animals, and it was so alive that I could almost feel the dragon's scales between my toes, the tip of the snake's forked tongue in my ear canal. Many tragic events took place in this story too, as I'd learned to expect from my father's tales. Yet still I hoped, every time I heard an unfamiliar story, I hoped and wished that this time nobody would die, perhaps this time everybody would get the ending they deserved and finally be happy.

The story follows a widower who had three daughters, and it goes without saying that a war broke out around them. The king had ordered all the men in the land to send their sons into battle, and at this the widower became very disheartened, for he was the only man in the realm who had no sons to send to the front. The youngest of his three daughters, Aldona, took pity on her broken father, approached him, and spoke.

"Do not worry, Father, I will go to war," she began. "Prepare me a uniform and cut my hair so that I don't look like a girl. Give me a horse and weapons, and I will fight as your son."

The widower did as he was told. He prepared his daughter a uniform and cut her hair, saddled his strongest horse and sharpened his best weapons, and meanwhile his daughter began calling herself by another name. Now she was Don, and thus she set off with all the other men.

"But remember," her father said. "You are a man now, not a girl in men's clothing. Do not tell anybody the truth, for my shoulders cannot bear such shame."

The following morning the men arrived in the town, each from his own village. At that moment a kulshedra appeared in the sky, a long, scaly, fire-breathing, silver-eyed, four-legged dragon that crawled out of its cave inside the mountain once a year to savage the people it saw, and it bellowed at the citizens from the skies above.

"If you never wish to see me again, give me the king's son."

The king's son was instantly locked outside the town's gates. The kulshedra swooped down behind him and began savaging him. Not one of the men present thought to help the boy as he pleaded to the kulshedra and his father for mercy, for people said that a kulshedra was invincible on the land, in the sea, and in the air.

Undeterred, Don pulled out her sword and ran to help the king's son, for she pitied him as she did her father. A few slashes, and the kulshedra's little wings and legs were thrashing on the grass like eels, and a moment later the dragon looked like a sliced loaf of bread served up on a green platter. The kulshedra's fatal weakness was the power of a woman's compassion.

The townsfolk were astounded, and so was Don, and together Don and the king's son marched to the royal palace to meet the king.

"In return for slaying the kulshedra, my father will offer you one of his kingdoms, but ask him instead for his horse, for his horse is one of a kind, the wisest creature on earth. It can think and speak like a man, and with that horse you shall be invincible," the king's son told Don, who duly refused the reward the king offered.

"If you wish to reward me in some way, Your Highness, please give me your horse," said Don, though she felt a pang of greed in her heart upon asking.

The king took great offense at Don's brazenness and decided to give her nothing at all. As Don left the palace, the king's son followed her, and when the townsfolk asked where he was going, the boy pointed at Don and said, "This is my new father. As my former father cares more about his horse than his own son, I will be better off as this man's son instead."

When the king heard what his son had said, he changed his mind and gave Don his horse. Don gave the king's son her own horse as a memento and set off with her new horse, and, true enough, her new horse was unrivaled, a great steed, wise and fast, and with a thick white mane.

They arrived in another kingdom, through which Don had to travel to get home. The king of this dominion had declared that the next man to ride through the city was to marry his ugly daughter, for nobody wished to take the horrible girl to be his wife. When Don rode in through the city gates, a group of soldiers stopped her, and the very next day she was wedded to the king's toothless, scrawny slip of a daughter.

A few days later the king's daughter was weeping on her father's shoulder because Don refused to consummate their marriage. "I am so ugly," said the girl, unaware that her husband was unable to consummate the marriage because she too was a girl. Because Don would not lie with his daughter, the king ordered her to be killed, by sending her into the clutches of another kulshedra, by urging wild mountain wolves to tear her to pieces, by poisoning her meals, but with the help of her horse Don survived each and every one of the king's malicious plans.

The king's soldiers would not allow Don to leave the kingdom, and naturally she could never reveal that she was in fact a girl. One day she had gone into the forest to weep for her tragic fate, when a snake appeared and slithered around her feet.

"Why are you crying, my child?" asked the snake, and tried to hold back its laughter. "Men don't cry."

"I am not a man," Don replied, and fell to the ground. "I am a girl, and I want to return to my family," she continued and revealed her breasts, flattened beneath the suit of armor like pectoral muscles.

"Well, well," the snake replied and began smacking its forked tongue. "If you give me your horse, I will grant you a wish, any wish." The snake coiled itself into a grey-black bundle, its head jutting up in the middle like a tulip.

Don began to think what to wish for, but the only way she could imagine escaping the situation was to ask the snake to turn her into a man so that she could lie with the king's daughter, then leave and visit her father. She gave the snake her horse and the snake turned her into a man, after which Don finally consummated his marriage to the king's daughter and duly appeased the king.

Don then traveled back home. He arrived at the family cottage, knocked on the door, and saw his father, who naturally did not recognize him. "What do you want?" his father asked, and though Don told his father everything that had happened, explained how he had conquered the kulshedra, how he had been given the king's horse in reward but had to give it to the snake to keep the hot-tempered king satisfied, and though his father believed him, he no longer wanted his child back in the family home.

"Silly child," the father said, disappointed, shaking his head and shutting the door in his offspring's face. "Why go to war if you are not prepared to die like a man?" came his voice from behind the door. "Why ask the king for a horse when you already have one?"

III

Tirana-Durrës

1991–1992

THE BEGINNING

We left the house early in the morning, all our belongings stuffed into thin plastic bags, long before anyone else had woken up. When I closed our front door for the last time and when Agim opened the gate leading out into the street, slowly so that its loosened handle wouldn't make a sound, I experienced a strange sensation, I felt at once light and heavy. I was angry, bitter even, at my mother and father and sister, I wanted revenge on all of them by disappearing, yet at the same time I felt a pang of guilt, as though I should have told someone about our departure in case anything happened. It wasn't right to simply disappear.

But Agim had come up with a plan, and we were going to stick to it. We wouldn't tell anybody that we were leaving, and we would take with us as much as possible, anything that we could sell or that might be useful, and I grabbed hold of his plan like a drowning man grabs a rope thrown in the water, because I had nothing else, no reason to stay at home except for my mother, and Agim had managed to convince both of us that a better world awaited us somewhere else.

"You are fifteen and I'm sixteen," he said. "Imagine everything we'll be able to do."

We had become blinded by our own imaginations; for weeks we'd spoken about our future with such clarity that it hadn't even occurred to us that our dreams might not come true. We would be together forever, we would travel to New York where we wouldn't be afraid of anything, to Spain where we would eat until we were fat, to Germany where everybody with a job was rich; we would go to the movies, to restaurants, we would drink coffee and eat pastries at cafés by the foot of glass skyscrapers. Then we would go to our jobs, he to his own and I to mine; he would be a respected brain surgeon who would save orphaned children, women, and the elderly, and I would do something else, I would assist him or get a job of my own unblocking drains, pipes, and sinks or building highways.

And then we would earn money, money would come from all directions, enough to fill every drawer and cabinet in the house, there would be so much of it that we would never be able to spend it all, we would buy things we didn't need, an enormous house, and crystal vases, ornaments to decorate our home, a room full of sweets or two stuffed tigers for our grand estate, because with that amount of money we could buy so much of anything we wanted that we'd need plenty of creativity to decide how to use it all.

Agim walked in front of me. The cold first light of the morning had painted the street brown and the edges of the light were tinged with all the shades of gold, and the plastic bags bulged around him like a donkey's packs, stuffed full. Agim had almost three times as much stuff as I did, because in addition to his own clothes he had packed up his sister's and mother's clothes too.

"I'll need all of these," he replied proudly when I laughed at him.

We then fell silent, and when I looked at the old men in rancid suits loitering in the street eating hunks of white bread either by itself or with a thin smattering of mashed onions or beans, bread upon which their dirty fingers had left dark smudges like crows' feathers, boys slightly older than me staring around smugly and who had pulled up their T-shirts so that their stomachs showed, girls walking briskly hand in hand from one place to another, it seemed as though of a journey that would take us hundreds of kilometers we had taken barely a single step.

We walked into the city center, and when we sat down on a bench in Parku Rinia, our knuckles and fingers white, I thought of the story my father had told me about the time he and my mother had met each other right here in this park. I realized that it looked entirely different in his story; around the rusted fountain there were flowerbeds that my father hadn't even mentioned. It was hard to imagine that anybody had ever walked through this park the way my parents had, let alone fallen in love like them.

My father had commandeered the park, made it his own, described it completely differently, added things that weren't there. Perhaps he did this on purpose, perhaps by mistake, perhaps his story was mixed with memories of other parks, or perhaps he thought that the park wasn't grand enough on its own, wasn't worthy of the love between him and my mother, and wanted to give us a more glorious version of events.

The heat and humidity of the day had gathered in the clutches of the park as though a spotlight were burning down on us, and it felt like the dust-stained streets would start to boil at any moment. The people smelled, the benches too. It was as though the sweat had been wafting around the city for so long that the smell had become an integral part of its being, its foundation.

"How much money have you got?" Agim asked, as though he had been holding back the question since the start of our journey. He propped his feet on the bench and began retying his shoelaces.

"What?"

"Money. How much did you take with you?" He repeated the question, put his feet back on the ground, and turned to look at me as he crossed his legs and seemed deliberately to stretch one of his legs as far in front of him as possible.

"None," I answered.

As soon as I'd answered I began to think how childish and stupid it was to run away. We had nowhere to stay and no idea where we should go. The police station? A foreign embassy? Should we find a SHIK official and bribe him or someone else to get us across the border? We'd been thinking about life after reaching our destination with such enthusiasm that the most important and difficult part, the journey itself, had fallen by the wayside and been forgotten like an unpleasant chore.

"Don't worry," he said, taking my wrist in his hand and pulling a bundle of bills from his back pocket.

At first I stared at it in disbelief because I'd never seen so much money, then the sight began to frighten me, as I was certain someone would see the bills in Agim's hand and rob us. Instinctively I closed the money in his hand and told him to hide it in his underpants.

"We'll be fine," he said with such confidence that I couldn't possibly admit to him that I wanted to go home to my mother, that I already missed her and that I hadn't really taken our decision to leave very seriously, that I'd imagined we'd be away for a few days, a week at most. I'd go home again once we realized this would all come to nothing, and it would give my mother time to recover too.

"I stole this from my father," said Agim, and gave an unconvincing laugh. "The idiot didn't realize I knew where he kept his money." He stuffed the cash into his trousers.

"Imagine," said Agim. "We can do anything now, we can be anyone, we can go anywhere." And I nodded as he spoke, slowly like a servant, and I only prayed that in his own mind he had answered all the questions that I was too shy to bring up with him.

Our first few days were like drunken evenings, and though there was always an element of awkwardness and disbelief in my conversations with Agim, I understood what was going on in his mind: we were invincible, it was as though we were on drugs, we were independent, free to do whatever we pleased amid the smells, enormous buildings, events, and people of the biggest city in the country. We could go anywhere we wanted, believe in whatever we chose. People in the city didn't seem to fear anything, though only a few years ago people had slept with one eye open, and when they were awake they were constantly on edge, convinced that war was about to break out, that the authorities would find out their most terrifying secrets, that men who believed in God or boys who were caught stealing would be wrenched from their families and taken far, far away.

Tirana was bustling with people, street vendors who wouldn't take no for an answer, crafty pickpockets, people traffickers whom you shouldn't ever look in the eye, toothless old men and their wives and daughters who brought them food. And everybody smoked, everywhere, incessantly, tobacco, tobacco, tobacco, young and old, men and women.

Very few people looked like they had a job, and attending school was as rare as it was wholly acceptable to ask what use there is for books in a time of conflict, to declare that we were at war and people were dying, though the war was going on hundreds of kilometers to the north and northeast of Albania, in Croatia and Slovenia, Bosnia and Kosovo. It looked as though the entire city was in a state of emergency.

Perhaps our curiosity at the prospect of boundless opportunities prevented us from seeing the city's dangers or what was really going on around us. Agim used up almost half of his money to pay for a hotel room next to Parku i Madh in the south of the city a few kilometers from Skanderbeg Square. He frittered away his money on macchiatos, clothes and jewelry, expensive food, things that not even people with a job could afford in this city, and all of this he paid for me to have as well. We ate huge portions in restaurants, drank lemonade in cafés, and pretended to be foreigners or the children of rich people. Agim even told waiters and shop assistants that he was a psychology student, and I imitated him, nonchalantly ordered us ice creams, new cups of coffee before we'd even finished the first, and we really felt like we were the people we pretended to be.

The days melted into weeks, slowly hauling themselves into the following days like fat old ladies. We had set up home in our hotel room; the things we had bought lay on the edges of the bed and scattered on the floor, unopened shopping bags were stuffed in the cupboards and the desk drawers. Most of it we didn't need at all, especially not the face creams and hairbrushes that Agim had bought, though at every turn I tried to remind him that our money wouldn't last forever and I wouldn't mind living so that we didn't constantly have to worry about tomorrow and beyond, at least for a while.

One night, just before we were about to go to sleep, Agim awoke to the fact that he had used up almost all our money. He sat on the edge of the bed, breathing in fits, and gripped my bare shin with his cold, clammy hand.

"Bujar," he began. "Something's wrong. I can't breathe." He turned his head to one side. The sharp tip of his chin pointed toward the white wall opposite. His mouth was open and his long hair looked like a wig as it flowed across his neck and shoulders like a lion's mane. I sat up in bed and took hold of Agim by his bony upper arm, and he huddled close to me. His clasped hands and legs, tucked up beside me, made him look like an enormous knot that could come undone at any moment. His chin sank in above my clavicle and he was breathing against my neck, his entire body trembling, and he wept.

———————

After a few weeks we found ourselves sleeping outdoors. Everything we owned was once again crammed into plastic bags, and it was constantly raining, and I was hungry like a viper just woken from hibernation, so hungry that I was ready to eat the sleeves of my jacket. We couldn't get to sleep, and in the mornings I felt as though I'd been run over by a car.

Though we both looked like stray dogs, Agim considered running out of money and having to sleep rough merely a temporary setback, while I was ready to go home because I was willing to believe that Ana and my mother would be waiting for me there and everything could go back to how it was before. For Agim, going back wasn't an option.

"If you want to go home, be my guest. Nobody's forcing you to stay," he said, scraping mud from his shoe with a stick.

I wanted to strangle him, because he knew that I could never leave him alone, have his well-being on my conscience, and spend the rest of my life wondering what had happened to him. Two people had already disappeared from my life at what felt like the flick of a switch, and I didn't want him to be the third.

"Don't be silly," I said. "But we'll die of hunger if we don't eat soon. Or we'll catch a disease if we don't wash. We could be beaten up too."

"Oh, come on," Agim scoffed, holding up one of his dozens of plastic bags.

Agim then shoved his hand into the bag, rummaged through its contents, and pulled out a pistol wrapped in a T-shirt. At the sight of it I hauled myself upright as though the thing had been discharged at my feet. *Where did you get that? Have you had it with you all this time? Why do you have a gun? Idiot, put it away.*

"Calm down," said Agim quietly, hiding the gun and beckoning me back to his side. "I stole it from my father. We need a weapon. Now sit down and don't give in so easily. Everything will be all right, we'll be fine."

I don't know why, maybe it was the way Agim was speaking, maybe it was his soothing voice, but when he said that everything would be all right as soon as we could sell some of these useless things, I sat down next to him again, wrapped my arm around his neck, and no longer felt hungry at all but laughed instead, and for the first time in weeks my foremost thought was not how I could get Agim and myself back home safely.

"Idiot," I said, and he smiled.

THE STONE CITY

In the evenings we hid in the bunkers across the city, and on colder nights we moved into the public lavatories, where the sinks were broken and the tiles smashed. With some rags he'd found in the trash Agim wiped a small area of the floor free of detritus, placed a couple of plastic bags on top of each other on the floor, and only then did he set our things on them and lie down. He handed me some small pieces of paper and told me to stuff them in my nose and ears so that I couldn't smell the stench or hear people banging on the door.

We came to know the city and its movements, we knew where there were the fewest people and which areas were the safest at which time of day. Agim felt no homesickness whatsoever, and any yearning I had felt had begun to fade from my mind. We washed our clothes wherever we could, in fountains or in the dirty sinks at gas stations, and we dried them by putting them on and lying down in the sunshine. We gathered clothes from trash cans, ate the food that restaurants had thrown away; sometimes we begged from the owners of restaurants or grocery stores, sometimes from customers as they sat eating. We lived at people's feet, surviving on the scraps they threw away.

A homeless old man had told Agim about an abandoned apartment building a few kilometers from the center of Tirana. We set off and eventually found the right building: a few rooms still had windows and doors that could be shut, but most of the doorways were covered simply with black garbage bags. The halls and corridors smelled of urine, but the fine brick dust hanging in the air made the smell more bearable than it was in public lavatories. Every room in the building was spoken for; in every hallway on every story sick, malnourished people sat or lay on the floor, people whom the city and the whole world had rejected. Some looked as if they had lived there for years. Agim and I glanced at each other in bewilderment, for though we'd seen poor people around the city, we hadn't realized that so many of them really lived this way.

In a hallway on the third floor we found a little corner where we laid out a few cardboard boxes we'd found in the dumpster behind a nearby grocery store.

"Poverty is a state of mind," said Agim, telling me to repeat it.

"Poverty is a state of mind," I said, and I tried to smile, and Agim told me to remember that a lack of possessions doesn't make you poor.

But the longer we lived that way, the more clearly we understood what poverty really meant. People think of poverty in three different ways. There are those who take pity on the poor and who occasionally might be willing to part with a few coins at the bottom of their pockets simply to buy a cleaner conscience. These people are generally plagued with guilt about a crime or some unforgivable act they once committed. Then there are those who are afraid of poor people and who might behave violently toward them for that reason.

However, the ones I remember the most were the great numbers of people for whom we were not even worthy of pity. Many of them might tense their shoulders, adjust the position of their handbag, or press their hands firmly into their pockets whenever they walked past the poor or the homeless. Every time we noticed someone doing that we became slightly more insignificant, and our self-esteem was in shreds by the time we realized that not even the human traffickers posed a threat to us any longer. Nobody wanted to come near us. People don't want the things they can achieve without any effort; that is what poverty taught us.

We realized we had been very much mistaken when, before we started begging, we imagined we should try and make ourselves as inconspicuous as possible, because by now we would have given the little that we had if only someone might stop, might notice our plight and try to alleviate it in any way they could. *That's the way people are,* said Agim. *They feel empathy only toward people who are like them.*

"And we're no better than they are," he continued, staring at the wall opposite, the gleam of disgust in his eyes, and handed me a tomato from which he'd cut off a piece of mold. "That's why we have to become just like them," he said, looking down at the black dirt beneath his fingernails and, frustrated, beginning to pick at them with a small stone.

In July, Agim and I began selling cigarettes and lighters in the street. We stole our first few packs of cigarettes from a small corner shop, which we decided deserved to be robbed because its owner whistled lasciviously and shouted demeaning comments at young girls walking past. *Want to taste?* he might say and grab his crotch, or *Want to come around the back for a spot of work?* Then he'd simply chuckle to himself.

I walked inside and asked if the man could sell me some corn flour. When he came out from behind the counter, opened the bag of flour, and began measuring it into a smaller bag, Agim shouted to him from outside and asked for a kilo of tomatoes. When the man didn't go straight outside to measure them, Agim informed him that he would go and buy them at the store across the street instead. The man leaped up like a jack-in-the-box and went outside to weigh tomatoes for Agim, and while he was out of sight I slipped behind the counter and pinched ten packs of red Marlboros and stuffed them around the waist of my trousers like a belt.

"I've changed my mind, thanks," said Agim once the storekeeper had put his best tomatoes into a bag. "My father wanted better tomatoes than these." Once the storekeeper came back inside, I too turned down the flour. *It's too lumpy, my sister will never be able to make anything from this.*

"Get out of here," the man said, first to Agim, then to me.

We walked back to the city center, laid out the cigarette packs at the bottom of an old fruit box, and began walking around restaurants, cafés, squares, and parks. Agim had his own area and I had mine. If we sold one pack for a fifth more than it cost in the store, after five packs we'd have enough to buy another pack, and in this way we worked out that before long we'd have enough money to buy food and clothes. Either that or we'd have a phenomenal amount of tobacco.

We roamed the streets from early morning until late in the evening. In the mornings it felt as though we had been glued to the stony ledges we called beds, and in the evenings our feet felt as though they had been mangled by the keel of a ship, but we soon noticed that a small amount of money was starting to build up. Our selection was widening all the time, and in addition to cigarettes and lighters we were soon selling chewing gum, watches, and air fresheners. We'd even managed to get some regular customers who came to like me and my banter so much that they didn't buy tobacco from any other street vendors.

And the more money we saved, the more courageously we talked about the future, of holidays at the beach in Ulqini or Durrës, of studying at the University of Tirana, of crossing the border into Greece and from Greece to the world beyond.

One man befriended me more than others. He owned a restaurant opposite a mosque; he was always sitting at the same table and he always bought a pack of cigarettes from me at around midday. His name was Enver, and in some ways he reminded me of Agim's father.

One day he asked me straight out, "Are you homeless? Where are your parents?"

In front of him on the table were a half-empty cup of coffee, a pair of sunglasses, and a lighter bearing the image of a soccer player. His voice was calm, but to me his every word was a blow to my ribs that pierced my stomach and shook my spine. When I almost dropped the box I was carrying he placed his right hand on my shoulder.

"Are you homeless, *djalosh*? Where is your father?"

His words seemed to drown somewhere. All I could see were his bushy eyebrows; I smelled the heady stink of his breath and tasted the dryness in my mouth.

"My father is dead," I stammered. "And I'm not homeless,"

I said, managing to swallow back my agitation and the images of my father. "Or poor."

"Very well," he said, and he asked to buy a pack of red Marlboros and a new lighter with a picture of the Albanian flag and the word SHQIPËRIA, which referred to all Albanians who had spread out across the Balkans regardless of where the borders had been drawn.

That evening I told Agim I wanted some new clothes and said I felt ashamed looking like this.

"I know. Me too," he replied, rolling his eyes with a deflated sigh.

We were still the same people, we still dreamed in the same way, and we still wanted the same things as before: soap and shoes with no holes in them, normal food, *pasul* and *pitë,* goulash and stuffed peppers, a soft rug or a mattress to lie on, a door we could lock, clean sheets and laundry detergent for our dirty clothes, trousers with legs that weren't constantly muddy and full of holes.

"But we mustn't waste our money before the winter," said Agim, and I nodded, content that Agim was resolute and committed to saving money, as we had sworn we would never be penniless again.

"We need every last coin we can put aside," he continued, taking me by the elbow and shaking me a few times as if to clear my mind so that I would see what was truly important.

Because there was only one thing without which we couldn't have survived. I needed nothing else in my life except him, and I knew that he needed nothing else and nobody else in his life except me.

THE LION'S BREATH

As we wandered around the city, we heard countless tales of the fate of the Albanians, of how splintered life had become. Poverty had broken families, split the bonds between husbands and wives, brothers and sisters, children and parents. Hunger drove many people to suicide or forced them to sell everything they owned for a pittance; some even gambled their houses away. Agim heard of a man who had come to an agreement with smugglers to sell his daughter to Italy. But the most tragic aspect of the story, however, was not the father's greed but his daughter's willingness to leave. She would rather sell herself for money than live in Albania—and when Agim told me this it didn't surprise me in the least.

When we learned that some people protesting outside foreign embassies had been granted visas to countries in Western Europe, we were envious, and there was nothing encouraging in the envy we felt, nothing to make us work harder to achieve what we wanted. It was a different kind of envy, demoralizing, the kind of envy that made us think that other people had taken something from us, stolen our options, our direction.

We imagined life in Germany and Scandinavia, the kinds of things German people do, what Germans think in the course of a day.

"Probably . . . ," Agim began, holding back a laugh. "Probably what to eat next."

"Or what to buy," I said, and we both chuckled.

"I know," he said, interrupting our laughter. "What are Swedish people like in the morning?" Agim asked and repositioned the jacket under his head.

"Well?"

"They feel sad because they have to go to work to earn money for a full eight hours."

Again we laughed but soon fell serious; the harshness of our mattress hurt my sides. I took a deep breath, and I heard him do the same. He was nowhere near falling asleep either.

"I know," he said again, placing a finger on my wrist. "What do Finnish people worry about before falling asleep?"

"Well?" I asked again, and looked at his slender fingers, silvered in the moonlight, the boom of my heartbeat ringing in my ears.

"Oh no, says the Finn, only seven hours until I have to get up again!"

Before my eyes closed I recalled the story my father had told me about a lion that was brought to a zoo in the middle of an old city. A group of men had gone to the lion's home, captured it by shooting a tranquilizer dart into its neck, and transported it to a part of the world where the lion had no chance of survival without help from humans.

The lion was locked in a cage at the top of a tall hill, and the locals were invited to come and look at it. When the lion was feeding they were terrified of its gigantic jaws, of its saber teeth that tore apart hunks of pork as though they were soft cheese; they watched as the lion slowly woke up to begin a new day, squinted its green eyes, and stretched its limbs like a cat the size of a house; they admired its giant mane and razor-sharp claws. The lion became an attraction; people wanted to see it while they still had the chance.

But eventually the lion fell silent and its roar was heard only on rare occasions, though the staff and visitors to the zoo tried to provoke the lion, sometimes throwing rocks at it, sometimes waving their arms or taunting it with fresh meat. Some people said that you should never look directly into the lion's green eyes because then you would die or turn into a statue; it would bring you unhappiness in love, work, or your family life. Others said that if you heard the lion's roar, it would bring you love and enough good fortune that you could share it around.

One day the lion escaped from the zoo. Nobody could tell how the lion had managed to do this, neither the zoo's staff nor the townsfolk. The animal's surprising, inexplicable disappearance whipped the locals into a frenzy: men took up their rifles, climbed on their horses, and rode off in search of the lion in the nearby woods, hills, and mountains, and the women shut their children indoors. *What if the lion finds our children and eats them?* they wondered. *It is a wild beast, after all, a creature that thinks of nothing but how to satiate its hunger. The lion surely can't have gone far,* they thought.

Weeks went by, and because nobody had seen a trace of the lion, people began to suggest that it must have died, its body would turn up before long, its green eyes must already be in the vultures' stomachs. The lion has to be so weak and hungry by now that it won't even be able to catch an old man, they reasoned with themselves, though they knew only too well that the lion was still alive. It had to be hiding somewhere, breathing as quiet as a mouse and prowling around like a newly married woman in a sleeping house, and in secret they believed that one day the lion would in fact return, for they still looked around anxiously and made sure to double-check that all their houses' doors were locked.

Some months later most people had forgotten all about the lion, so when it finally reappeared on the outskirts of the city people could hardly believe their eyes. That isn't the lion we know, people said disdainfully, and they mocked the lion's slovenly steps, its sagging hide and protruding ribs, its dirty tangled mane. They laughed at it. The lion proceeded toward the foot of the hillside and stopped for a moment to look at the hill that it would have to ascend to reach the zoo. It breathed heavily and closed its eyes, and when it finally raised one of its paws to take the first step toward the summit the lion felt a bullet sink into its flank like a wrecking ball, and slumped to the ground.

With a weary, glazed eye it saw the crowds of people gathered behind it, a man with a rifle in his hand; it saw the children dangling from their mothers' necks, and it heard the growing sound of the crowd, saw the man with the rifle lifted up like a hero, and there was relief in the women's sighs as they lowered their children to the ground.

Europe was our America; everybody around us wanted to be European, to belong to the European family, to stand on the other side of the invisible but insurmountable fence where people were people, at the forefront of humanity. But Europe wasn't a place you could get to all that easily, and the more difficult the authorities made the process of getting there and the more we read and heard about how other countries, especially Italy, were helping Albania get back on its feet, the more determined we were to reach Western Europe.

At school nobody had told us anything at all about the other countries of Europe. Instead we learned all manner of useless information about communism, Enver Hoxha, the Five-Year Plan and Albania's military arsenal, individual warriors from our history, their lives, their wives and children and victories in bloody battles whose moral was always the same: that the Albanians were great heroes, warriors without equal, and that thousands had died for our freedom.

Agim and I began collecting newspaper articles about Albanians who had moved to Europe or who had tried to get there. Earlier that summer thousands had sailed from Vlorë or Durrës and reached the Italian ports of Brindisi and Bari, where they were offered food, accommodation, and legal assistance. The newspapers featured images of Albanians penned into camps set up in military barracks and parks and harbors; there were even some photographs of Italian families who had opened their doors to fleeing Albanians. At first the Italians seemed to like us as they criticized the efforts of their own government: the situation had been handled badly, the tragedy had lasted too long, and the Albanians had not been provided with adequate living conditions.

"It's because we look the same as the Italians," Agim commented. "If we didn't fit into the crowd so well, they probably wouldn't like us that much."

"You're wrong. People always help others in need," I said

loftily, but when the newspapers began running stories about the petty crimes committed by Albanians, shoplifting and robberies, the Italians' attitude soon changed.

Agim read the paper to me and I listened. Soon the Italians were worried that people would start flooding into their country not only from Albania but from farther afield too, Yugoslavia, Turkey, and the Middle East. Italy is not a charity but a country in a state of emergency, someone said, and another added that the Albanians are barbaric, like wild beasts, violent criminals whose unabated bloodthirstiness put the security of our civilization at risk. There was mention of how much this had cost the Italian taxpayer, with fifty billion lira a month spent on pampering the Albanians. They said the Albanians were in Italy looking for work and a better life and not political asylum, which cannot be awarded on the basis of poverty alone. And I wondered why poverty wasn't reason enough to allow people to move from one country into another, why looking for work and a better life in another country was somehow wrong. Why couldn't people do that? Doesn't everyone deserve a job that pays enough money to make a living?

Eventually Agim and I began to think along the same lines as the Italians. Didn't these criminals understand that, apart from worsening their own opportunities, their bad behavior impacted the chances of their compatriots who wanted to make a fresh start? Didn't they realize how shameful it was?

By August there were once again tens of thousands of people trying to enter Italy; it was as though the country's scent had settled in the nostrils of every Albanian. On August 7 a crowd of thousands commandeered the cargo ship *Vlora,* and the very next day the captain, Halim Milaqi, steered the ship out of the port of Durrës toward Bari. For the next few days the newspapers were filled with images in which the *Vlora* looked less like a ship and more like an anthill. Desperate Albanians had filled every deck, some had climbed up its pipes and ropes, some dangled precariously from the railings, and so the ship set sail like an enormous, tattered sheet. The newspapers showed pictures of people who had fallen into the sea, people who couldn't fit into the ship, images of those who had disappeared in the water and whom the ship's propellers had shredded into food for the ocean's own creatures, images of weeping children and happily waving men.

"Do you think those people will ever come back?" I asked Agim.

"Not on your life," he replied cockily, as though the mere suggestion of such a thing was ludicrous.

"But their families have stayed here," I said. "They might come home one day."

He wasn't listening. "What would you take with you?" he snapped. "Exactly. Nothing," he said, answering his own question before I could get a word in, and I decided not to say anything at all because I sensed that, right now, that was what he most needed from me.

When the *Vlora* arrived in the port of Bari, the Albanians disembarked onto the dock. Some jumped from the decks into the water and swam ashore, and when I first saw those images I was convinced that those men had jumped into the water because during the journey they had wet themselves or defecated in their trousers. At first the Italian authorities didn't allow the Albanians outside the harbor complex; the new arrivals were given some food and blankets but nothing more. Then they were escorted to the soccer stadium in Bari. There a helicopter dropped them food and clothes, but when it became clear that they were to be deported back to Albania a riot broke out; some managed to escape the stadium, others returned to Albania voluntarily.

When I heard these stories I was more ashamed than ever before, more ashamed than when my own father had caught me telling a filthy, selfish lie, and I don't think Agim had ever been so furious either, because one August evening he folded up the newspaper and declared that the Albanians were shocking people, they were animals, then he tore the paper to shreds as though it were a photograph of his worst enemy and said with the conviction of boundless confidence and extreme frustration that when we finally reach Europe we will never tell anyone we are Albanians, that's what we'll do, we are no longer Albanians, and I agreed because it suited me perfectly.

THE SENSE OF SNOW

The days grew shorter, wet snow wrapped itself around the city like a silken sheet, icy winds blew in from across the Adriatic Sea and silenced the city, and bright glowing lights lit behind the windows. Tables outside cafés and restaurants were carried inside, the market stalls disappeared, and eventually we found ourselves once again with no money.

At first the chill appeared almost unnoticed, but soon the frozen air hit us right in the stomach and gnawed at our limbs as though they had been stuck into a meat grinder. The first sub-zero days almost paralyzed us, because there was nowhere for us to go inside and warm up. Even huddling tight against each other didn't keep us warm enough. Café owners didn't allow us to sit indoors without paying and we couldn't afford to order anything. Before long the cold burrowed beneath our skin and deep into our bones where it resided, merciless and omnipresent; it was an ardent, noble cold that not even standing by an open fire could banish. My lips became so chapped that they cracked in two; I couldn't feel my fingers or hear when people spoke to me, because the cold had numbed my thoughts too.

I wanted to die, and so did Agim, so that the cold might be replaced with something else, anything at all, because it had become the only thing that we could sense. Even hunger was easier to tolerate than the cold.

We had two options: we could either die or we could do something about it. Because we had nothing to sell, we decided to try to get jobs. We would work for free if necessary— anything to be indoors.

I wandered around dozens of cafés and restaurants in my half of the city, and Agim did the same in his half. I asked the owners if they needed help and told them I was hardworking and did all kinds of labor, everything from washing dishes to waiting tables. I asked only for a very modest wage and said I was eager to commit to the job and learn new skills, but nobody wanted to take me on, and again I was convinced it had something to do with the way I looked, my ripped down jacket, which was covered in grime, my face, dried so much with the cold that it was impossible to show any expression, my lips, which looked as though they had been attacked with a saw.

As evening fell I roamed the windy streets to the restaurant owned by Enver. There he was behind the counter, the man with the familiar, friendly, broad face. He walked up to me and offered his hand. Because it had been some time since our last meeting, he apparently thought it proper to introduce himself formally, giving his full name. After shaking my hand, Mr. Selim stood staring at me with his grey-brown eyes.

"Are you looking for work?" he asked, pushing a hand into his pocket.

I noticed that he began wiping the palm of his hand against his thigh. Yes, I replied in almost a whisper. The aroma of freshly brewed coffee, the steaming, almost intoxicating scent of fresh bread and the mouthwatering smell of french fries cooking in the fryer almost knocked me out.

"I can offer you work," he said and took his hand out of his pocket when he realized my eyes had fixed on it.

"Thank you, sir," I said. "I'll do whatever you ask, and I thank you for allowing me to do it."

At this he scoffed and managed to look even a little self-important: his large gums protruded and his thin lips almost disappeared from view. He told me he had lived on this street all his life, he'd had the same restaurant for years and would soon leave it to his son, if only the son stopped teasing girls and loitering around with his friends.

Mr. Selim showed me along a narrow corridor and into the room at the back. The only way to walk along the corridor was sideways, as tall cupboards lined both walls, their shelves filled with flour, jars of spices, pasta, preserved fruit and vegetables, tomato purée, olives, cheeses, beans, and peas; the sight of all this made me feel faint. We eventually arrived in a large room at the back where there was a gas stove, pots, knives, chopping boards, fresh fruit and vegetables. The air was heavy with the sweet smell of onions and raw meat. I was soon so warm that my palms and legs began to tingle, as though the frost had burned my skin so much that it had turned into a single, giant piece of scar tissue that covered my entire body.

Mr. Selim showed me to my workstation. In front of me was a large sink full of cutlery and plates, some still bearing left-over food. Mr. Selim quickly showed me where to find cleaning equipment, explained what temperature the dishes should be washed at and how to dry them properly, but I couldn't clearly hear his words as my mind was filled with those half-eaten pizzas and *byrek,* meat pies served with *bibër* and cabbage salad, fresh bread and peppers cooked first in the oven, then in a frying pan, towering hamburgers layered with slices of tomato and salad, their edges almost gleaming.

"When can you start?" he asked, and though this was a perfectly natural question under the circumstances, it seemed to come from above and entirely out of the blue.

"Straightaway," I said humbly, and I could hear the pleading note of hunger in my voice.

Mr. Selim took a deep breath, rested a finger on the sink, and began wiping it pensively, as though he were trying to put his thoughts into words.

"You'll have to clean up a bit first," he said. "You can use the shower in my apartment upstairs. My wife and daughter will serve dinner soon."

A moment later we stepped out the back door of the restaurant. Next to the door a set of concrete stairs led up to the living quarters above, the railings decorative and painted white. The cold outdoor air felt fresh and bracing; for once it was wonderful to move from the warmth out into the cold.

His home was large and set on three floors. The restaurant was on the ground floor; on the second floor were Mr. and Mrs. Selim's bedroom, a large bathroom and a large kitchen opening to a dining room attached to a living room filled with old-fashioned, valuable-looking furniture, and on the third floor lived their children, sixteen-year-old Gëzime and eighteen-year-old Gëzim, who now and then waited tables in the restaurant.

Mrs. Selim, a tall lady in her forties with wide hips, welcomed me graciously but was somewhat standoffish with her husband. Their life together seemed tired; they spoke to each other slowly and with fatigue.

Mrs. Selim guided me into the bathroom and left me alone, popping her head around the door only to tell me that dinner would be served in half an hour. Their hospitality made me feel awkward and I couldn't understand how they could be so kind to a complete stranger. I could have been anybody, could have stuffed my pockets full of their belongings and run away. And yet the only thing I wanted to do was to show them I was worthy of their trust.

I took off my clothes, hopped over the edge of the bathtub, and stood beneath the warm shower for almost half an hour, and I couldn't recall a time when I'd felt as content as when I saw the grime peeling away from my hardened skin like dust from a counter, as I felt the clean water running down my body and gathering at the bottom of the bath like dark, foamy glue before disappearing into the depths of the sewers forever.

After I turned the water off, Mrs. Selim knocked on the door and said she'd left a pile of her son's old clothes by the door and asked me to leave my own clothes in the tub. When I stepped out of the shower, I opened the door as quietly as I could, reached my hand outside like a tired snake, and grabbed the pile of clothes on the floor. Mrs. Selim's son's clothes smelled of peaches; they had been ironed and felt as soft as cotton wool.

I pulled on the blue jeans, the black long-sleeved shirt and white tennis socks, stuffed my own clothes into a plastic bag, and made my way toward the smell of food and the cozy sounds of family life coming from Mr. and Mrs. Selim's living room. The closer I came to the doorway, the more fiercely my heart began to pound. All at once I felt terribly warm.

"Take a seat," said Mrs. Selim before I'd even reached the living room.

Mr. Selim was already sitting at the head of the table and stirring his soup with a look of impatience. Mrs. Selim put down her dishcloth by the sink, pulled out a chair from beneath the table, and again gestured for me to sit down. Then she approached me, snatched the plastic bag dangling from my forefinger, and called out to her daughter, who appeared instantly and took the bag as her mother whispered something to her. At that I realized I'd forgotten to leave my clothes in the bathtub as Mrs. Selim had asked, and this made me feel all the more ill at ease.

I wanted to apologize, turn the clock back, and correct my mistake, but instead I sat down next to Mr. Selim and waited for his instruction to start eating. But Mr. Selim didn't move; he simply looked at me, his eyes expressive as they shifted from me to the basket of bread, the pot of creamy soup, the fried eggs, and *suxhuk* topped with spiced oil. I looked at him, awkward again, and wiped my sweaty forehead until Mr. Selim opened his mouth.

"You are a guest in our house," he began finally. "Please, start with the soup." And with that I poured two large ladles of soup into the bowl in front of me.

The first spoonful of soup was perhaps the most wonderful thing that had ever passed my lips, and I ate so much and with such speed and appetite that I almost choked, then ate more still; I simply couldn't get enough. I decided I would not become full. I decided that instead of a stomach I had an empty cellar into which I would store food like a bear—everything laid out in front of me. I tore the bread with my fingers and stuffed it into my mouth, and I didn't care what Mr. Selim thought, didn't care upon hearing the sounds of Mr. Selim's daughter washing my clothes in the bathroom.

After the meal I felt as though I had expanded to three times my normal size. Moving was slow and difficult, my legs felt heavy, and my stomach was hard as stone. My desire to fall asleep was so great that I thought it wouldn't matter if I never woke up again. I thanked Mr. and Mrs. Selim many times over and said I would arrive for work at noon the following day just as Mr. Selim had asked during our meal, and Mrs. Selim said I would find my clothes in the storeroom in the morning.

Agim hardly recognized me. He stood in front of me, bewildered; I noticed that he wanted to touch my face, but it was as though he was ashamed of his filthy fingers. He admired my new clothes and wanted to hear the same things over and over, how Mr. Selim had invited me into his home to wash, what the warm water had felt like on my skin, what the clean clothes smelled like. Then he told me he too had managed to find a job at a local laundry.

"I'm so proud of you," he said. "Everything's going to turn out just fine."

"I think so too," I said.

We went to sleep, huddled against each other, and the cold didn't seem to plague us as it had before, because tomorrow, the day after, the spring that would soon burst into flower was growing within us like the most exciting movie.

At first working at Mr. Selim's restaurant felt tough and tedious, but with surprising ease I became accustomed to the mechanical work and to how slowly time passed. The flow of dirty dishes never seemed to end. On busy days I might not finish work until late in the evening. I soon became ill and had an allergic reaction to the dish soap, my hands became dry and started to itch, but I was paid a wage for the work I did and I was allowed to eat as much of the leftover food as I wished, and because I had permission to use the toilet at the back to wash, I didn't complain to Mr. Selim about anything and didn't even ask for a pair of rubber gloves.

I never spoke to Mr. Selim about where I'd been before I started working for him. He never asked about where I lived and never sent greetings to my family the way he did with the other staff. From the way he looked at me when I said I was going to stop for the day or that I would wash up the plates as soon as I'd finished with the pots, or when I said I needed the bathroom before my shift or asked to take food home to give to Agim later in the evening, I understood I was somehow special in his eyes. I imagined he probably pitied me, that he knew the truth of the situation but was too discreet to mention it out loud.

One morning, a few weeks after I'd started working there, Mr. Selim appeared at my workstation. He didn't say anything, he simply stood on the spot and looked at me, a strange smile masking his face. At first I thought he was drunk, because he was breathing heavily the way drunkards do.

Then he took a few steps closer—it felt as though the floorboards trembled beneath the force of his heavy steps—and pressed himself against my back. I could feel his stomach against my lower back, the tremor of his thick, knobbly thighs, and his hardened penis against my bottom. Then he grabbed my sides with his stumpy, hairy paws, slid them down my hips, and began rubbing my backside.

"Don't stop," he instructed me.

I was terrified and continued scouring the already clean

plate with a sponge. That man, I thought, I don't know what I thought, I was too afraid to notice among the plates a knife I could have stuck into his repulsive chest or with which I could have slit his throat, too afraid to run away and steal the cash box, too afraid to say anything, to ask him to stop.

Mr. Selim pulled my pants down and began slapping my back and legs. Then he began grumbling obscenities, *Take that, you little whore,* he said, and he turned me around, placed his hand on the top of my head, and pushed it downward like a knife into a soft lawn. Open your mouth, open it, now, he said, slapping me across the face with the palm of his hand, and I opened my mouth and shut my eyes and resolved to do as he asked. He thrust a salty finger in my mouth, and as he pulled me to my feet with his finger I banished all thoughts of where I was at that moment from my mind and thought only of where I wanted to be: it was a hot summer's day, Agim and I were on a white sandy beach, sitting side by side looking out at the ships as they grew smaller and finally disappeared into the mists of the horizon.

Mr. Selim turned me around again and pressed me against the sink. He spat into his hand and spread the spittle over himself and over me. *Quiet,* he growled, though I hadn't said a word, and when he pushed inside me I thought I would die, right there, in this man's arms, those greasy hands that he used to whack my buttocks would be the last to touch me, because I hadn't known that such pain was possible, let alone that you could survive such pain, and I couldn't speak, couldn't breathe, couldn't move or shift position, and my hands slipped from the edge of the sink and into the dirty dishwater, into which I submerged my face and screamed.

.   .   .

He humiliated me like this for the next few months, and I let him. I reasoned with myself that this was a small price to pay for the work I was allowed to do and the money I earned. Though I bled every time I went to the bathroom and though my body was constantly in pain, it became easier each time, I learned to relax the right muscles and I began eating fresh lemon after each encounter.

Over time it became more and more subtle and discreet: Mr. Selim might ask me to stay behind after a shift to help him, sometimes he asked me to take a break in the middle of the day while Mrs. Selim was running errands and their children were out of the house. Then he would ask me to follow him up to the bedroom, where he pulled the thick floral curtains in front of the windows, locked all of the doors in the house, and started ordering me around. *Change position. Fetch me some water. Clothes on. Clothes off.* Sometimes he even followed me into the toilet at the back of the restaurant before the other staff had arrived.

Some days he was so rough with me that I began thinking of different ways to kill him. I loathed him, his disgusting face, his small hands, his thick hair, I wanted him to drown, to fry in cooking fat, to burn in an oven, to suffocate in a gas chamber.

But I lived this way for months without doing a thing, allowing him to do whatever he wanted to me, with me, and I didn't say anything to Agim because I knew that if I told him the truth, Agim would have run to the restaurant, pistol in hand, and emptied the chamber into Mr. Selim's backside.

———

Agim never thought of home. He never even used the word *home,* and before long he gave up the words *Albania* and *Alba-*

nian too. He didn't believe in God, his own people, or the idea that there was a place where people could build a home. I remember him once saying that all life on earth is war and that death is the end of one battle in that eternal war, and thus in his mind even home was a place where wars occurred. Once he even said that all Albanians and all gods will die one day; before long everything will disappear.

Perhaps this was something he had read somewhere, but it had the effect that I too started thinking about my life from the outside, I began to understand him and why he found it so easy to deal with adversity: when you don't care about your life, you don't worry about death either, and when you don't care about life in general, you can see its inexorable, merciless end as bright as day, flooded with light.

I began to agree with him on most things, but still I wanted to think that though there is much sorrow and suffering in the world, things we cannot affect at all, there are some things where we can make a difference. I tried to make Agim understand that we should concentrate on the things we can change instead of worrying about the things we can't. It doesn't help anyone to think that one day everything will be destroyed anyway.

Sometimes I really worried about him. He had always been buoyed with a certain melancholy, shielded with a certain exterior; there was a certain slowness in his movements though he was quick to talk and act. Still, he retreated into his own thoughts as he might into an unpleasant dream, and often he looked as though he didn't know where he was, though he knew more about the world around him than anyone I knew. I was afraid that Agim would lose all hope, the desire to live, that our plight would make him give up altogether and pick up the pistol, stick the barrel in his mouth, and eventually pull the trigger because as long as I'd known him, for some reason I'd been convinced that his life would end in the most dreadful way possible: by his own hand.

Through the course of that winter he asked me, just as he had asked me in the past, what the point of all this was: *What's the point in living, Bujar? Wouldn't it be easier if you shot me first, then shot yourself, or the other way around? Would you have the courage to do it?* he asked. *Would you do that for me if I asked you to? I know I would if you asked me.*

As summer approached I suggested we get a change of scenery, because his talk was becoming darker all the time, his movements slower, he would spend longer and longer without saying a word, his gaze fixed on the same spot, the joy that had once lived in his eyes now seemingly extinguished. If we didn't do something today, I thought, tomorrow he might not exist.

"Let's get out of Tirana. Let's go somewhere warmer," I said. "Durrës, maybe." He agreed, though at first he seemed somewhat skeptical about the idea.

On the day we left I emptied the cash box at Mr. Selim's restaurant as he tidied himself up in the toilet at the back. The chlorine taste of his sperm was still in my mouth, and once I'd emptied the register of all its cash I ran off, I ran and ran back to my Agim, grabbed him around the neck, and I was so profoundly relieved to see him, for on the way home I'd become worried whether he would still be alive, and I pulled his forehead against my own, he held my agitated hands still, and I was in such a frenzy at the sudden rush of excitement that I almost kissed him.

"What have you done?" he asked, his voice quavering.

"Let's go," I said, closing my eyes, and for a short moment we simply stood there, motionless, holding each other like lovers.

Soon we stepped onto a bus. This time we would ration our money more sensibly, we would sleep in boats, ships, and abandoned buildings, we would sell ice cream, jewelry, and cigarettes on the beach at Durrës and along the seaside boulevard all summer, we'd sell so much that we'd be able to save enough money to allow us to move abroad and start afresh.

We stepped off the bus; the air smelled of almonds, of oil and olives, and all around us was the sound of lively chatter laced with emotion.

"I'm happy," Agim said on our first night there as we sat on the beach. "I'm happy we came here."

"So am I," I answered.

THE UNDERWATER WORLD

Selling knickknacks in Durrës was noticeably easier than in Tirana, even though there was much more competition, because the city was awash with tourists. People came to Durrës from all across Albania, even from Yugoslavia.

There were Italian businessmen in the city too, but they were far more difficult customers, and I was sure that their impression of us was every bit as bad as I'd heard. They were constantly gloating at us with an air of superiority, constantly questioning the authenticity of the trinkets we were selling and laughing in our faces. Of course the designer sunglasses, hanging on a wooden stick and which we'd picked up at the bazaar for next to nothing, weren't real, and neither were the gleaming wristwatches and designer handbags. They shooed us on our way like flies. These were the same men who shook their heads as they passed Romany beggars with their children placed in the middle of the pavement and wrapped so tightly in dirty sheets that they looked like a wasps' nest on which someone had drawn the wrinkly face of a baby. There they lay, bundles in the street, dying beneath the hottest of suns, and when I saw how disparagingly the Italians looked at them, I imagined their relief as they thought, *Thank goodness Italy isn't like this; only in places that are fundamentally rotten do people live in such misery.*

Agim told me that people in Italy weren't forced into arranged marriages. In Italy, he said, men constantly buy their wives gifts, men listen to their wives in family matters and invite the entire family to celebrate the children's birthdays. I started to get annoyed at Agim always talking about Italy as if everything there was better than here in Albania.

"Nobody is perfect," I said.

We walked along the shore side by side. Agim was eating a roasted corncob, and I was waiting for him to eat half of it and give me the other half.

"What?"

"I've had enough of listening to you talking shit about the Albanians. You can see for yourself how badly the Italians here behave. They drink and harass the girls. They're pigs."

"If you lie down with dogs, you'll get up with fleas."

"You're an Albanian too, whether you like it or not. You can't escape that fact, no matter how much you try."

"I am not like them," he whined, munching on his corncob so that there was less than half left. "I'm not like other Albanians."

"You might not be like them, but you're their compatriot," I said and held out my hand, where I expected him to place the remains of the corncob. He bit into it again. "You can't just decide not to be the way you were born."

"Yes, you can," he almost shouted. "Of course you can decide. Why on earth shouldn't you?"

"You just can't," I said, watching as again he munched on the corncob. "Give it to me."

"What?"

"The corn."

"Sorry," he said. "I forgot." He placed the tattered remains of the cob in my hand. "But you're wrong, Bujar. People change all the time. We don't leave the same way we arrived."

"Of course we don't, but you can't just change your country or your name to something else."

"Yes, I can."

"You cannot. You can deny it and lie about it, but you are an Albanian too, you always have been and you always will be, Albanian is your mother tongue and your name is Agim, and you'll always know that, even if you never tell anyone the truth."

He shook his head, gritted his teeth, and gave a deep sigh.

"You're jealous. That's what this is. Admit it."

"I am not," I said. I looked at the sky, then threw the gnawed corncob on the sand.

"Yes, you are. You always have been."

"Jealous of what?"

"Of the fact that I'm better than you."

"What?"

"I am better than you. At everything. I can do more than you, I know more than you. You can't stand the fact that you're not my equal."

"Stop it."

"Admit it. I am better than you. You don't know anything and you don't know how to do anything. You're stupid. An idiot. Worthless."

I knocked him to the ground, gripped his neck, and trapped his thrashing legs with my thighs.

"What did you say?" I shouted, raising my fist to his forehead.

When he started to cry like a child who has hurt himself I climbed off him and helped him up with both hands.

"Silly," I said and brushed the sand from his clothes. "Everything's fine," I continued, when I noticed that he still hadn't pulled himself together but stood with both hands shielding his face, his fingers trembling.

For the first few weeks we slept outdoors in shifts, sometimes down on the beach where we washed our clothes, sometimes on the rocks along the shore where we dried them.

One day Agim met a young local man who promised to allow us to use the attic of his house for a small monthly fee. He showed us the way up to the roof of the apartment building using a ladder and opened the door leading into a stale-smelling corridor. From there we went down one flight of stairs and found ourselves in a small storage room full of dirty rags and bottles of detergent. A broken lamp dangled from the ceiling, the wooden floor was rotten, and the corners of the room were covered in grime and shrouded in cobwebs. There were three doors in the room: behind one were the stairs leading up to the roof; judging by the noise, behind another was a generator, while the third door opened into an empty storage room. Agim glanced at me and held out his hand. I took his hand in mine and laid our plastic bags on the floor.

The space was at most ten square meters in size. Agim found some rusted old tin signs, which he used to make us a floor. In the trash cans he found old newspapers, a dirty mattress, two ripped, yellowed pillows and two woolen blankets; then he stole some glasses and napkins from cafés along the beach and a lantern from a general store. He didn't give a shit about getting caught.

He began stealing books too, which he read to me in the evenings. One evening he pulled out an Albanian-Italian dictionary. He wanted us to know at least a bit of the language by the time we finally set foot on the country's shore.

"What if I never manage to learn Italian?" he asked, frustrated, laying the book down between us.

"Agim," I said, picking up the book, "you're the most intelligent person I've ever met. If anyone can learn Italian, it's you." I placed the book back in his lap.

He picked up the book and flicked through the pages, as though he were no longer afraid of its contents, and began reading out loud the pronunciation guidelines and simple examples at the beginning of the book. *I drive a car,* he said in Albanian and then in Italian. We were sitting with our backs against the wall; though it was midday it was almost dark in the storage room and nobody knew of our existence, but now we had a place we could call home, and what's more we had a dictionary and his brains, a plan and a goal.

Once he became tired of reading, Agim placed his hand on my thigh and allowed his fingers to slide around the back of my leg. He edged his hand upward in such a way that I felt a tingling sensation in my groin, then he turned his head and started to kiss my neck, and how wonderful it felt when he slid his hand into my trousers and started to rub, and I closed my eyes and it didn't occur to me for a second to ask him to stop.

We lived like this for weeks. In the daytime we sold as much tobacco and junk as we could, and in the evenings we drank lemonade or beer on the beach, smoked cigarettes, and feasted on paprika-flavored potato chips, chocolate bars, and *llokum,* and as we sat on the beach one orange-red evening Agim started talking about crossing the sea.

"Damn it, I'll swim across if there's no other way. I'm not going to stay here, that's for sure," he said as though he were licking the words, and his voice was so serious that I had no reason to doubt that he would do it. He really would swim across, and he'd probably make it, with that unflinching confidence of his and the power of determination, he'd do it.

It bothered me that for the first time he'd started talking about himself in the singular. Didn't he realize I'd left everything behind for him? I wondered. Didn't he know that I didn't have anywhere else to go now either, that I'd always stood by him and always would, because I could never leave him? I took his hand, which was somehow both dry and clammy. He turned to look at me and said he was serious. I squeezed his hand, closed my eyes. *I know you're serious,* I said.

"I'll come with you," I said, wondering whether he spoke about himself in the singular because he thought the same as I did about the two of us: that I was nothing without him, nothing at all. And I feared that he might ask himself what he needed me for or wonder in what ways I was useful to him, and I feared this the way people fear their worst nightmares coming true, feared that the answer to my question would be *Actually, I don't need you for anything at all.*

He sneered, clasped his other hand around mine, and answered by asking why I was saying things like that. *Of course you'll come too,* he said, *because we . . .* He paused briefly, though it seemed as though he didn't need to think about his next words. *Because we'll always be together, right?*

"There's something I've been meaning to ask you," I said eventually.

"What?" he said slowly, as if he realized I'd been mulling over the matter for months, years.

"Are you . . . ?" I stammered. *"Peder?"* I managed to spit the word out, and as soon as I'd said it I felt a great sense of relief that I'd finally asked him directly, and now his only options were to answer or not to answer; there was no way of escaping such a direct question.

Agim stood up, reached his long arms behind his head, and let down his hair, which he hadn't cut for years.

"It doesn't matter if you are," I added. "But I'm not. You know that, don't you? Though we sometimes do . . . those things in the evenings."

Agim looked at me quizzically for a moment, propped a hand on his hip, leaned against it, and stared out to sea. With every day that passed he seemed smaller and thinner.

He turned back to look at me, this time with a curious smile, then dug his toe into the sand and flicked it up in my face.

"Me neither," he said, laughing. "A girl can't be a *peder,"* he continued, and I began to smile too because I'd known the answer to this question ever since I'd met him.

———————

We began planning how to cross the Adriatic Sea. Several passenger and cargo ferries sailed daily from Durrës for Italy. However, at both ends of the journey the authorities painstakingly scrutinized the passengers' documentation, so we knew there was no way we would be able to enter the country legally.

We had both attended school until eighth grade, then struck out on our own, so it was obvious that in the Italians' eyes we weren't exactly desirable immigrants. What's more, we didn't have passports or other identification: there was no official documentation of our existence.

One evening we took a walk down to Parku Buzëdeti, from which you could look out across the whole of the port of Durrës, shaped like an eagle's talon. The ships sounded their horns, and we saw metallic containers that looked like the backs of trucks hanging from cranes. This side of the harbor was like a small town all on its own. Half serious, I suggested to Agim that we could break into the harbor and hide in one of the containers.

Agim was startled and glared at me, his gaze razor-sharp, and I realized straightaway how silly it was and how useless I was at making plans.

I had consciously been trying not to think about my sister's fate. Her sudden disappearance meant there was still a small chance she was safe somewhere else, married and living in a remote mountain village or working somewhere in Greece and perhaps not in the clutches of the traffickers after all.

I didn't want to think about her or how she might have been smuggled out of Albania in a metallic container filled with other young women who had met a similar fate, I didn't want to think about how easy it was for the traffickers to bribe the dockworkers in the harbor, how corrupt the police were, and how the authorities, travel agents, and bus drivers were all involved in selling and transporting people, because it didn't help anybody—least of all my sister. If you're rich, there's nothing you can't get, and if you're poor enough, there's nothing you wouldn't do for money.

Now I felt teary, and Agim wrapped his arms around me.

"The traffickers aren't interested in boys our age. We're not good enough for those fat pigs," he said.

I felt sick. Albania and the Albanians, what miserable, small people they were, how unpleasant—me and Agim too, for we were just as much to blame as everybody else. We had befriended human traffickers, sold them sweets and cigarettes, they'd smiled at us many times, doubtless flattered that we didn't realize we should live in fear of them.

They were all around, they stood watch on the streets looking for young girls, who disappeared all the time, it happened every single day. It was as though they stuffed their prey into jam jars, then the jam was shipped out like cargo, and from that point onward the girls belonged to people they didn't know, they were slaves in an illegal factory, dancers in nightclubs, or prisoners in dark basements, with no belongings or language skills, powerless to do anything about it.

And we were all complicit in their fate: I was guilty of it, Agim too, because we accepted the world around us as it was, unchanged, and we didn't lift a finger to change it for the better.

When I awoke the next morning, Agim had fetched me a can of chilled Coca-Cola. I asked if he would like to taste it, but he declined though we normally shared everything and though I knew he loved Coca-Cola like he loved everything American.

"Come," he said.

"Where?"

"Let's go to the beach."

The foaming water tickled our feet; the day was cloudless and the sun looked enormous; it was hot and from somewhere came the squawk of birds. The buildings along the shoreline and the mountains behind them breathed in the sand like lungs inhaling moisture after a downpour.

"Don't think about it," said Agim. "You can't do anything about it. It's just one of those things you can't affect. Right?"

"I know," I said. "I don't care."

"Have you ever thought . . . ?" Agim began cautiously. "Have you ever wondered what death feels like?"

"No. Don't think about things like that," I said.

I could see in his eyes that he knew perfectly well I had wondered about it, I'd thought about it every day since we decided to leave home. What would happen if we died? Or if only one of us died—what would the other one do?

I pulled his arm toward my chest and kissed the back of his hand, and he laid his head on my shoulder.

"I love you," he said, and held his breath.

For a moment I said nothing, simply stared into the distance as far as the sea would allow.

"I know," I said eventually. "I love you too."

"Do you?" he said, letting out the breath he'd been holding inside. It burst from his mouth like air from a balloon. "Really?"

"Really."

ON THE ROAD

We began putting even more money away. We aimed to set aside at least half of our earnings and to live as frugally as possible. Sometimes I sold more, sometimes it was Agim; it didn't matter because everything we managed to save was shared. When we arrived home each evening we counted the amount of money we'd earned, he counted it and I counted it again, then we counted it all together, and my worst fear was that Agim would no longer be beside me when I awoke the following morning, that he would leave me and take all the money that we hid in a crevice in the wall. I began to dread losing him, yet my constant doubt felt almost like I was betraying him.

The quicker we got the money together, the more detailed our plans for the future became and the more enthusiastically we started learning new words in Italian.

Our first plan was to bribe the dockworkers to let us board a cargo ship and find a hiding place belowdecks where nobody would find us. Only when the ship arrived at its destination and the people on board disembarked would we step ashore, look for a police station, and seek asylum. However, our hopes of carrying out that plan were soon dashed.

We knew that many people had crossed the Adriatic Sea and that even more people wanted to attempt the crossing: the journey to the Italian ports of Brindisi or Bari wasn't long and some people said you could get there in a matter of hours, depending on the ship and its speed. Some people's plans to get across were so tragic that we couldn't help but wonder what on earth they had been thinking. How desperate they must have been to cram their entire family into a simple wooden boat and start rowing out to sea. That was the most ridiculous of the methods we heard about; it was almost certain suicide.

Sometimes there were stories in the news of empty boats found drifting at sea, their holds full of clothes, tools, and children's toys. Some of them had run out of fuel halfway across; in other boats people had started arguing during the trip and ended up destroying one another. Boats overturned in storms and heavy rain, people drowned in the open sea. And if you did manage to sail ashore, there was always the risk of being deported straightaway.

Others had sold all their belongings and paid the traffickers a small fortune to get them to Italy.

"We won't be doing that," said Agim. "You never know what they will have agreed to with the Italian authorities."

A few days later Agim announced that we would cross the sea in a motorboat.

"We'll buy a boat and set off," he said calmly.

I didn't want to discourage him by saying it was a crazy idea, it was dangerous, and neither of us knew the first thing about boats. Besides, buying a boat wasn't that simple.

He began to explain his plan. A small motorboat will be perfect for us, he said, one made of plastic or fiberglass, because there are only two of us and we don't have that many belongings. We would have to follow the weather forecast: we shouldn't set off if the wind is too strong. We should reserve at least one full day for the journey, but we should take enough food and drink to last several days. According to his calculations, we had saved enough money to be able to afford a small motorboat.

"What do you think?"

"Are you sure this is going to work?" I asked.

"Everything will work out," he said. "How hard can it be? Besides, I've read a book that listed everything people should take with them on a fishing trip. And the man in that book was really old. Don't worry, I'll take care of everything. And when we get there, I'll do the talking because I know what to say to the authorities."

He took a pack of Wests from the bottom of his box of wares, opened it, pulled out a cigarette as though it were a sword, then handed me the pack, and in an instant our little cubbyhole was full of smoke, and I wondered how he even knew to take all of these things into consideration.

Neither of us dared carry around all the cash we had amassed, and if we were to buy something as expensive as this, someone would certainly start following us. Agim said that for that reason all preparations would have to be carried out on the day of our departure—no, on the same afternoon and evening, within the space of a few hours, he clarified, and we would have to set sail at sundown when the sea winds calmed.

When the day before our departure finally arrived, Agim went off to buy us some new clothes, and I went out to sell what was left of our knickknacks. Eventually I gave most of them away for next to nothing. In the afternoon Agim came home with bags full of clothes. He had bought us both a pair of jeans—dark ones for himself and a lighter pair for me—two pairs of standard black leather shoes, and two shirts, light blue for himself and white for me.

"Do you like them?" he asked, though he could see how much I liked the clothes.

"I love them," I replied.

"Don't get them dirty," he instructed me. "We want to look good when we arrive."

Then he threw me a lump of soap, which I held beneath my nose with both hands and sniffed.

"You can only take one bag with you," said Agim. "I mean it. The lighter the boat, the quicker it will travel and the less fuel it will use," he explained, perhaps more to himself than to me.

Agim got up early the next day and bought us six large bottles of water. We climbed up to the roof of the house and poured one bottle of water over each other, then we thoroughly lathered ourselves with soap. Agim scratched at his groin and armpits and looked as though scrubbing himself made every cell in his body itch. We were both white as snow and somehow freezing cold, and we hated having to walk barefoot down the stairs to our things.

We left the apartment before midday. All we took with us were the money, the dictionary, one change of clothes, the lump of soap, and the pistol. Walking along the streets felt suddenly wonderful. As we traversed the same Durrës streets we had walked before, we were now met with long, friendly glances, especially from the women but also from men of all ages. The vendors called out to us, trying to sell us their wares, calling us beautiful boys. I imagined that they must have thought we were the sons of local officials or Italian tourists. Agim seemed to enjoy the attention far more than me, because he loved moments like this, loved being on display—it seemed that he had built his entire life around these types of moments, moments in which he could appear as the person he wanted to be, the person he truly was beneath those broken shoes and dirty clothes.

I, on the other hand, was worried about him, frightened that we would be found out or that we might attract the wrong kind of attention. I tried to talk to Agim about it as he walked around like he owned the place, but he didn't seem to care, he simply smoked cigarettes one after the other and paraded around with his shoulders held high like a dancer.

"Be quiet," he snapped. "Allow me to have this."

And so we wandered around Durrës all day like tourists, and at some point it felt as though we really did own the entire city, the whole world: tucked deep inside my plastic bag I had a wad of banknotes and walking beside me was someone without whom I simply could not imagine my life. We ate ice cream and burgers; I whistled to girls walking past, who looked back, timidly at first, then smiled at us; we smoked cigarettes, sat in cafés, and talked about the same things we always did, as though that evening we were not about to begin the most important journey of our lives.

A little before sunset, when most shops were about to close

their doors for the night, Agim and I walked up to a boat shop. We'd agreed that he would do all the talking and I'd stand beside him, smile, and behave as normally as possible, because he knew that I wasn't as good of a speaker as he was.

"Good evening, sir," Agim greeted the man behind the counter, who had already begun locking the cupboards in the store.

"Evening," the man replied bluntly, as if to prevent a time-consuming conversation that probably wouldn't lead to a sale.

"My father, Shaban Hoxha, needs a small motorboat this instant. He sent me to find one when he learned earlier today that he cannot get the boat he had rented for his fishing trip with Italian businessmen tomorrow," said Agim as clearly and surely as he could.

"Shaban Hoxha," the salesman repeated, glancing at me, at my hands, which I had stuffed into my pockets, at the plastic bag hanging from my wrist like a life buoy. The man probably knew all the families living in the area, and I realized that using the name Hoxha had always been our only option. No other name would have done, because no other name instilled people with such dread; no other name would have stopped him from asking further questions.

"Very well," the man said, his brow furrowed as though he knew precisely why we were buying the boat, and he stepped out from behind the counter.

Keeping close together, Agim and I walked out to where the owner kept his boats. Some of them were so big that we would never be able to carry them. Others, meanwhile, looked so rickety that I thought they probably shouldn't have been on sale at all and certainly wouldn't have lasted for such a long journey. Agim's eyes fixed on the same boat that I had spotted: a small open boat in fairly good condition with two benches and rowlocks for the oars, and equipped with an outboard motor.

The man told us how much the boat cost and scratched his beard. A few moments passed, Agim suggested another price and the man declined, Agim suggested a third price and a fourth, at which the man laughed and stroked his mustache between his thumb and forefinger and said that for that price you can have the worst boat I've got and a kick up the ass. Agim seemed to win the man over because eventually he gave in, walked over to the boat we had chosen, and started its engine to demonstrate that it really worked.

"Very well," said the man, and I handed Agim the plastic bag and followed them, watched Agim count out the money for the man, and watched the man count it back.

We carried the boat and oars out of the store—at that point it didn't weigh very much at all—crossed the street, and placed the boat on the sand. There were still a few people out on the beach and they watched in bewilderment as we tripped and stumbled, but by this point we no longer cared about anything: we had come this far and we were without a doubt leaving tonight; if necessary we would blow our plastic bags full of air and start swimming.

We took turns fetching full canisters of fuel from a nearby gas station, three trips each, and loaded them into the hold of the boat.

Once we had pushed the boat out into the water and clambered aboard, I felt as though I loved Agim as much as it is possible to love another person, with a passion that cut deep into my heart, with the power of my every thought.

We rowed until the city was nothing but a hazy strip of lights behind us. Then Agim picked up the cord attached to the motor and began pulling. The motor growled a few times, but at the fourth tug it started to purr like a cat. Agim remained crouched over, his knees against his chin, as though he hadn't heard the sound of the motor. He pulled a compass out of his pocket, and as the boat headed west he pressed his hands against his forehead and began letting out a series of strange whimpering sounds—he was sobbing—and I held out my hand to him and he took it. Then he pulled out a pack of cigarettes and a lighter, and we sat next to each other on the bench, beneath the silky black sky and the bright white moon, and lit our cigarettes, and for a while we didn't say a word, for enslaved by the darkness we could barely see each other, we simply glided forward, at times he kept hold of the rudder, at times I did so, and together we broke the sound of the quiet night and the gently rushing sea, its surface like a freshly lacquered floor.

It didn't matter where we ended up, I thought then, because every place I had ever been with him had been a home.

IV

I knew it was the end of my life. And yet I had only wanted to return home; I absolutely had no wish for death, nor for crossing over into the new life.

ORHAN PAMUK, *The New Life*
(trans. Güneli Gün)

7

People in Helsinki are terribly stylish. That's my first impression of the city. You'd be hard-pressed to find a better dressed city than this. People's clothes look new, they are tall and beautiful and extremely white, their blue or green eyes make them look innocent, affluent, healthy, clean, pure. At the same time they appear cautious and withdrawn, because when I say hello to the assistants in grocery or clothes stores they barely look at me, and when I ask for directions many of them seem somehow agitated or embarrassed, as if I were too eager to get to know them.

The drunks are a spectacle to behold. Over my first few weekends in the city I watch them, a look of disbelief on my face. I step on the bus and they are drunk, and nobody does anything about it; they can hardly stand upright and they urinate in the street or over themselves, and nobody does anything about that either. It's unpleasant, disgusting, and unforgivable, especially for people who live in such impeccable surroundings where everything is in perfect order and nothing ever runs out. Why do they drink so much? I keep asking myself.

I imagine that if I had grown up in a country like this, I would have read so many books that I wouldn't have been able to keep my eyes open, I would have gotten myself a university education and joined a respected profession, I would have lived the best life possible and made those closest to me positively burst with pride.

In my apartment there's a shower that you can turn ice-cold or boiling hot, even in the middle of winter, and even if you run the warm water for a long time, it never runs out, there are no boilers anywhere, water could gush from the pipework all day long if I wanted it to. I am amazed at the products in the supermarket, displayed with military precision, at the quick and orderly lines, at how rarely people speak to one another on the bus, in parks or offices, as though everybody is living in their own little vacuum.

In public places people talk to one another extremely quietly, as though they were constantly saying something criminal. Making eye contact is challenging, like trying to solve a complicated mathematical equation, because people here don't look other people in the eye, or if they do their gaze is generally dismissive and cruel. There's no mistaking it: *Get out of my way,* it says, *why are you standing there?*

Many people here seem hostile toward foreigners; it's as if they'd prefer the country to remain unchanged, to be constructed of only certain elements: people who look a certain way and speak certain languages. Somebody slips an anonymous letter through my mail slot telling me to go back where I came from, and when shop assistants follow me in stores as though I were planning to steal something, it makes me almost want to do what they expect.

I wander around the city in a state of melancholy: I don't feel at home here, it feels like I am carrying my suitcases everywhere I go. Finnish people can't see what a privileged life they lead, as though they've never heard of a world outside their borders.

I'm already planning to leave and start over again somewhere else, but then I meet her. One evening I go to a gay bar, and there she is, and she is beautiful. She is sitting near the entrance, shoulders hunched, her head drooping as she watches the handsome white men around her and timidly turns her glass on the table like a coffee cup that's too hot, her forehead wrinkled like the surface of an old leather bag.

I notice her the minute I step inside, and I watch her out of the corner of my eye as I order a drink. She's wearing a pair of skinny red trousers and a tight white T-shirt, a thick golden necklace with a dangling cross, her slender arms are limp as overcooked spaghetti, and she has a long giraffe's neck, black hair tied in a bun behind her head, and small breasts.

I walk up to her, and when I sit down next to her I say hello and introduce myself—with my real name, to my own surprise. She takes a quick gulp of her drink and only then takes my hand. *Tanja,* she says, and I almost laugh, because she doesn't look like a Tanja, though her movements are feminine and though she has the form of a woman, and before I can say anything she explains that Tanja isn't her real name. It's Tom, *you know,* she adds and glances nervously around her for a moment before opening her mouth again and saying she likes my bracelet.

I thank her and say I know what she's talking about, *You don't have to explain anything,* and from that moment on our conversation flows naturally, I ask her questions and she seems happy to answer them, she is proper and polite, harmless and kind, and can barely speak loud enough to be heard above the music blaring around us. She is captivating, and I feel the urge to hold her close to me, like a set of keys in my pocket.

I learn that her doctor parents hoped she would become a doctor or a lawyer, but that she decided to study theology at the University of Helsinki instead, because on a religious retreat at the age of fifteen she'd learned that God humbly loves and accepts everyone, even her, exactly the way they are. She tells me she would like to become a priest and that her parents find this more difficult to accept than her transsexuality, because neither of them believes in God. I learn that she comes to this bar several times a week because it's essentially the only place in the city where all kinds of people are welcome.

After a while she receives a text message. Tanja looks at her phone and tells me she has to leave. Nice to meet you, I say, really nice. It would be nice to see you again, I haven't got any friends in Finland yet, and once I've said it she gently touches my shoulder and says with a faint smile, *I can be your friend.* She asks for my phone number, says she'll be in touch the following week, and disappears first into the line of people at the cloakroom, then out of the door, and in her long woolen coat she takes lengthy, quick steps as though someone were chasing her.

The following day I travel from my studio apartment in eastern Helsinki into the city center, walk from the central railway station up a small hill, and arrive at a gloomy, clinical shopping mall and begin wandering around its different stores. I'm looking for a pair of skinny red trousers and a tight white T-shirt, but everything is either the wrong size or doesn't fit in quite the right way, and all I buy is a golden pendant with a cross.

I then cut across the only street in the city that ever feels busy and pass the door of a large department store, walk along a street lined with lighted wreaths, and arrive at a white church with a green roof standing glumly on its platform at the top of a hill. I walk up the steep steps to the main entrance and stop to admire the view, the graceful old buildings whose bright colors shine in defiance of the growing darkness. Farther off I can see the harbor, where cruise ships growl like dogs, and in front of the church is a small square, in the middle of which is the statue of a man standing in a stupid position with his back to the church as though he were about to reveal his great ignorance to the gathered crowds.

The city is like a fusion of Western Europe and the former Soviet Union. The buildings are low and small like the relief patterns on a coin; it doesn't require much time to take everything in, and the city's inhabitants walk around as if they are always in a hurry, as if they lived in a city far bigger than this.

I step inside the church, and its interior is a disappointment to me. Judging by its grand façade, I would have expected something more decorative than the plain wooden pews, the few arched ceilings and statues, the nondescript altar, on both sides of which gilded angels have descended and kneel in prayer and behind which a gold-framed painting depicts a man dying. But in some ways the church fits the modest essence of the country.

I sit down at the front of the church, pull my new pendant bearing the cross from my bag, and place it around my neck, and when a priest greets me by nodding in my direction with the subtlest of gestures, like a barely perceptible brushstroke, I feel as though I understand something essential about Finland: people here are not impolite, they are lonely, they like to be left in peace, and they don't need anything extravagant around them.

I walk down the church steps and regret feeling so stubborn earlier because in fact I enjoy living here. I take a right and come to the steps of a building painted yellow, steps even steeper than those of the church, like a set of fake eyelashes, and I step inside a luxurious square lobby with yet more white statues, and judging by the few signs erected in the corners, I realize I am in the university. I can hear a group of people approaching: they are speaking very fast and all walking in the same direction, leaving the lobby echoing once they've gone. I decide to follow them, and before long we are in a lecture hall with heavy mahogany desks and people start laying books and papers out in front of them.

I sit at the end of a row of chairs, near the door, and I too pull a pen and notebook from my bag. I don't look at anyone and nobody looks at me but I'm still as nervous as if I were in a police interrogation, and eventually a woman clearly older than us walks in and starts saying something and the students begin taking notes. The woman speaks at great length and in a monotonous tone, as lifeless as the dying man in the painting behind the altar; sometimes she clasps her hands, sometimes holds them clumsily at her sides, and for the next hour and a half I just sit and write in my notebook whenever the other students do, scattered sentences in different languages, names I have used and places I have visited, and I imagine I too am a student of theology and prepare myself to give my new name if someone asks for it. *Tanja*.

8

The following week I receive a text message from Tanja. Would you like to go for coffee tomorrow? the message asks, and it ends with a smiley face. Yes, I reply, and the following day I arrive early at a café near the university building and she turns up late and apologizes profusely, looks around nervously as though the walls are about to cave in on her, and suggests we take our coffee with us and go for a walk. The sun shines so rarely here in winter, she says.

We step outside, walk along a short boulevard, and arrive at the harbor, and we talk—not about me but about her, as I get the impression that she wants to talk about herself at length. I don't dare ask her whether she was alone in the bar that night like me or who sent her the text message. A boyfriend? Or a girlfriend?

We walk onward, heedless of the cold, at first without even really noticing it, because when she starts telling me about her sorrowful life I remain silent and she speaks as though she knows she is telling me something captivating, there in her long black coat and leather combat boots and thick scarf, half of which she has wrapped around her head like a helmet.

Tanja is a girl in a boy's body, incomplete and still on her way to achieving her final form. This is why she is depressed, she explains, as though she's talking to a dear friend, and she tells me all about her difficult childhood, the name-calling, the bullying, the violence.

"It's hard being like this," she says, dispirited.

"I understand," I say, and I feel like hugging her.

"I've been meaning to ask you something," she says after a short silence. We continue along the shoreline and up a small hill, at the end of which stands a giant white ship that looks like a snow castle that will soon melt with the spring.

"Yes?"

"Are you . . . ," she begins. "Gay?"

My teeth start to ache in the frozen wind, my chest tight, as if an iron hoop were wrapped around it.

I don't know whether I'm gay or straight, I feel like saying. I want to tell her I've never thought that I might like men who like men, only men who like women and who could therefore never like me, but I've been with women too, and I want to tell her that I find it impossible to become aroused, but I have still had sex with both men and women when the men and women in my life have wanted it.

"Yes," I reply. "Among other things." She laughs brightly and I smile, too, as I glance at her, the deep dimples on her cheeks and her dazzling white teeth glimmering like untouched snow.

"I know what you mean," she says, and leads us to a park on a hill opposite the harbor.

At the top of the hill is a small, round bunker that looks like a saggy breast, and there are only a few people in the park, old ladies out walking their dogs.

"It's the first thing people notice," she says despondently. "Difference. As if it's a crime."

She sighs again and begins telling me about the last few years.

I've given everything to become a girl. You can't even change your name if the authorities deem your new name to be the wrong gender. Can you imagine? she asks angrily. *You can't change it by yourself, you have to fill out a hell of a lot of paperwork instead and get a doctor's certificate. It's ridiculous. You can't change your name but you can get pregnant and then decide you don't want to keep the life growing inside you. You can give your child away to be raised by the state or someone else. You can leave your family and your hometown without any repercussions, because people have the right to disappear and be forgotten. You can ask not to be resuscitated, to donate your organs to someone who needs them, but you can't decide on your own name though it's something that doesn't affect anyone else. You can even decline cancer treatment and take your own life, but not live your life bearing the name that is yours.*

"Isn't it just ridiculous?" she asks as she comes to the end of her monologue, which spills out of her as though she'd practiced it in advance.

"This is a shitty place to live, I want to get out of here," Tanja says, agitated, as if in revenge for what she has had to endure, and she looks at the piled snow around us as though it were a trap of some kind.

"What do you do here? Are you on holiday or do you live here? Where are you from?" Her questions are like rapid fire, as though each of them has only one possible answer.

I swallow.

"I don't know," I reply. "I'm here for the time being because I don't want to go back home."

"Why not?" she asks instantly. "Where is your home?"

"In Italy," I say. "It's an even shittier place than this. You wouldn't believe how hard it is to be different there."

She sighs again, *I understand,* and the steamed air coming from her mouth dissolves around her face.

Soon she tells me about the hormone treatment she has started and about how she had to visit the doctor countless times before starting the treatment because the doctors had to be sure that she really wanted to live as a woman and that her desire to live in the other gender had lasted at least two years and that she had no history of mental illness.

Once she has told me her story, I feel as though I've been touched inappropriately, as though I, too, had been stripped of the basic right to exist and live the way I want to. Heavy clouds begin gathering across the sky, and I don't know what to say.

"It's really strange," I say. "Anyone could lie and say they've felt like they belong to the other gender their whole life, and give them the answer they want to hear."

"Exactly," she says, perked up by my empathy, and she tells me there's another large park nearby, as though going there were a condition for continuing our conversation, and I feel an inexplicable sense of unity with her and certainty that she feels the same toward me—why else would she talk about herself so intimately?

"Have you been there?" she asks, and she says the park's name. I haven't, I tell her; there seems to be nothing but parks in this city, a park for everyone.

She has already started walking decisively toward the other park, and I follow her though I'm eager to get indoors. And she talks and talks, now barely pausing for breath and without letting me get a word in, explaining how her body has changed since she began the hormone treatment, *Fat started to build up around my breasts and hips and my body ached all the time, my bones and muscles ached and I was constantly thirsty, I would wake up in the morning to find that my mouth had dried shut overnight, and it felt as if something were chewing on my organs, I lay awake with pain all night and tried to get through the day without fainting, some nights I prayed that I might die, then in the morning I'd cry for no reason and every reason.*

Why can't you simply decide to be a man or a woman by wearing men's or women's clothing? I wondered as I listened to her. Why can't everybody present themselves the way they want to? If I want to use a woman's name or a foreign name, I can simply say so and nobody will ask me to prove why.

"What happens now?" I ask.

"I'm still waiting for the surgery," she says. "Until then I'll just have to get by, as I have done until now."

Tanja walks slowly beside me, almost falls behind, and when I turn to look at her I see she has lowered her eyes to the ground, the bottom half of her face seems tensed. She looks so sad that I wonder whether anything brings her happiness.

"Do you have any hobbies?" I ask.

"Yes," she replies and looks up. "I'm a singer; I used to sing in a choir. I've sung all my life, and I want to get a record deal, but that will have to wait."

"A singer?"

"Yes."

"That's fascinating," I say, envious that she knows who she is, what she wants, and that it's going to be possible for her to go and get it.

"But I don't want to start a career like this. I can't," she says mournfully. *You know?*

I know, I understand, I reply. I suggest that we leave the park and she agrees, and as we walk along the path back to the café the envy I feel toward her turns to pity.

She has powdered her face carelessly, and you can tell she is a boy in girl's clothing. She has an awkward, boy's posture, large pores, and a big Adam's apple, a boy's voice and height, she's well over six feet tall, far too tall to pass as a woman, despite everything she's been through she's just too carelessly put together to be a believable woman, and I'm relieved to be so much shorter than her, that my genes are different, that I can change myself just the way I want.

I wonder what it would be like to be her, how nervous I would be about going outside.

It would be winter, dark, there would be snow along the streets and across the bodies of the parks, and I would grip a black leather bag over my shoulder with both hands. At first I would avoid public places; everything would feel so new that I'd worry about being found out if there was too much light. And I would avoid speaking too, I'd simply walk to the bus stop, to the end of the street and back again; I'd sit down in the park for a while and walk back to the busy bus stop, where I would stand for hours pretending to wait for my own bus.

I would be unable to do anything else, because at this point I wouldn't understand that I can decide who I am, the way I am, and I wouldn't yet know that I don't dress in girls' clothes in order to be a girl, but to have the same advantages as girls.

I wouldn't yet realize that all human activity is motivated by the desire to be better. People move from one country to the next to secure better living conditions, and nothing is said or done unselfishly, every action entails the promise of a greater tomorrow, the wish that I'll get something I want, something

I think I can't live without. I wouldn't yet understand that it would be best to stay right here, hanging from the edge of my own desire, ablaze, mindlessly longing for something I can never attain.

For what I would understand the least, and what she doesn't yet understand at all, is the nature of desire, the numbness that follows when it's fulfilled. Getting what you want feels like sleeping in a windowless room or standing at the heart of a foreign city, defeated by triumph. The one thing you have given everything to become—a lawyer, a writer, a woman, a doctor—so that you could touch the silver crown of desire: the moment when that happens, when everything comes true and your face is bared and your body lies outstretched on its back like a hollow cadaver encompassing all the happiness in the world, the bottomless joy that springs from the fulfillment of a wish, the sound of a dream, a smell like a fresh sheet fluttering onto a bed. That's the worst of it, when nothing is the way you thought, when you realize you've been living a lie, telling yourself a story, and the disbelief—how could I have wanted something so much that I wept for it so many times, you say to yourself, that I felt the razor blades of envy slice so viscerally between my ribs and smelled their scent like burnt gasoline—and the revulsion you sense when you realize that you hadn't expected to feel sadness when you should have felt joy; the feeling when you return home and switch off all the lights behind you, pull the curtains across the windows, and can no longer hear the motions of your heart; the feeling that you would give everything away to go back to the beginning, to revive your story's origins.

Tanja doesn't know there's nothing worse than that.

9

Over the next few weeks Tanja and I meet almost every day. We visit quiet little cafés and museums and see the city's attractions, generally just as they are about to close for the day, and she helps me to fill in forms and teaches me Finnish, buys me textbooks, and points me to classes available at various schools. *How about a painting class,* she asks. *Or you could become an interpreter, that would be a great profession,* she says, as though she considers Finland my permanent home and sees herself as someone whose responsibility it is to plan my future, a future in which she will inevitably play a part.

I meet her friends, young adults studying at the university, people my age, and one of them says she cares about Tanja so much that she simply has to ask me, *You do care about her too, right?*

Of course I do, she's wonderful, I say, and I accompany Tanja to a party at one of the university's student unions, where she refuses to dance or drink alcohol and where she shyly but proudly introduces me to her people. When we visit clothing stores, she never tries on any of the clothes she finds but buys them, says she'll try them on at home and return them if they don't fit. Sometimes I try to take her by the hand, as we sit next to each other on the tram or as we walk side by side, and sometimes I try to slide my arm around her waist, but she pulls her hand away and slips free as though she doesn't want anybody to see me touching her.

Perhaps it's because on some level she believes everything her mother has said. Tanja told me how her mother had once said she would never find a partner because nobody wants to live with somebody like Tanja, *You look disgusting, you sound disgusting, I already have a daughter and I don't need another one.*

She is twenty-two years old and too sensitive for this world, I can tell from the way she moves, the way she behaves, from the fact that there's no point asking her anything when there are people around, that she doesn't like me talking to her on crowded buses or trains, and that she deliberately arrives late for her lectures in case the students are asked to introduce themselves.

To her I am a twenty-seven-year-old immigrant, an Italian man who prefers not to speak his native language. I am an only child and my parents died in a car accident, Tanja learns about me, and says that this is the one thing we have in common, both of us have a difficult past, and this is why we get on so well. *People like us always understand each other, don't you think,* she asks. *Of course,* I reply, and she says she cares about me. *You're probably my best friend, I'm so glad I've met you,* she tells me. *It's so easy to talk to you,* she says after we've eaten lunch on a restaurant terrace and enthused about the spring, talked about all the things we'd like to do once it arrives.

One day I invite myself to her apartment, and somewhat

reservedly she allows me into her home. I want to see the way she lives, I want to look in her bathroom mirror, see which products she uses and how she takes care of herself. She lives near the university, a short walk from the city center in a top-floor apartment with a view over the sea on one side and a city view on the other. As she walks ahead of me along her long hallway, Tanja explains, almost ashamed, that the apartment belongs to her grandparents, *I wouldn't be able to live here otherwise, and this isn't my furniture,* she adds as she stands in front of a large white sofa and begins to tuck her tight white top into the black skirt reaching halfway down her thighs.

The apartment looks like something straight out of an interior-design magazine, as though every painting, every piece of furniture, is an artistic unit of its own. Large white chests of drawers are dotted throughout the apartment, each of them featuring showy decorative items.

She asks whether I'd like to watch TV or a movie or whether we should eat something, she takes the remote control from a glass coffee table then puts it down again, pulls the curtains to one side. *Or what would you like to do,* she asks and lowers her hands awkwardly to her hips.

I look at her and the apartment around her, the life she lives, the place where she belongs, how dispossessed she seems despite everything. Studies at the university, an apartment and furniture like this, friends who care about her, yet she cannot see what she already has and sees only that which she is still lacking, presumably because she doesn't want what she already has as much as she wants what she cannot have.

I walk toward her and take her by the shoulder, pull her against me and draw in her smell, the scent of lavender soap, and for the first time she does not resist me at all.

I love you, I say, only a few centimeters from her face. She has lowered her head and closed her eyes, then she raises the hand from behind her back, slides it between us, and places her fingertips on my chest. And when she says *I think . . . I love you too,* I raise both hands to her ears, run my fingers through her hair, and press my lips against hers, and for a brief moment I can taste her salty tears against my upper lip.

I push her onto the sofa and kiss her, my eyes are open though hers are closed, her face is red and her limbs stiff, and she begins making movements with her arms and legs as though she were being attacked, and when I place a hand on her stomach, her muscles tense, and when I touch her chest she clenches her fists and curls up.

But then I understand what it is she wants: when I don't place my hands near her groin or chest, the redness on her cheeks disappears; when I don't ask her to take her clothes off, she kisses me all the more passionately; when I don't touch her at all, she gives herself to me completely to the extent that she can at present.

"Should you . . . ?" Tanja begins to say. I've just returned from a language class and she's come home from a lecture; we are drinking fresh coffee from glass mugs, a rainy June day droops on the other side of the window, and she has just been thinking out loud about ways to avoid going on an annual holiday with her family. Tanja explains that the entire family is locked away in three small cottages in the middle of the woods for a full week, there isn't even an indoor toilet, there's nowhere to escape, and the rest of the family constantly bombard her with questions, as if they were mocking her.

"Move in?" She completes her question and stands up from beside me, walks to the other side of the living room, picks up a magazine on the table, slides it into the magazine rack, and stands with her back to me. I place my mug on the coffee table, and the clink startles her; she moves her weight to her left leg and rests her right leg across it.

"You know what?" I say. "I've been thinking the same thing."

"Really?" she asks, then turns, giving a coy smile in that unique way of hers, so that I cannot see the landscape opening up behind her, the rain brushing across the sea like a broom.

"Yes," I reply, and she walks back to me, sits in my lap, kisses my lips, then slips out of my arms again.

She decides to call her mother, grabs the telephone almost violently, and scrolls for the right number, overjoyed, barely breathing. Her mother picks up and a moment later I can hear her mother shouting something; I don't understand very much but I recognize the pathos, the frustrated tone of voice used to coax a child, for in her eyes Tanja is still a child, and Tanja listens for a moment, the nail of her right forefinger in her mouth, before she starts shouting back, *I hate you*. She hangs up, and when the phone starts ringing again Tanja glances at the screen, puts it back on the coffee table, and lets it ring until it eventually stops.

She sits down on the sofa, and I pull her into my arms with a smile, sense her pulse gradually calming down. "Good," she says, as though to steady herself, and sighs deeply.

"Good," I reply.

"I'm happy," she informs me. "I'm happy you're going to move in."

"So am I," I say, my lips against the top of her head, and I start stroking her arm, but she pulls it out of reach as soon as I feel the stubble on the skin of her wrist.

The following week I move my things to her apartment, only a few cardboard boxes of clothes and miscellaneous belongings. *Is that everything?* she asks in astonishment, then apologizes for the question.

Sorry, a word she keeps repeating, sorry I'm walking too slowly, sorry the television is too loud, sorry I woke you, sorry I went to the bathroom last night, sorry I didn't buy milk for the morning, sorry it's such a mess here, sorry, sorry, sorry I'm so ugly, sorry, I look awful in this outfit, sorry, I fully understand if you don't want to introduce me to anybody. She's sorry about everything.

I don't understand why she thinks she's in my way all the time, why she has stopped finding herself meaningful, and why she gives me so much space, half of all the closet space and two-thirds of her enormous bed, where she lies awake all night at the edge of the mattress, her body stiff, as though she were tensing every last muscle. She often listens to music on a set of headphones, so quietly that she hears if I say something or ask for something, and she obeys me as though I owned her—when I say I'd like to go to the movies, she buys us tickets, and when I see a pleasant-looking restaurant, she calls them, books a table, and pays the bill.

While we live together she does everything like an Albanian wife: she prepares food and launders our clothes, cleans the apartment and buys the things we need, and she never asks me for anything except my presence; *I have enough money for both of us,* she explains when I mention it to her, and I don't mind being a part of all the luxury we enjoy. On the contrary.

In the evenings she sits quietly next to me reading romance

novels or magazines, sometimes she watches television with me, and when one evening there's an ad on TV for a singing competition to be filmed later in the autumn, I tell her she should participate.

"No way," she says, but secretly smiles: she has wrapped herself in the cloak of my suggestion, I notice it in the way she always puts a hand up to her mouth every time I mention the competition and tries to hide her enthusiasm in a yawn.

Share your story, the ad encourages. It runs often, and every time it appears I suggest she should take part, as if to tease her, to see her naked in the face of my question, and after a while she clearly starts expecting me to ask her again, because she always comes up with a new reason why she could never take part in the competition. *I'm too ugly, they wouldn't take me looking like this, I don't have time because of my studies, I don't want to look like this if or when I ever do anything like that,* but still she starts singing her favorite songs in the kitchen, she sings and plays them so often that they begin playing in my mind too.

When she's not at home I walk around the apartment as though it were my own. I admire the black marble counters, run my fingers through the chains of the chandeliers hanging from the ceiling, fondle the valuable ornaments displayed throughout the apartment. I imagine I'm famous, imagine that I've earned all this, a closet half the size of the bedroom bursting with shoes and clothes, a large hallway with a mirrored wardrobe running the full length of the wall, a dining room with an eight-seater table that we never use, a guest room into which Tanja has crammed her bookshelves and all the excess junk in the apartment as though it were a storage room and where she sometimes sleeps, especially if she is aware that I slept badly the night before.

One day I spot a shoebox on top of one of the bookcases. I pick it up, open it, and see a pile of printed pages: images of genital reconstructive surgery, articles on how a vagina can be constructed using skin grafts, the penis, the scrotum, or the intestine, pictures of different kinds of breast implants, and presentations of various hair-removal techniques. The images are unpleasant; they look more like shots of roadkill than human genitalia.

Another day I play "Like a Prayer" on her computer and try to read her diary entries, but I can understand only a few words and scattered sentences, such as *sad* and *every day the same shit* and *I hate them.* After listening to the song a few times, I begin to get a feel for its rhythm and understand more of Tanja's diaries, and by listening to a version in which Madonna doesn't sing, I start to learn when I should open my mouth and sing. I listen to the song so many times that I memorize every single word, the way it starts and ends, at what point the tempo gets faster and at what point Madonna starts singing at the top of her lungs.

Tanja arrives home; she's bought us fresh berries and peas— there are many different ways to eat them, she says of the latter. You can run the sides of the opened peapod across your mouth or pick out the peas with your fingers and eat them straightaway or do as I do and collect them in a bowl so that you can eat them one at a time like candy, she explains, but for the next few days I cannot concentrate on her or anything she says.

I toss and turn in bed all night, restless, unable to fall asleep, *I close my eyes, oh God I think I'm falling out of the sky,* I say to myself. *I close my eyes, heaven help me,* but something about the song feels wrong. Tanja is sleeping soundly beside me, on her stomach; she never rolls onto her back or side, as though even her subconscious is protecting her, making sure she never gives herself away. Then, all of a sudden, I remember the boys sitting on Skanderbeg Square with their cassette player and the way they sang *I think I'm falling from the sky* instead of *I think I'm falling out of the sky*.

I sit up in bed: it's already getting light outside, specks of yellow and blue tinting the pink sky. I realize that, despite what I'd thought before, the sky in the song isn't a metaphor for the world, it isn't a place from which people fall to the earth, but these words are spoken by someone for whom the sky and the act of falling from the sky is in itself a place to be, and that Madonna is really singing about what happens if you fall but don't have a place to land.

I run through the chorus in my head. I realize that Madonna is not in fact praying in this song, though I've thought so for as long as I can remember. People like Madonna don't need to pray to anyone, least of all to God, and I wonder whether this is why she sings about God, because though God is present in the lyrics, God's absence runs through the whole song.

I get out of bed and dash to the window ledge. Tanja's breath pauses for a moment, then continues; I stretch my leg out against the cold surface of the glass and look out the window and see my collarbone reflected there, as slender as a violin string, my fragile skin wrapped around my bones like a translucent film.

Has her lover left her, I wonder, and is that why she sings the way she does? Because in the song she is on her knees, cowed by love or something similar to love, perhaps by the desire to take her lover somewhere she can no longer take him, and soon it will be midnight, followed by the coldest hours of the night when she is utterly alone and can perhaps feel the full force of her lost beloved like a shock wave.

I switch off the light and return to Tanja; I don't want to close my eyes, don't want to see her moving with the rhythm of her dreams. For tonight I will dream of him, his face, his touch, the kindness of his heart; I know it, because he has been with me these last few days, more present than for a long time, and I've tried to push him away, shut him behind the window like a ghost, because I fear him though he's no longer here, hasn't been for over a decade; I'm afraid of how I'm still trying to keep him alive.

————————

Tanja loves me. I know that, I can feel it.

She loves the way I wake in the mornings, the sounds I make as I stretch before getting out of bed, the way I breathe; she loves my neck, so passionately she kisses it, and my lips, I can see it in the way she watches my mouth when I speak. She loves my eyes, eyes that don't look at her the wrong way; she loves the way I leave the room when she starts changing her outfit; and she loves my voice, that and the fact that I never ask her why she takes a change of clothes into the shower with her, never ask her to bathe with me, never ask her what all those pills in the bathroom are for or why she needs them. She loves how perfect I am for her when I tell her *You are beautiful* before she walks out the door, loves it when she can reply by saying *No I'm not, you are so handsome,* and she loves the fact that sometimes when she's clearing up after dinner she can barely contain her smile, loves those little moments when she finds herself wishing this will never end—that is what she loves the most.

10

The auditions for the singing competition are held in a local theater. Once Tanja has wished me a good day and kissed me on the cheek as she walks out the door, I go to her closet and take out her best outfit.

The theater lobby is full of people and the line outside the door twists along the nearby streets; scaffolding erected in front of the building holds television cameras that move back and forth across the crowds. I'm extremely nervous: all these people have turned up to perform, I think, to make their dreams come true, to present to the world the best versions of themselves, to become the people they believe they truly are, and I worry that someone else's light may be brighter than my own.

Some of the hopefuls have brought alcohol with them and sip it like water, others have come in ridiculous outfits: one is dressed as a pig, one as a chicken. One woman is wearing nothing but a bikini, though the amount of makeup on her face and body more than compensates for the lack of clothing; there's a shirtless muscular man whose torso is disproportionately large compared to his feet and who tenses his muscles in front of the camera as though he were trying to overcome a bout of constipation.

I've put on a pair of black panty hose, a tight black woolen dress, a pair of low-heeled black leather ankle boots, which are two sizes too big; on my shoulder I have a plain black leather handbag with a silver zipper. As I look at the others, I think that many of them are wearing entirely the wrong kinds of clothes, the kind of outfit that they think will make them stand out from the crowd.

I arrive at the registration desk set up in the lobby, where I am given a sticker with the number of my audition. After this we are escorted into different areas of the theater to wait our turn.

There are thousands of applicants: in the same windowless room as me there are dozens of people who must be at least sixteen and no older than twenty-eight, and I know that similar auditions are being held in other cities too and on several different days.

Sitting around me I see sixteen-year-olds with Mohawks and men in suits who must be over twenty-five. After a while the door opens and a woman in her thirties walks in and introduces herself as the show's producer. She speaks loudly but in a friendly tone and informs us that we will be called to perform in front of the panel of producers one at a time. *The producers?* someone asks. *Aren't we going to perform for the judges?* The woman explains that the producers decide which singers will get through to the next round, and that only then will we sing for the judges. *Just be yourself,* she says encouragingly, and wishes us good luck.

The atmosphere in the room becomes even more electrified;

the competitors peer at one another as though they've just been asked to fill out a lengthy, complicated form. Then we wait and wait: we are locked in a room and can do nothing but wait for what happens next. All we know is that someone else will eventually decide our fate. Someone in the corner of the room swears out loud, and I wouldn't be surprised if the competitors started to fight with one another.

Finally the door opens again and we are informed that we will be taken somewhere in groups of ten, and I am in the first group. I walk through a number of decorative halls and rooms and arrive on a stage, where several booths a few square meters in size have been erected.

Soon it's my turn. I am asked to step into the booth and to follow the instructions on a screen attached to the wall. *What is your name?* the screen asks in a man's voice. *Tanja,* I reply. I notice a camera above the screen and wait for the next question, which comes after a short pause.

Tell us something about yourself, the screen instructs me. I cross my hands over my stomach and realize that the panel of producers must be sitting on the other side of the screen, because I can hear the sound of breathing and faint chatter from the speakers. *I believe I am what this show is looking for,* I say in English. I think my eyes must be twitching with nervousness. Inside the booth it's terribly hot and there's little room to move, and it's in this cell only a few square meters in size that I am to prove to them that I'm a decent singer. *Okay then,* comes the voice. *Please sing,* the man says with a hint of boredom.

Without a backing track, I sing for what must be only about twenty seconds before the same voice interrupts me and asks me to step out of the booth. Somewhat baffled, I follow his instructions. *Thank you for your time,* says the woman who guided me to the booth as she urges the next competitor onstage and beckons me back the way I came, as though she were overseeing a line of pigs strung up on meat hooks in a slaughterhouse.

Just a minute, I say instinctively and ask her why I didn't get through to the next round. *I didn't do anything wrong, did I?* I ask, and in my frustration I grab her arm and beg her to give me another chance. *Let go of me,* she says, but I can't hear her; I simply repeat over and over, *Please, please, please.*

The producer takes me to one side. I look her angrily in the eyes and she explains that they can't put me through to the competition phase because I'm not interesting enough, because they are looking for something different, and because my singing wasn't good enough. *Besides, this show is aimed at a Finnish audience, so speaking English might become a problem.*

The woman walks back to her own place and I remain standing behind her. I'm livid, and I struggle to keep my emotions inside. *I'm a trans woman,* I say, but my voice is lost in the hubbub, it disappears into the space between the rows of lights, drowns beneath the sound of hundreds of steps across the stage, into the musty fabric of the thick velvet curtains. *I'm a trans woman,* I repeat, louder this time, and this time the woman hears me and turns her head just enough that I can see her profile, her lips pursed forward as if to take a bite out of the most sumptuous of desserts; I can just make out tiny capillaries that look like vines twining across her eyeballs.

Really? she says, and walks back toward me.

That's amazing.

I am restless all evening; I can barely eat though Tanja has prepared my favorite food, rainbow trout with roasted vegetables.

"You know . . . ," I say as she carries the dessert from the kitchen, a tray laid with cheeses and crackers, fig and apricot jam.

"Yes?" she says, placing the tray between us on the table.

"I'm not really Italian," I say calmly.

"What?" she asks and sits down on the chair opposite me.

"I'm not really Italian," I repeat.

I'd imagined that saying this would have felt more shameful, that the words wouldn't be able to withstand being spoken out loud, that all the time I've spent hiding would no longer leave any room for the truth.

For a moment she is silent; she lowers her eyes to the cheese platter and clasps her hands, and suddenly there is a distance between us, a space that could fit the sky and an entire ocean.

"I don't know what to say," Tanja says sullenly, lowering her gaze from the platter to the floor. "Where are you from then?"

And so I tell her. About Albania, the country I have not once visited since I left, about the first few months in Italy, which I spent in a military barrack in Bari. *It was terrible, you can't imagine how terrible it is when you can't speak the language, you can't talk to anybody or tell them what you're feeling and still you want them to accept you, and how horrible it is to watch as other people simply get on with their lives while you are stuck, wrapped in see-through plastic, in the wrong language, the wrong skin, you can't imagine how shameful it feels though there's nothing you can do about it, and how infuriating that shame can be, so infuriating that you feel like bashing your head against the wall and knocking over statues, punching someone in the face and stealing their handbag, because you are too helpless to do anything else.*

We were assigned feeding times like dogs, I say angrily, and by now she has raised her eyes and looks at me, almost frightened. They said food would be available between six and seven. You can't believe how humiliating it is to walk up to a hatch at a certain time to fetch the food they had prepared; they decided when we ate and what we ate and when we had showers, and we were given strange people's clothes to wear, shoes with someone else's sweat in them, shirts yellowed at the armpits and trousers ripped at the crotch, and like prisoners we were allocated an area we were allowed to use, and the most laughable part of it is that, despite all this, I wanted nothing more than to be an Italian, I wished that by putting on their clothes I would change and become them, that the smell of the clothes I was given would become my scent, too, though all the while I hated them with all my heart.

Tanja stands up, steps behind my chair, places her hands on my shoulders, then slides them down my chest toward my stomach, presses her cheek against mine.

"I'm so sorry," she says pityingly, and she sniffs. "I'm sorry if you've felt you can't tell me this," she stammers and presses herself tighter against me.

"No, don't apologize, I should have told you straightaway," I respond. I stand up from the chair, relieved, take her hand, and pull her with me over to the living-room sofa, where we sit at opposite ends.

"I understand, I really do," Tanja says, picking up a pillow and clasping it in her arms. "It's awful that you had to experience that," she continues. "Why haven't you visited Albania since you left?"

It's not my place, I tell her. *That's why I left, that's why I've never spoken about it to anyone but you,* I say, and she nods sympathetically. *And from then on I haven't had a homeland, only other lands, strange countries in which I've had to make a home,* and when I tell her about all this I can't control the slight tremor in my hands; my entire body goes into a state of disorder, as the weight that has pressed down on my stomach all my life rolls to the floor, rolls across the floor to her feet, climbs up her long legs and into her hands, into the cushion that she holds tighter against herself, and all the way up to her shoulders, which she leans forward as though a hand were pushing her upper back toward me.

"I'm sorry. I love you," she says, as though she were nothing without me, as though I could say anything to her and always get the same answer, an apology and all the love that she has to give.

11

The following week I return to the theater. I can't help myself; I want to find out where this will lead, how far I can go—and everything seems to happen of its own accord.

The competitors who have gotten through to the next round were asked to arrive at the same theater at eight o'clock in the morning and are instructed to wear exactly the same clothes as at the audition. Even our hair has to be the same, we have to wear the same jewelry, every detail must be as it was a week earlier, right down to the shade of lipstick. This time we wait in the theater lobby, where chairs have been set up like in an airport lounge and there are drinks and snacks on tables lining the walls.

We are then taken to another room in groups of thirty and told to wait to be called up in front of the judges one at a time. *And the most important thing,* says one of the men. *Don't be nervous about the cameras. Imagine they are pieces of furniture. Don't pay them any attention.*

Again I'm in the first group. We don't have to wait long for the show's host to walk in, followed by a camera crew and sound engineers. The host starts speaking to us and unctuously touching the competitors on the shoulder and hand as if he knew us.

The first competitor to be called is an overweight young girl. She stands up with surprising ease, takes off her thick scarf, and accompanied by her mother walks up to the handsome host dressed in a black suit, a black tie, a grey shirt, and shiny black leather shoes. The girl and her mother look mountainous next to him.

The cameras start rolling and the host asks the girl if she's nervous. *Yes,* she answers, clearly embarrassed, her forehead gleaming with sweat. She looks at the cameras around her, places a forefinger to her lip, presses her eggplant-shaped legs together into a curious-looking position, and turns her head away from the cameras. The girl's mother proudly explains to the host that her daughter is very nervous about meeting one of the judges in particular, as he is her idol, has been for years. The girl walks into the judging room, and once the door shuts we can't hear anything.

We wait and wait, which gives the host the chance to ask the girl's mother all kinds of things, like how long she has been singing and what taking part in this competition means to her, and the girl's mother explains that this competition means the world to her daughter because she's been singing since she was a little girl. Then, after a full three minutes, the girl steps out of the room, collapses into her mother's arms, and starts crying inconsolably. The host touches her shoulder, his fingers sinking into the girl's doughlike skin. *What happened, what did they say,* he asks over her wailing, as though he's trying to keep a straight face, and all the while the cameras roll, the girl doesn't answer, and the cameras zoom in on her as though this moment were the most fascinating thing about her.

The girl begins pacing around the room, her cheeks scarred with tears, and the cameras follow her and the men behind them seem to deliberately provoke her, ask what she thinks of the judges, and try to cajole her into singing for the cameras again: *Out here we heard how well you sang, will you sing for us again,* they ask.

The girl's mother chases her and the cameras begin following her too, though she asks them to stop filming, but the girl continues screaming and by now everyone in the room is following her movements, bewildered and amused.

One of the cameramen thrusts his camera right up to the girl's face, and at this the girl finally loses it: she calls each of the judges an idiot, says that the show is stupid and the other competitors are talentless, and eventually she informs the cameras that she is about to sign a recording contract and starts singing—or hollering—for a few seconds, after which she takes hold of every sign and empty chair she can find and knocks them over in a rage. Then she defiantly walks up to her mother, grabs the handbag her mother is still holding for her, and disappears from the room, as the cameramen follow her all the way out into the corridor.

Well, says the host, raising his eyebrows in such a way that the whole room bursts into laughter. *Do we have a Tanja here,* he asks, and looks around. For a brief moment I wonder whether to quietly sneak out of the room or answer.

Then I stand up. *That's me,* I say, and I apologize for not answering immediately.

As I stand in front of the judges, the muscles in my arms and legs feel limp, atrophied, and when I see them smiling at me encouragingly from behind the long table, I clench my teeth together so hard that my gums ache.

I've seen their photographs in advertisements, but they look far smaller in person, like scale models or copies of what I thought they would look like, and I think of the attraction I feel toward them: Is it because they are famous, because they've done something significant in their lives, something they will leave behind after they are gone, that gives a reason for their existence, or is it simply born of my desire to make an impression on them, to sing as well as I can? Merely standing in front of them makes me feel something I've never experienced before, as though I were exceptional and special, the most beautiful person in the world.

There are three judges: a bald, handsome music producer dressed in the latest urban fashion; a short, slim woman with curly red hair who has released many records of her own; and the charismatic main judge, a bearded man in his fifties who works for one of the large record labels. They sit opposite me in an open space that resembles a gymnasium.

I stand on a yellow sticker on the floor; there are cameras and props everywhere, cables scattered across the floor like autumn leaves in the street, loudspeakers, microphones, lights, and I can't help but wonder how much equipment and how many people it takes to make this situation intimate for the viewers, who see only a fraction of it all.

Tell us something about yourself, the bald man asks in English. I exhale all the air gathered in my lungs and the judges laugh. *Relax, there's no need to be nervous,* the curly-haired woman says with a friendly nod. *My name is Tanja,* I say. *But that's not my real name, you know,* I continue, looking through them, at a poster hanging behind them, and then the judges look at each other, smiling brightly. *And where do you come from, Tanja,* asks the bearded one.

Turkey, I answer after a short pause, and I instantly regret that I couldn't think of any other country when I told the producer about myself after my performance in the booth. *But I'm not a Muslim,* I blurt out spontaneously, like a drop of spittle accidentally trickling from the side of my mouth. Everybody is silent for a moment, the bearded one twiddles a pen in his hand, and the bald one casts his eyes meaningfully at the papers laid out in front of him.

It says here you're transgender, says the bearded one, and I have barely had time to answer *yes* when he continues. *Tell us something about that,* and all of a sudden my legs are about to buckle, what I've said has been filmed, I begin to tremble, and I feel as though I'm about to vomit out a bowling ball. I raise my hands to cover my face. *I'm sorry, I'm so sorry,* escapes from my mouth, and the words push me to an even more unmanageable state of mind: I have no control over my movements, my legs feel as though I have a pair of stilts taped to my ankles, my nostrils and sinuses feel blocked. I apologize a third time, a fourth time, until I sense the smell of the curly-haired judge, who has gotten up and is now standing next to me.

She hugs me. *You're so beautiful,* she says, and she pushes me away to see my tearstained face. *Everything is going to work out just fine,* she assures me. *We're all on your side,* she says, cooing as she might to a cute baby in her arms.

Thank you, I whisper, and I manage to pull myself together, though the agitation is still coursing through my body. I wipe my palms on the back of my shirt. *It's so difficult,* I say, and I blow my nose on the tissue one of the staff hands me, *being like this,* I continue.

"Like what?" the head judge asks.

"A trans woman," I say, my voice still shaky.

"We don't care about that," says the bald judge. "People are so much more than what they look like on the outside."

"That's right," says the head judge, and sits up straight. "As far as we're concerned, it doesn't matter whether you're a man or a woman," he continues, and looks at the other judges, who all nod first at him, then encouragingly at me.

"We're not here to define you, we don't judge a book by its cover," says the bald judge meekly. "Don't ever let it define you or stop you from doing things like this," he says, and asks if I'm ready to start.

I take a deep breath, but my voice seems to come from the wrong place entirely. I know as soon as I've started that the song doesn't sound the way it should, the way it sounds in my head, and after ten seconds I'm ready to stop and vanish from their eyes.

The bearded judge interrupts my singing after a few phrases and thanks me. *That went rather well,* he says. *We'll have to work on it a bit, but all in all you sang really well,* he adds, and by the time it's the turn of the curly-haired woman to speak there are already tears flowing down her cheeks. *I'm so happy you decided to take part in this competition. It's because of people like you that shows like this exist,* she gushes, and I feel almost as though it's my turn to console her. *You're such a unique individual, the world needs more people like you. So beautiful,* she says. *I loved the way you sang. Promise you'll always be yourself. We've been looking for someone like you,* she says. *Always stay just the way you are.*

Once the judges have given me their positive feedback and

handed me a piece of paper, my ticket to the next round, I smile at them, thank them, and hug them, and all the work I have done to come closer to what I want, or what someone else wants of me, to fit into their group, all those hours spent lying in the darkness calculating my next move, the oceans I have crossed and the people that have disappeared from my side, the cities I have visited and the stations in which I've slept, for a fleeting moment I remember none of it. *I am one of a kind*, I convince myself. *One of a kind, here, in this life.*

As I step out of the room, the host hugs me ecstatically and asks how I feel. *I feel really good now,* I say, glancing up at the cameras and slipping free of his arms, though he's trying to hold me on the spot and ask me more about what the judges said. I visit the bathroom, look at myself in the mirror as I scrub my hands under the running water, and I feel as though I have done something irrevocable, something fateful. Then I latch on to the female judge's words again: *We've been looking for someone like you,* she told me, and I dry my hands and swear to myself that I will do everything I can to live up to her words, to be the person she sees in me.

That evening I arrive at a restaurant where the production team is waiting, a short blond woman and a tall dark-haired man. I have dressed in my own clothes, and because of that I'm extremely nervous; for some reason I expect them to comment or ask something about my outfit, but to my relief they simply help take off my windbreaker and lead me to a table for four at the back of the restaurant, set slightly apart from the other tables. The woman pulls out a chair and asks me to sit down.

A waiter arrives and hands us the menu, and with that the

man orders us champagne and says tonight we will celebrate. I look around at the white tablecloths and tall glasses with slender stems, soft chairs and waiters in white shirts and black trousers, crystal chandeliers and old paintings of landscapes on the wall.

Could you tell us something about your home country and how you ended up in Finland? the man asks once we've placed our orders. And then I tell them the whole story, precisely the way my imagination has begun to draw it:

I was born as a boy in Istanbul in 1975. My Christian mother was a seamstress and my Christian father worked as a waiter in a restaurant. We lived in a poor area on the outskirts of Istanbul. I am an only child and my parents died when I was fifteen. It was a car accident, a truck veered out of the other lane and hit them, and they died instantly, I'll never forget that day, the rain that plummeted like bullets from the sky, the fog and the damp hanging in layers over the city like rose petals, I'll never forget how I had to identify my parents' bodies in the hospital morgue, the soda machine that swallowed my coin and that I started rattling so furiously that the staff called the security guards, I'll never forget the sound of the zipper as the body bags were opened, the repulsive smell and the gleam of all the metallic equipment, it was worse than looking at the sun with the naked eye.

I'd always excelled in school; I wanted to learn a good profession in order to give my parents financial security. But then they died, suddenly they were just gone, and I went to live with my slightly senile widowed aunt, changed schools, and made new friends. When I started to realize I was different from the others—a girl in a boy's body—in some ways, a sick way perhaps, I was glad my parents were gone, because I know, I know better than anybody else, that they would have never understood this or me.

I lost so much weight I almost disappeared, and for years I kept to myself, and it was only once I was accepted to the university to study psychology that I began to dress in women's clothing. But in a place like Turkey it was impossible to be like me, you know, I lived in constant fear for my life and my family disowned me, though my aunt was indifferent because by this point she couldn't remember anything, she barely knew who I was.

Then I fell in love and everything started to go downhill, though I'd expected the opposite to happen. The man I fell in love with was an Italian doctor; I met him at an event organized by the university where he was giving a talk about the Italian health-care system. I was beautiful and I'd dressed up for the occasion. After the presentation I went to talk to him, and that same evening he asked me out for a drink.

We talked all evening, his eyes glinted and so did mine, *I've never met anybody quite like you, such a mature young lady,* he said and I smiled, we didn't care for the food in front of us or the noise around us, didn't heed the calls to prayer from the city's countless mosques, and didn't pay any attention to the looks we got when he leaned across the table and kissed me: a fair-haired Western man and me, this creature, blazing with lust.

From that night on I loved him, and I felt that he loved me too. He walked me home and kissed me in the middle of the street before he flew back to Italy. I wrote him letters in which I told him about my parents, my studies, and my loneliness. The man always wrote back to me and told me about himself, his family and parents, and after a few months he sent me a plane ticket to Rome, and by this point I loved him so much that there was no room in my head for anything else, and I truly believed that he loved me every bit as much, just as unbearably as I loved him.

I packed my suitcase and left, and the man was waiting for me at the airport, with his white smile, clean-shaven face, expensive-smelling cologne, and clothes that said success; and when he embraced me in the airport lobby and said *I'm so happy you've come,* I almost lost my mind with love.

We went to his apartment, where the first thing he wanted to do was sleep with me. But when I stripped off my clothes and stood naked in front of him, the man cleared his throat and said *What's this, I want you to leave, right now, and never come back,* and just like that I no longer meant anything to him, even though I knew sensitive things about him—that he had once tried to sabotage his colleague's work because he was jealous of the colleague's promotion, that his father had cheated on his mother—even though there was nothing I wanted in my life but to have him as my own. He erased me from his life like a badly written sentence.

I decided to stay in Italy, because I didn't want to return to Istanbul and I'd never felt at home in Turkey. And thus began a drawn-out battle with the local authorities. *Why have you come here? What are you doing here? Do you have a partner? Do you have a job? Do you have any particular reason to be here? How well do you speak Italian?*

At first I thought they were asking these questions because they were worried I would be a burden on their society, but though I later got a job at a restaurant and was able to pay for my own apartment and support myself financially, the questions never stopped. It was then that I realized it was personal, that they didn't like me simply because of my nationality, and when people don't like you, you don't like yourself either, that's the way it goes, you learn to give certain answers to certain questions because that's the answer the person asking the question wants to hear, and before long you are inevitably caught up in a web of lies, lies that people are forced into telling because the truth doesn't make an impression, because the truth always fails, because it's never good enough.

What can you do if your story, which is so tragic that you imagine it will awaken people's sympathy, instead elicits hatred and violence? Where can you go if returning to your homeland is not an option?

I moved to Germany, and from Germany to Spain, from Spain to the United States, and for years I was so lonely that I almost took my own life. I didn't know what to do with all that loneliness, and I couldn't get rid of it because it was the air itself, the gulf between me and the person sitting opposite; it was the faces of all the people I looked at but who would not look back at me, it was every back turned on me and every word not spoken to me directly.

When I heard from a friend in the United States what life is like in Finland, such as that education and health care are free, I wanted to come here immediately, because I thought that here I could have a fresh start, as myself, finally—and here I am, I'm in treatment, and I'm hoping I'll soon be scheduled for gender realignment surgery. That is what I want, more than anything, for my life to finally begin.

The man has taken notes throughout my recitation, and the woman is drunk and crying. *Could you tell us all this again tomorrow?* the man asks. *We'd love to film you at home, if that's okay.*

I'm reluctant at first, but when the man says how important

it is to talk publicly about subjects like this, how beneficial my story could be to people struggling with the same issues, and when I remember that Tanja will be studying at the library all day and all evening, I agree.

The following day a camera crew arrives at Tanja's house, they set up their equipment in the living room and admire the décor, move pieces of furniture and position me in appropriate lighting at the corner of the sofa, leaning against a blood-red cushion like royalty.

Once I've recounted my story in almost the same way as I did the previous evening, I learn that I will be introduced to viewers in the first episode, to be aired in a few months' time.

Then they start asking me about my thoughts on transsexuality, what it feels like to be a trans woman, what people tend to say when they hear the truth, what kinds of situations I've found myself in as a trans person. Are you in a relationship, do you like men or women? they ask. What's your sexual orientation?

I decide not to tell them anything about my partner, I lift the cushion and place it on my stomach, and for a second I lose the ability to speak. The man explains that the viewers will want to know how it feels to be me and what my everyday life is like.

"I don't really want to talk about it," I say, clasping the cushion in my arms.

"Where's your wardrobe?" the woman asks suddenly. "Could we film that, too?"

I say yes and lead them to the closet, where I show off Tanja's finest clothes, her ball gowns, sequined tops, and high heels, and they get excited, as though they'd just won a great prize. *Amazing*, they exclaim as I hold different dresses up against my body, *Where did you buy that and that, would you put on those shoes and that scarf for us?* they ask, and then I explain that this scarf is from Paris and these shoes from New York, and I bought this Prada handbag in Stockholm.

Once they have taken all the indoor shots they need, we leave the apartment. We walk along the nearby streets: they want to film me in my local grocery store, where the shop assistants look awkwardly at me and the cameras; they want to film me in a clothing store and by the sea; they want to watch how I walk in women's shoes, how I move around in women's clothing, and how I get by with my few words of Finnish.

"What would winning the competition mean to you?" the woman asks.

We have crossed a market square and are now in a park walking along the water's edge, and they have stopped me at the spot where the trains heading north can be seen behind me.

"Winning the competition . . . ," I repeat and try to imagine what a winner looks like, and in my mind's eye a winner would smile, a winner's smile is permanent and piercing, a winner's teeth gleam in photographs so brightly that nobody could take such happiness away.

"I would finally be happy," I say, and with that they stop filming.

"This is great material," the woman says to her colleague and the cameramen, who have started packing up their equipment and checking their phones.

"It certainly is," says the man. Then to me he adds, "Finland is going to love you."

And so, barely thanking me, they disappear.

12

Tanja spends money as though it will never run out. At an art gallery she buys a new painting for the living-room wall; she has arranged to have it delivered and the painting arrives carried by two men. The men tear the wrapping from around the painting and hang it above the television. *Thank you, thank you very much,* says Tanja, and closes the door behind them.

The painting has a white background, and against the background are a black square, a yellow circle, and a red star. The shapes are arranged in a triangle so that the star is above the circle and the square. The pattern looks vaguely like a human face, either upside down or leaning to the side, a bewildered, surprised, or angry face. If you turn your head you can see three expressions in the painting, a set of eyes made up either of the circle and the star, the square and the star, or the circle and the square, and a mouth formed by any of the three shapes.

"Isn't it great?" asks Tanja, satisfied.

"I don't understand it," I say, though the painting is certainly impressive, its refined white frame lending it a feel of stateliness, and its geometric shapes fitting perfectly with the rest of the interior.

"It's contemporary art," she explains. "It shows all human expressions, everything a person can feel," she adds. By now her tone of voice is almost disparaging.

"It's ugly," I say. "Anybody could paint that."

"It's not ugly. I'm sorry you don't like it."

"How much did you pay for it?"

"That doesn't matter," she says.

"Yes it does, it matters a lot."

"Two thousand nine hundred euros," she replies quietly, then mumbles that the painting is by a famous young artist, that it's an investment, and that one day it will be much more valuable.

"You're stupid," I say. "Who spends that much money on one painting?" I shout. "For the same amount you could have painted hundreds of similar paintings yourself!"

And I continue shouting, though she has curled in on herself, lowering her head, wrapping her arms around her body the way she does, raising her shoulders and crossing her legs. *Don't you fucking understand you can't just throw money around like that,* I say, and she turns her back to me and walks into the kitchen. *People are starving and dying, and you buy a goddamn painting that costs almost three thousand euros,* I rave on and hear the lock on the bathroom door click shut. *You're so fucking stupid, you can't even tell when someone's taking you for a fool,* I shout, and I hear the sound of water rushing from the tap. *People treat you however they want and you never stand up for yourself, you fawn over people and let them walk all over you.*

When she eventually opens the door, she goes straight into the guest room and spends the night there, and the next morning she has gone before I wake up. When I arrive home that evening the painting is gone and Tanja is sitting upright in the armchair as though she were full of air, and when she begins to speak the words burst out of her mouth as though pushed by an immense pressure as she says, *You were absolutely right about that painting, I should never have bought it without asking you first, I'm sorry, I had it taken back today.*

I listen to her words but walk right past her, through the dining room and into the bedroom, and close the door behind me, but I can still hear the long, oppressive flow of her breathing and sense the aura of a body filling up with misery.

_____

I tell Tanja that I'd like to meet her family.

"Families should stick together in case something happens," I tell her. "Nobody knows you as well as they do."

"No," she says at first. "Under no circumstances." She seems determined, but once I've brought the subject up often enough and strongly enough, she acquiesces, though I can see how much the thought plagues her, how nervous she sounds on the telephone as she tries to arrange a time that suits everybody.

"I don't want to do this," she says more than once. "Please, I don't like them, I don't want to see them."

"We're doing this," I reply firmly. "How else can we build a future together?"

We meet in a café: Tanja and I sit on one side of the table and her siblings sit opposite us. Tanja is the youngest of three children; her sister is stunningly beautiful with blond hair and has just graduated from law school and works for one of the best legal firms in the city. Her brother too is devilishly handsome: thick blond hair slopes across his forehead from left to right; he has graduated from business school and works as an investment banker. They both look healthy, affluent, amenable, open-minded, and approachable, as if they know precisely what they are going to do the following day.

As I look at them, I realize why Tanja is such a disappointment to her parents, why she didn't want me to meet her siblings, and why she hadn't told them anything about me except my name and that I am her partner.

At first we chat about the weather and the café décor to break the ice, and after a short while her sister finally asks:

"So, you met at the university, is that right, Tanja?"

Though the question isn't aimed at me, I answer on her behalf.

"That's right," I say. "I came here as an exchange student from Sapienza University in Rome, and then I met Tanja."

"That's nice," her brother says, and looks at his sister, who nods kindly toward us. "What did you study again?"

"Psychology," I reply, and I glance at Tanja, who picks up her coffee cup with both hands and raises it to her lips.

"I've always been interested in psychology too," her brother says. "Luckily I can study anything I want in my free time," he continues, smiling.

Our conversation seems to be going swimmingly: sometimes I laugh at their jokes and childhood memories, and sometimes they laugh at my experiences in Finland, how strange I find it that cars here stop at the pedestrian crossings, how rare it is to find table service in cafés, how slavishly people here follow rules and regulations, and when I compare the line-number system in waiting rooms to a farm where the animals are waiting to be slaughtered, they laugh.

"I speak a little bit of Italian too," says her sister. "But not very well," she is keen to point out when I ask her in Italian whether she likes the coffee.

For most of our meeting, Tanja remains quiet, though her siblings genuinely seem to like her and care about her and regularly ask what she thinks about things, and I realize that Tanja doesn't like her siblings because she doesn't like herself in their company.

We say goodbye outside the café and I kiss her sister and brother on both cheeks.

"It was lovely to meet you," says Tanja's sister.

"Likewise," I reply and try to smile in the same way as she does.

"Really nice to meet you," her brother adds.

"Yes."

"Let's go for coffee again soon," he continues.

"Yes, or perhaps we could go for dinner," suggests her sister.

"Absolutely, that's a good idea," her brother replies. "Well, see you again."

"That went well," I say once they have disappeared around the corner. "Don't you think?"

Tanja shows me her broadest smile and takes my arm, something she has never done in public before.

13

The next phases of the competition take place over the space of a weekend. The competitors are brought in from all across Finland to an arts college; the show pays for our rooms at a nearby hotel and all our meals at the hotel restaurant.

I've told Tanja I'm going on a weekend excursion to the archipelago with my Finnish class to learn about Finnish landscapes and ways of spending free time, and she believed me and said simply that she'd miss me. *This is our first weekend apart, but it's good that they organize things like that, you'll probably make a lot of new friends.*

In the next round of the competition we have the opportunity to sing a song of our choice without a backing track for thirty seconds, and I get through even though I sing the same song in almost the same way, and at every stage the producers want to interview me both before and after my performance.

We can ask the production team for anything, and they bring

us the things we ask for as quickly as they can. *It's really important to us that you're happy and that you have everything you need,* they say. They wait on us so much that sometimes I feel as though I owe them a favor, and as they wipe the sweat from my brow before I step onstage or double-check with me that everything is fine, I pay my debt by replying to their questions as exhaustively as I can.

Now when they ask me what it's like to be a trans woman, I know to tell them it feels like constantly being an outsider, always being misunderstood, carrying the wrong ID. I give them examples from my day-to-day life, tell them how humiliating it is to travel with a man's passport, to have to defend my appearance at airport security, how hard it is to talk sometimes, especially if there's phlegm in my throat because then my voice comes from the wrong place and sounds like that of a man. And that feels like I've been found out, like walking around naked.

I explain to them, just as Tanja has explained to me, that only through examples like this can you gain people's compassion, and they film my every word. *First I have to be pitied, and only then can I be accepted,* I say. But that happens only with those who accept people like me to begin with. Unfortunately not everybody is like that, I say sorrowfully.

In the end, most people think I'm ill, I say, mentally unstable. People think that beneath this shell there's a flaw that can't be fixed or evaded, that I always have been and always will be less of a woman and less of a human being than they are. I have to live with that fact, every day. *That's amazing,* they say time and again, and stroke me on the shoulder.

Throughout the weekend, I don't make any attempt to get to know the other competitors, though the judges and the production team encourage us to do so. The remaining contestants have found others like them, they hug one another, praise one another, and pretend to wish one another the best of luck, though each and every one of us has the same goal, a goal that only one of us can achieve.

Only one competitor can secure a recording contract, only one can win, only one is better than everybody else—and for that we are prepared to stay awake all weekend if need be, to use all the time available to practice. Everyone is prepared to do whatever is necessary to win the grand prize.

I want it too, every bit as much as the others, and I truly believe in my chances, for the further I get the clearer it becomes to me that they are not interested in finding the best singer but something else entirely.

In the weekend's final round I sing a song from start to finish, a simple song that the show's vocal coach advised me to sing. My performance goes badly wrong; I forget the words right at the beginning and can't find my way back into the rhythm of the song.

Despite my failure I still believe I will get through to the next round, because I've been filmed far more than any of the other competitors. The judges have always put me through, no matter how badly I've screwed up, and sent home singers who are far more talented than I am. In the final round there are only twenty-four men and twenty-four women left, and the judges call each competitor individually to hear their fate.

When it's my turn, I walk into the room lined with dark curtains, where there's a brightly lit stage with four chairs. The judges are occupying three of them; I step up to the stage and the judges gesture for me to sit down in the empty chair opposite them. *How are you doing?* asks the curly-haired judge, and I tell her I feel fine, *a little nervous, that's all*. I look her in the eyes and she looks back compassionately and eventually says, *I'm afraid we haven't selected you to join the finalists at the live TV broadcasts.*

"What?" I ask, dumbfounded.

I stand up and begin walking out of the room, and before I step down from the stage, the curly-haired judge takes me by the arm and asks if it's all right to hug me. I let her wrap her arms around me, and with ripples of disgust on my face I listen as she says, as though to comfort me, *I wish you all the best for the future, thank you so much for being on the show, I'm convinced that your story will inspire thousands of people.*

Don't they understand that everything is over now, I wonder as I walk out of the room, that there's no going back anymore, I think as I gather my things under the consoling gazes of the host and the other competitors and briefly say to the cameras that I'm sad and disappointed but okay.

I walk down to the shore. Seagulls arch across the sky and dig their beaks into the trash cans; somewhere farther off ships dock at the quays and the wind whips the trees so much that the leaves rubbing against each other sound like a broken radio.

I begin walking home, and as I approach the door to Tanja's apartment in the quiet stairwell, I know that I can no longer be with her.

Late that evening I inform her that I'm leaving, that I'm breaking up with her. It is a Sunday and only the last, red-brown vestiges of the day are left when I break it to her. At first it's as though she doesn't hear my words, she rushes instead from room to room, so I say it again, sometimes to her back and sometimes to her face. *I am leaving, we can't be together, I don't want this any longer, I don't want you anymore.* I try to follow the impact of my words, but her face remains expressionless and colorless.

"Did you meet someone in the archipelago?" she asks after a while. I am sitting on the sofa staring at my numb hands; she has appeared at the living-room door and stands leaning against the doorframe, her legs crossed, her shoulders raised so high that her neck has disappeared, her arms wrapped tightly around her upper body, and when I look at her I can tell she is about to collapse, that she is unable to say anything else to me, cannot even look at me.

"I don't love you anymore," I reply without looking up at her. She turns in the doorway, and I can hear the scratch of the wall in the hallway as she slides along it to the floor.

At first her moans are tight and short, like a cat before it is dropped in boiling water, then she sounds as if she is having a heart attack, her breathing becomes rapid and shallow, air gushes uncontrollably in and out of her mouth, and I walk up to her, watch her as she leans against her knee, her other leg wrapped under her, how she grips her ankle with both hands, her head bowed humbly, her face hidden.

I grip her armpits and try to lift her up, but she is completely limp and seems to weigh many times her bodyweight because she does not want to get up, so I leave her and walk into the kitchen. She gasps for air violently as though she has just woken from a nightmare and starts sniveling like a child, and I let her sit there, in the hallway, where she remains slumped for hours, neither moving nor speaking to me.

I tell her that I am going to sleep and that I'll be leaving in the morning, and when she doesn't respond to this either I walk up to her and crouch down next to her. *Please stop crying,* I implore her, and my hands touch the damp at the back of her head and I can feel her tremors throughout my entire body. *I'm sorry,* I say. *Good night.*

I climb into bed, and after a while I hear her; I am about to fall asleep when I feel a soft breeze on my cheek as she walks through the room; I can smell her as she creeps into the bathroom, hear how carefully she switches on the bathroom lights, the way she always does when she thinks I'm asleep. She fumbles with something for a moment and runs water into the sink, and I open my eyes slightly and see a strip of light beneath the door and a skirmish of shadows as she moves around. Stripes of grey light make the floor look like a zebra's coat; then she switches off the lights, tiptoes out, and quietly lies down on her half of the bed, her back to mine.

When I wake up there's a strange draft in the room, as though the window has been left open overnight. I turn to look at her and she is cold and colorless; she no longer looks like herself, like anybody, she is nobody though her body is right here; and when I go into the bathroom to fetch a tissue I see that the contents of the bathroom cabinet have been laid out around the sink; and when I return to wipe the white froth that has bubbled from her mouth and across her face and neck, I notice a scrap of paper that has fallen from her hand to the floor, her arm twisted as though she had been holding a stone.

I love you, and I will love you forever.
I'm sorry.

14

It is early morning when I arrive back in Tirana. The city looks almost the same, though time has scraped away parts of the buildings, some of the rooftops; where once there was nothing there are now modern apartment complexes, but the same old men are still smoking in Skanderbeg Square, their faces still furrowed. The air is filled with the same sounds, the same children sitting bored by the tables set up along the pocked streets.

People talk about the same things as before, about the West, about moving abroad, about poverty, unemployment, money—they want to get out of here, to start a life they have already built in their minds, because they don't understand how much they would have to give up if they actually left. I know that in this situation they do not need words to see the hopelessness of the past in one another's eyes, the unpredictability of the future, all that suffering that the sheer impossibility of starting afresh causes them; they still cautiously peer over their shoulders as they walk, as though wishing that the past staring back at them was not their own.

But to their good fortune they don't know what starting over is really like, they don't know how it feels when things that once made you proud turn into things that cause you greater shame than any pride you have ever felt.

I look at the familiar streets and buildings and allow my thoughts to return to my childhood: waking to the sounds of my mother clanking around in the kitchen or my father warming up his voice or my sister's sighs as she awoke next to me. Soon we will eat breakfast and then each of us will go off in a different direction, as we do every single morning, and in my stupidity I don't realize that this is happiness, me with my best friend, my father in his old dark suit and black leather shoes; then in the evening we all come home and eat again and my father tells me a story about the birth of Albania, of how an entire land hatched from an eagle's egg or about men who fight and fight, how they defend themselves when someone threatens them, and in my mind all this happens like in a movie. My father is so skilled at telling me about the world, about conquests, warhorses, invasions, as though every element of the world is part of a movie: a spotlight, an ornament, or a moving wall.

I walk up to my former home: the general store on the ground floor is closed, its windows covered with old newspapers and a rusty padlock hanging from the door. Save for this, nothing else has changed; some houses in the area have been painted and some renovated, but our house has stood here all this time almost untouched, simply gathering dust over the years like an abandoned attic. I step in through the gates, walk up the stairs—there are small, familiar-looking puddles of water on some of the steps—and I knock first at one door, but nobody answers. Then I hear shuffling behind another door, and the sound of boiling water; I knock and eventually the door opens.

Are you broke? a woman's voice asks from inside the apartment. *I don't have any money,* she says, having appeared in the hallway like a lifeless militant before I can say I don't need money, before I can start the conversation in a different way, before I can take in how much she has changed: how emaciated she is, the bones in her back and her whole posture like a twisted hanger; her greasy hair, her grey, veiny skin and hardened feet; her yellowed bathrobe and toothless mouth. *There's nothing here for you, nothing,* she says. *Who are you, are you coming or going?* she continues and slaps herself on the forehead, squints her eyes, and disappears into the kitchen.

I walk up to the kitchen doorway, rest my suitcase against the wall, and notice how much junk she has collected in the hall and living room: tightly closed plastic bags, old packaging and empty cigarette packs, dirty clothes, paper plates and cardboard boxes on every surface. I don't recognize her movements as she picks up some eggs in her white fingers and throws them onto a plate, peels off their shells like a squirrel opening a nut, casts the shells to the floor, grabs a fork and a bottle of vinegar, and begins mashing the steaming eggs, *Yes, yes, yes,* she says, throwing the fork at the wall and slapping herself again, and I don't recognize her voice either, her sudden sounds or the words she lets pour from her mouth with astonishing speed, *Yes yes yes, yes yes yes.*

What's your name? she asks, crouching on the floor as she begins shoveling the eggs into her mouth. I take a step forward. *Bujar,* I say, and when she hears the name she seems startled, frozen on the spot. *Bujar, Bujar, Bujar, I know that name,* she says, and she grins so widely that I can count her teeth on the fingers of one hand. She places the plate on the floor, swimming with scraps of old newspaper. *That's right,* I say. *Hmm,* she mutters, *I have a son called Bujar, but he's much younger than you, yes yes yes, same name as you, he'll be home soon, yes.* I decide not to tell her why I've come, and not to apologize for leaving the way I did, because I know that's the most appropriate thing to do.

I walk her to the shower, where I wash her. She is very timid and resists me at first but little by little begins to trust me; she probably recognizes my voice. The bathroom is full of junk, rolls of paper and plates, newspapers and scraps of cardboard, and as I wash her I wonder how she has survived here for so long—does anyone visit her?—and how does she remember to eat, how is it possible that she hasn't gotten sick or died yet, how can she have lived in this stench all these years? Has she been alone all this time?

I take her to her bedroom, clear a space on the bed, dress her in old clothes from the wardrobe, a clean white shirt and a pair of blue pants I find as I wade through the clutter. She holds on to my shoulders as I pull the pants up; *Yes yes yes,* she says and stares out of the window, and so I spend the day with her, listening to the things she tells me about the stuff she's collected, how she found plastic containers in the street a while back and stored them in one of the kitchen drawers, how the cats meow at night, how quickly the evenings turn to night, and how slowly the next day dawns, how hard it is sometimes to find decent dishes or wearable clothes, how beautiful a certain shampoo smells, how the kids in the neighborhood gather behind her door, laugh, and ask for money, and how their mothers sometimes visit, leaving clean clothes and groceries at the door, and at the point when her words run out she falls asleep, and I'm not sure if she will ever wake up from the dream she has fallen into, so quietly and gently my mother sleeps.

I close the bedroom door and open the door to my own former bedroom. It is the only empty space in the apartment, only a tattered mattress on the floor wrapped in a white sheet and black curtains pulled across the windows.

―――――――

And in the morning my beloved appears as a horse beside my bed, like a gigantic, gnarled hunk of meat. There he is, transformed, looking exactly the same as all the horses in my father's stories. His worn, chipped, black-brown hooves are the size of my head, and the grooves of his ribs are like closed lips. His velvet-black hide and tapered muzzle and enormous black eyes, tainted with sorrow, appear etched into his gleaming head, held in place by a dark-brown bridle, a white stripe running its length.

The horse wearily turns his head, his damp mane spilling to the floor like a waterfall; he is on his side in the middle of the room like the ruins of a thousand-year-old building, though you rarely see a horse lying down. *What are you doing here?* I ask the horse, looking him in the eye, and for a moment the horse does not reply but instead stares languidly back at me, gives a faint whinny, smacks his dry lips, flashes his browned teeth, and like a whale exhales the carbon gathered inside his lungs.

"Tell me a story about myself," the horse says, facing the wall. Slowly he stands up, and only now do I see his rock-hard muscles, the hardy tendons binding them together, his round rump raised like a throne on his hind legs, arched like a pair of scythes. "Would you be so kind?" the horse asks, and his words sound distant, like the war cries of an entire army from beyond the valley.

"About you?" I ask the horse, avoiding his piercing, desperate stare when he turns to look at me.

"Yes, a story about me," the horse replies. "Surely you remember it?"

I stand up and begin telling the horse a story about a horse, and he stands next to me listening as you would to an ancient tale, nodding, encouraging, bemoaning, rejoicing along with the protagonist. Side by side, we walk out of the house, and suddenly the horse is dragging his heavy limbs like a pig scuffing its trotters, his long tail sweeping the street behind him, and I feel so terribly ashamed of the horse and I don't know whether it's because of the way he is walking or because he imagines he deserves an entire story of his own. Before long we arrive at the foot of a mountain and together we climb up onto a high jagged ledge where legend has it that the greatest eagle in all my homeland has been seen many a time.

Everything plays out just the way my memory recalls, and how familiar it all seems: the changing hues of his skin, the sound of the sand beneath our feet, the smell of the mountain, his voice as he whispers my name in the dark, *Bujar*. And all this I remember, that we have traveled in this lightlessness so far and so long that I am about to lose my mind, but he is not. I remember how relieved he is to grab me by the knee, though we haven't been able to see anything for hours, for what feels like a lifetime, though I'm sure we are about to die. I remember how he slides his hand down to my stomach, farther still, though the power of the shuddering motor behind us seems to be fading. We truly are going to die, I know it, I remember thinking it, ready to become one with the night.

I remember how he slips his hand into my pants and how I grab it, how I ask him to turn back but he refuses, how I grip the rudder, how he shoves me to the front of the boat so violently that I almost fall into the water, and I remember how I then push him and he topples overboard and bobs in the sea like an apple, and how at first I pretend not to hear as he cries out my name in terror, and how I seconds later shut down the engine and step across the boat to look for him and see only darkness.

There on the grass, shining with fresh rain, the horse rests his chin on my shoulder, and through his marble eyes I can see into the horse's past: I see the moss-covered lands through which the horse has galloped, the paths he has ridden, paths that have gobbled up soldiers fallen from his back and swallowed the blood that oozed from his hooves, and now I understand why the horse never speaks of his most gruesome memories, why he always banishes them from his mind, drops them from the window like children from a burning home.

ACKNOWLEDGMENTS

Thank you to Antti Kasper, fiction editor at Otava, for all the help and support I have received throughout my writing career. For this I would also like to thank Leenastiina Kakko and Silka Raatikainen.

Thank you to Iina Akkila, Venla Hiidensalo, and Krista Lehtonen, the irreplaceable readers from whom I received much invaluable, thoughtful feedback on this manuscript. Thank you to my family. And a special thank-you to my friends, particularly Tua Harno, Meri Kuusisto, and Pasi Pekkola.

I want to thank David Hackston for translating my work with uncompromising diligence and sensitivity, and Tim O'Connell and Anna Kaufman at Pantheon, as well as Laura Macaulay and Adam Freudenheim at Pushkin Press, for publishing my work in English. It means the world to me. Thank you to Josefine Kals and Michelle Tomassi at Pantheon and Tabitha Pelly at Pushkin Press for sharing such beautiful words about my books with the world. And thank you to my agent, Sarah Chalfant, for everything.

Once again, the greatest thanks of all are reserved for my editor, whose ability to read and see I admire most profoundly. Without your patience and trust, this novel would never have been completed. Thank you, Lotta Sonninen.

ALSO BY

Pajtim Statovci

MY CAT YUGOSLAVIA

In 1980s Yugoslavia, a young Muslim girl is married off to a man she hardly knows, but what was meant to be a happy match goes quickly wrong. Soon thereafter her country is torn apart by war and she and her family flee. Years later, her son, Bekim, grows up a social outcast in present-day Finland, not just an immigrant in a country suspicious of foreigners but a gay man in an unaccepting society. Aside from casual hookups, his only friend is a boa constrictor whom, improbably—he is terrified of snakes—he lets roam his apartment. Then, during a visit to a gay bar, Bekim meets a talking cat who moves in with him and his snake. It is this witty, charming, manipulative creature who starts Bekim on a journey back to Kosovo to confront his demons and make sense of the magical, cruel, incredible history of his family. And it is this that, in turn, enables him finally, to open himself to true love—which he will find in the most unexpected place.

Fiction

VINTAGE BOOKS
Available wherever books are sold.
www.vintagebooks.com